IF THE OWL CALLS

IF THE OWL CALLS

a novel

Sharon White

SANTA ROSA, CALIFORNIA

This is a work of fiction. Names, characters, places, and incidents are either the product of the author's imagination or are used fictitiously.

Edited by Peg Alford Pursell
Designed by Mike Corrao
Author portrait © Joseph V. Labolito

Library of Congress Cataloging-in-Publication data is on file with the Library of Congress.

ISBN: 979-8-9923690-1-4 (paperback)
ISBN: 979-8-9923690-2-1 (ebook)

Published by Betty
WTAW Press
PO Box 2825
Santa Rosa, CA 95405
www.wtawpress.org

Betty is an imprint of WTAW Press, a not-for-profit literary book publishing press. This publication is made possible by the generous contributions from individual donors, public arts organizations, and private foundations.

For Scott

CONTENTS

(NOVEMBER)

HANS

1.

HANS RUBBED THE TINY window with his fist. It still took his breath away. The wildness of the vidda. They were not very far up, maybe four hundred meters, and he could see reindeer running in a long line toward the coast. Wisps of powdery snow kicked up around their hooves and then swirled away. The low hills stretched to the horizon, clusters of dark willow brush in the valleys along the frozen streams. The highest hills were bare rock. Wind scouring the snow off.

A mail bag was wedged behind his seat. Across the narrow aisle a woman sat in another seat, a larger mailbag stashed in the space behind the pilots. She was huddled in a bright orange parka.

The rivets on the cabin vibrated, one of the fat de Havillands they fly from Tromso to Alta with two or three seats, most of the cabin filled up with mail.

It was almost too loud to talk but the woman shouted at Hans, "Where are you going?"

This wasn't going to work, he thought. But he shouted back, "The construction site at the dam."

"Engineer?"

"No, cop."

"Too bad," she said, "It was sad. They were just trying to make a statement and now Paulsen has blasted his hand off and most of his arm."

Hans shook his head and pointed to his ear. "Too loud to hear."

"Later," she said.

Her face was familiar. Intense brown eyes. A TV reporter from Bergen maybe.

He rubbed the window again with his fist and looked out. The dim light glowing. The blue darkness of the north. Early November. Soon the sun would disappear for weeks.

Just a couple of months or so before, he would have been tempted to break the window. Take off. Run as fast as he could out of his life in Oslo. But he was checking out the sabotage at the construction site for the massive dam at Alta, a pitiful attempt to destroy a bridge. It was a thoroughly botched job. Eric Paulsen had blown up his hand. Olav Elstad brought him to the clinic. They were morons. A waste of time. Someone had seen another man running away from the bridge.

He flipped open a folder with the report about the sabotage from the office in Tromso. There was a picture of Paulsen's mangled hand.

He wondered if Malin Lund, his supervisor, should have sent someone else, someone not so attached to the north. Someone not so burned out. More patient. Less prickly. She thought it made sense, since he'd been the bad cop at the protests in Oslo against the dam. Later, everyone jumped on the bandwagon. Greens from all over Europe gathered in Alta. Hans didn't understand what was wrong with a hydro dam in the north. More electricity would mean streetlights so the kids could walk to school safely in the winter. He would've loved a ski track lit up through the darkest months.

His field was homicide but the department had trotted him out whenever they needed a Sami cop to negotiate in Oslo. He was more like a traffic cop at the protests, instead of a detective.

"Kari Finstad," the woman yelled across the aisle.

He turned toward her. "I recognized you," he said.

"That's a relief. I was hoping you knew who I was."

She was very pretty, very cool in a rough kind of way. A bandana neatly tied around her neck.

"It took me a few minutes but then it clicked," he laughed. She'd been in Oslo during the protests covering the news for her TV station.

"Almost there, folks," the copilot yelled. "Make sure those seat belts are fastened."

They'd be bouncing all over the plane if they weren't belted in. Even the mail bags were secured with several straps.

THAT NIGHT HE SLEPT in a sleazy hotel on the edge of Alta not far from the dam site. Hans hadn't been to Finnmark in over a year. The dark funky curtains in his room were closed tight. The room smelled like a gym. He couldn't remember where he was in the middle of the night, and he patted around for his cigarettes on the bedside table, blurry-eyed, coughing. He hit the glass of water, then found the package of gum and slipped a piece out of the thin paper.

He was trying not to smoke. He'd given it up when he married Astrid. She said it was a disgusting habit.

"The gum's just as bad," his boss said, the first time she saw him pull a stick of Dentine out of his pocket.

IN THE MORNING HE opened the heavy curtains and looked out at the wet cliffs. Rough-legged buzzards made their nests there in spring. Now a light snow was falling.

He'd been concentrating on birds for months. Mostly hawks, owls. Fierce birds. Birds with yellow eyes and knotted talons. He discovered the Botanical Gardens near his apartment in Oslo had a family of peregrine falcons. Their nest wedged on a ledge of one of the university buildings. He'd bought a pair of binoculars as a present to himself, and in early May, he watched the male bring bloody pigeons and bright green birch leaves to the chicks perched in their nest. Such a great breakfast for the kids.

He stepped out of the hotel into the cold morning air and pulled his collar up. He'd gotten so soft in the south. Felt the cold a lot more than he used to. An officer pulled up in a dented Saab and parked in front of the hotel. He got out of the car and handed Hans an insulated snowmobile suit.

"Put this on, Inspector. We'll guard your coat at the station," he chuckled.

Hans handed him his coat, the wind whirling around him, and struggled into the heavy suit. The car was warm. He wondered if this was some kind of initiation for the cop from the south. He rolled the window down.

The officer said, "Yup, that moon suit's pretty toasty."

Another officer was waiting for them at the site. He was dressed in an identical suit and leaning against a military surplus Mercedes truck with a trailer.

They hopped on the machines, flying across the low hills to the edge of the river. Hans couldn't remember the last time he'd been on a snowmobile. He was trailing behind the local cop in the wake of his machine. The two-stroke motor smell was comforting for some reason. When they reached the bridge, it was so small, arched over the ice-thick river. Out of place. The river had gouged a channel through the flat hills, arctic birch edging the banks.

They parked at the spot where Eric Paulsen had set off the bomb near the bridge, covered with crusty tracks. There was still blood on the frozen surface of the snow. It would have been hard to ski: new snow had blown away in the biting wind.

"Paulsen's gone now," the young officer said. His smooth face pink from the cold.

"I heard," Hans said.

"Is that why you're here?" The officer kicked at the frozen snow.

"In a way, yes."

"Stupid bastard. As if we didn't have enough to do without dealing with something like this. Just a flash in the pan."

"You've been taking the brunt of the protests around here, haven't you?"

"Yeah. But we've had a rotating bunch of city slickers to help out showing up."

"Just like me," Hans said.

"Not quite like you. I hear your family lives near here."

"I grew up here," Hans said and shrugged.

"Paulsen's in Leningrad now, the Interior Minister thinks, somehow smuggled out of the country with his family. He'd have to be in a hospital, attached to an IV. Doctors amputated his right arm below his elbow in the clinic. He didn't eat in the prison hospital in Tromso. They'd put him in solitary confinement. He wouldn't eat meat and asked for fruit. He threw pears and apples the guards brought him at the walls; he refused to drink water."

Hans knew the police had been holding Paulsen as a terrorist, charged with attempted homicidal arson. But they let him go. Out on bail. The office in Tromso wanted to review the case. The Labour Party didn't want more of a mess than the one they had already. All those pictures in the papers from the protests at the dam site. Flashing images on the news of fur-capped officers wrestling with hundreds of people in *gåktis*. Chained together, draped with blankets, huddled on the ground in the frigid cold.

Hans walked around the patch of blood-stained ice, bent down to touch the snow. He couldn't get the photo of Paulsen's severed hand out of his mind. He was lucky he hadn't killed himself.

"Ready to head back?"

The wind had gotten stronger, and his gloves were too thin for this kind of cold. "Sure," Hans said.

They loaded the snowmobiles on the trailer and drove back to the station. The officer dropped him off.

"Take care," he said. "Thanks for the ride."

"No problem, Inspector."

The place was humming. Big news for a small town. But the Alta police had been dealing with this kind of thing since the construction started on the dam almost two thousand kilometers north of Oslo. His coat was hanging on a hook in the staff room. Hans unzipped the snowmobile suit and slipped it off, then pulled his coat off the hook and replaced it with the heavy suit.

He took a seat and waited until the desk sergeant was ready to let him talk to Olav Elstad. It was definitely a sign the local police weren't happy the Minister had insisted a detective from Oslo look into the case.

Elstad was being held in Alta, but the police didn't have any reason to keep him much longer. There was a lack of evidence he'd been at the site. The chief said he was cooperating. He refused to tell them, though, the name of the third man. He wouldn't even admit there was another person involved.

This was admirable in a perverse kind of way. It seemed like it wasn't something that made much sense. Not telling the truth would just complicate matters and get them all into more trouble. Paulsen was a musician turned saboteur. Not something anyone could have predicted. His band was popular in Karasjok and Tromso. They toured coffee houses and played bars as the warmup band as far away as Bergen.

He'd looked at photos of the pieces of the bomb sealed in plastic bags in the evidence locker in Tromso, trying to figure out why they'd done this. What did they hope to accomplish? Just two or three men. Thousands protested against the dam in Oslo and at the construction site, and the government still decided to go ahead with the project.

He searched in his coat for the picture of Paulsen's hand, bloody, on ice in its own bag in the freezer of the medical examiner's lab. He thought he might show the picture to Elstad. Seeing his friend's hand might trigger a response. The fingers were long, skillful. There was a ring on one of them, a beautiful ring with interlocking circles like some of the Viking silver.

It could have been a ring Hans's brother made. Mikael was a drunk but a terrific artist even when they were kids. And that made his mother love him and his father praise him. His work was displayed in the cultural center, the silver hammered and twisted with a hangover, Hans figured, most days. But he produced a lot of work. He lived not far from their parents with a woman he'd met at a craft fair.

Lately, Mikael was fired up by friends who saw themselves as militants. Tough guys. They talked about cultural genocide. The state stealing land, language, religion from the Sami. He could imagine them involved in more subversive acts than the small bomb detonated at the bridge. They were bad news. Hans was relieved his brother didn't seem to be part of any of the events at the dam site. It would upset his mother and the warped image she had of Mikael.

The desk sergeant brought him a cup of coffee. Hans nodded and gave a thumbs up, pleased the sergeant would go out of his way to do something for him.

"Just a few minutes more," he said, adjusting his belt, "and then you can talk to him. He'll only speak Sami."

He gulped the coffee, lukewarm, and put the cup down on the table next to him. It was covered with magazines and brochures for pistols. An ashtray full of butts was spilling over onto the magazines. He opened the local paper folded on top of the pile. It was dated a few days after Iranian students occupied the US embassy in Iran. He glanced at the photo of demonstrators burning the American flag standing on the wall of the embassy, and then pulled on his coat and waited some more.

OLAV ELSTAD WAS SITTING on a chair in the tiny cell, a small man, but powerful. His face very animated. Full of light. Mysterious. His dark blue ski sweater was zipped up to his throat.

"Do you have any idea where your friend Eric is?"

"I didn't know the whole plan," he said.

Would he try to deflect each question, Hans wondered. Elstad was somewhere else, not paying attention to the detective in the Sorels and long woolen coat. Elstad rubbed his neck and then fiddled with the zipper on his sweater, pulling it up and down. Up and down.

The cell was narrow. Hans didn't like being there with the door locked. He knew it was irrational and took his coat off. Ran his hand through his hair. Popped a piece of gum out of its wrapper. Someone laughed outside the door. The space heater popped on in the room. A ticking sound like an egg timer.

"I've been notified by my office in Oslo that reindeer herders found a body in a ravine near Lismavarri." Hans leaned forward in his chair. "The remains had been there for a while."

"When?" Elstad asked. "That's very surprising."

Elstad was hard to read. Hans paused a second and then said, "Yesterday. It seems like someone should have found the body earlier. Villagers told the police you went on several long walks in the forest with an American girl who worked at the farm."

Elstad rubbed his hands on his thighs as if his fingers were cold.

"And a German boy was there too this summer?"

"Yes, Kathryn Cole and Gunter Schmidt. What does this have to do with them? I'm sure they didn't kill anyone. The girl's in Wales now."

"I know it seems like a strange thing to ask," Hans said and leaned forward, "but were you sleeping with the American girl?"

"What?" Elstad asked and shifted in his chair.

"Some of the villagers told the police they thought something was going on. Some kind of romantic attachment. They thought you'd be married soon."

Elstad shrugged. "No. What does this have to do with the death?"

"A body in a village always has something to do with the people in that village. It was your sister-in-law who reported the body."

Elstad's face twitched. "Listen, there's no reason for anyone in the village to kill someone like this. You'll just end up with information that makes no sense if you keep looking."

Hans wondered if this was a warning. Suddenly Elstad started laughing. "But that's your job, isn't it?"

Hans placed the photo of Paulsen's hand on the table between them. "I'm trying to understand why Eric Paulsen would risk losing his hand by setting off a bomb at the bridge. He's a musician, isn't he?"

Elstad shrugged. He wasn't looking at the picture of the severed hand. The brutal image. Instead, he changed the topic.

"I hear you're from here," he said.

"Near here."

"What's someone like you doing in Oslo? You were one of the cops at the protest at *Stortinget*. What was a detective doing herding legitimate demonstrators?"

Hans didn't flinch. Elstad would be very good at interrogating a suspect. He seemed to know how to get under someone's skin. Needling, a little threatening.

"Word gets around here quickly, doesn't it?"

"You know how people are. Always a story to tell." Elstad smiled.

"I'm sure we'll talk again," Hans said, and got up and walked toward the door and let a long breath out. He'd slipped so easily into speaking Sami.

2.

He met Kari Finstad that night for a drink in the hotel lounge. She was staying in the Thon Hotel, too, with her cameraman from the TV station. He wanted to say no when she asked. He'd stopped drinking and didn't want to sit in a bar, but he was curious to find out if Kari had talked to Elstad. She might have noticed something he missed.

The bartender, a thin man in his late thirties or so, just about Hans's age, wiped the grimy wooden bar with a damp cloth, polishing the surface. Kari was sitting there alone, a beer half-finished near her hand. In the summer the place would be packed with fishermen.

The lounge was small. Just a couple of metal tables with a few chairs. The stained linoleum looked like it needed a good scrub.

He sat down next to her.

"Ah, the mysterious detective sent to check up on those nasty troublemakers. I wondered why they held up the plane in Tromso."

Hans laughed. "Yeah, the flight from Oslo was late."

"Draft?" the bartender asked.

"Just coffee."

Kari touched his hand. "You're cold, very cold."

"No, I'm fine. Old frostbite, I think. A long ski trek with my wife."

When they were caught in the hut during the blizzard, Hans thought they might die but he wasn't afraid. It was a kind of Zen thing. The snow piled up against the wooden boards until they couldn't see outside. Just a glow of white. Like being buried in a ship. Astrid was sure they'd make it out alive. "It can't keep snowing forever," she said.

Whoever had stocked the hut knew what he was doing. Cans of sardines and containers of water. Flashlights and matches for the oil lamps. Wood piled in the corner of the tiny hut. On the third day the wind stopped blowing enough so Hans could shovel a path out from the door. Before that, they could barely open the door to pee.

"So there's a wife," she said and smiled.

"She died almost a year ago." He reached for his coffee. His wrist hit the handle of the cup and the coffee spilled onto the sticky wood. The bartender dipped his white towel into the spill and sopped it up. Kari was talking but she sounded far away. Meeting her was a mistake.

For a long time after Astrid's death, he was old. Bent like a question mark. He couldn't shop. Couldn't sit at his desk. But he did. At home, surrounded by the walls of his flat, striped curtains pulled back from long windows. Astrid loved them like that. "Just like Paris," she said. Her work was piled on the polished table until she died. And then someone came and swept it all away. Like their home was a crime scene.

He saw the apartment through a stranger's eyes every time he came home from work. The stained cotton cover on the futon. Matisse's favorite place to sit. Dog drool. Coffee stains. Magical lamps Astrid's mother designed. Sparkling and delicate, tiny globes full of light. A map of his marriage in the jars of shells on the wide windowsills. Feathers in tiny vases Astrid collected. Her favorite pot in the kitchen, heavy and red. Jars of beans and nuts lined up on open shelves. The scratched wooden floors of the living room.

He wasn't there. He was somewhere, anywhere. Her face, her hands disappearing. Her long neck, the way she tilted her head when she laughed. He expected her to be sitting at the table, her pencil running back and forth on the typed pages she was editing.

Those first months he drank. Cheap aquavit in a heavy shot glass. One night he threw the glass against the kitchen wall. He wanted to be covered with splinters of glass, but the glass just bounced. Tipped on its side in a puddle of booze.

A good friend he'd known the whole time he'd been in Oslo wouldn't talk to him anymore. His wife told Hans it was too difficult for them. She'd worked with Astrid at *Klassekampen,* where Astrid was the editor of the sports page. They loved Astrid, too. It was frustrating to listen to Hans going on about how he felt and seeing what a mess he was still after all these months and not thinking about what it was like for them. They had their own pain to deal with.

Kari told him she wanted to interview Ingrid Morland, the next Joni Mitchell, before she became famous. "She sings in a Sami-language band sometimes with Eric Paulsen. She's here now for some concert in Karasjok. Most of the time she lives in Oslo."

"Paulsen wasn't very smart," Hans said. "There's nothing they could do about the dam. Once the minister decides on a project, the government gets behind him. Paulsen must regret what he's done. It's an empty gesture."

The waiter set another cup down in front of Hans.

"Sorry," Hans said. "Long day."

He shook his head, "Not a problem."

"Oh come on, just a couple sticks of dynamite. And an alarm clock. It was just bad luck the bomb exploded too early," Kari said.

"This doesn't happen in Norway. They're not the IRA."

The bartender winked.

She wanted to know about Hans and his family. What was it like growing up in such a wild place? The last wilderness in Europe. Her short blonde hair falling across her forehead as she leaned toward him.

"Not so wild," he said.

Kari was surprised there were some families who still followed the reindeer. "But they use snowmobiles now. I wouldn't have guessed that."

"Yes, we're infinitely adaptable, aren't we?" Hans chuckled. "I'm reading a book by Johan Turi, *Muitalus Sámiid Birra. An Account of the Sami*."

"And why read that?"

"He was my great uncle." Hans touched the top of his coffee cup, checking the rim for chips. A habit he'd gotten into at some point.

"I suppose that's a good enough answer."

Kari waved at the bartender and smiled, pointing to her empty beer glass.

"Paulsen's the descendant of one of the people who killed a shopkeeper and a constable in Kautokeino in 1852. A revolt against the government that Turi writes about in his book. Turi's father saved a priest who was tied up by the protestors. The rebels shot at his father with the constable's rifle but missed."

"So was your ancestor a hero, or a coward?"

"I suppose he could have been a hero. He had enough courage to go against most of his neighbors."

The bartender brought Kari her glass of beer and she took a long sip. "It must be the sea air. I'm so thirsty," she said. "But it sounds like he was a collaborator, a kind of traitor."

"Turi didn't see it that way, but my mother feels the same way about me." Hans laughed. "She said I arrested four of her friends in Oslo, and not one of those women would harm a fly. She wouldn't speak to me for months."

"Oh wow," Kari said and laughed. "So you were a traitor? On the wrong side."

"She thought so."

A man wearing grubby clothes and a stained cap sat next to Kari and leaned close to her. He smelled like stale beer and wet wool.

"I'm a fisherman," he said.

"I can tell," she said. "My father's a fisherman, too."

"And where's he got his boat?"

"Bergen. He doesn't go out anymore."

"You're a sweet girl," he said, "to be so kind to such an old man." He winked and slapped the bar.

The bartender patted the man's hand. "You've had enough, you know, Knut. Time to go home."

Hans was afraid he was drunk enough to start a fight, but the man got up from his stool and shuffled to the door.

"That was clever of you not to rile him," the bartender said, nodding at Kari.

"I volunteer sometimes with my dad at the seamen's shelter in Bergen. I'm used to it."

"Another on the house?" the bartender asked.

Kari shook her head. "I didn't get that interview with Elstad. But you did, I hear," she said and touched Hans lightly on the shoulder.

"Yes, but you know I can't tell you anything. It's an ongoing investigation." Hans finished his coffee and pushed the cup away. Coffee simply wasn't working. The trip had caught up to him.

"I do know about the body in the ravine not far from Alta."

Hans turned to face her. "And I can't talk about that, either." The coffee was like a sleeping potion. Instead of it pumping him up he just wanted to sleep.

Her voice drummed against his ears. "Probably because you don't know anything about it yet. Or at least that's what my source told me. But it sounds like it might be a murder investigation now. Right up your alley."

"You know as much as I do, then," Hans said. The bartender was about to pour more coffee into his cup and Hans shook his head.

THE NEXT MORNING, AS Kari was standing in the lobby with her bags, she told him she had a driver to take her to Karasjok to interview Ingrid Morland. Hans shifted his duffle to his other shoulder and pulled out a stick of gum. He wanted a smoke. His hand was shaking, and everything seemed loud in the lobby. Crowded. Hot.

His boss knew about his emotional problems. He figured she'd sent him north not just because he'd been the officer at the protests in Oslo. But to give him something to think about. A new case near where he grew up, instead of a domestic dispute gone bad or a sour drug deal. She also probably guessed he could ferret out the truth because people would trust him. He spoke Sami, he could look the part. This made him uneasy.

"You're blinded by your affection for the north," Malin had told him before he left. "By the way you feel about your family, but I think it's okay. It lets you see things others would miss. They don't understand the culture."

"Ah," Hans said, "but I don't understand the culture either. Do I?"

"You've just been on a long vacation from your past."

Hans thought about that. This urge to know more about Turi's life suddenly. Something he couldn't imagine almost a year ago when Astrid was alive.

Kari was stuffing a red knitted scarf into her suitcase. "It just gets in the way sometimes," she said and pulled the zipper of her parka up.

Could the musician Ingrid Morland have anything to do with the sabotage at the bridge? It didn't make any sense, but she was close to Paulsen. She'd been around off and on in the summer. Kari had told him many of her songs were political.

Perhaps the other man was not a man at all, but a woman.

He was waiting for his ride to the copter pad. He fished a battered business card from his pocket as the officer pulled up in front of the hotel. Detective Inspector Hans Sorensen printed in the center, and, in very small letters, the address of police headquarters in Oslo. His telephone number was directly under the address.

"Call me anytime you're in Oslo," he said to Kari. The card was part of a masquerade. Since Astrid's death he'd lost track of who he was.

3.

Hans travelled from Alta to Lismavarri in a US-made Huey helicopter with an ex-army pilot. The kind he'd seen in the news from the failed American war in Vietnam. They flew close to the tops of the gnarled trees, the rocky outcrops. A crust of snow on most of the terrain. A white glow as they neared the river. He wanted to climb down into the ravine before the local cops moved the remains.

Four cops from Tana Bru, already at the scene, were waiting for him. He was sure they were annoyed he was involved in the investigation. Two were managing the ropes at the rim, two below to load the body onto the stretcher. They'd been waiting for an hour. Young, laughing even in rotten weather. He helped the two officers unload the stretcher, the body bag, and a pair of skis. His ski boots were in a pack on his back.

His hands slipped down the orange rope as he balanced his legs, pushing off lightly on the wet rock. He was clipped into a harness with a karabiner. The rain sluiced into his mouth, down his face, seeped into his collar. He was more alive than he'd been in a long time. This is what it feels like, he thought. Like sleet rushing through his veins. On the vidda in a gorge rappelling down to the river. Twenty meters or so. A fierce river, clotted with slush, half covered with ice where it fell from the lip of the cliff.

He could see the body by the edge of a pool, bent over the dark rocks. The two officers at the bottom leaned into the heavy mist. One was very tall and bearded, the other shorter with a pinched face. Their webbing harness belts were pulled over their ski clothes.

"Not in uniform?" Hans laughed.

"In this weather? About time," the shorter cop said. "How do you rate a ride in the copter?" He crouched to unzip the body bag.

"Just one way," Hans said. "No room with the body, is there?"

The other two cops on the rim of the ravine sent the stretcher down in a sling. There wasn't much to see. Hardly any trace of what happened, but Hans moved closer to the body and bent to look at the face, the hands, the coat. The face was yellowed, thick like leather. Then the arms and legs, the pieces of the torso pulled apart and worried by buzzards. Only doing their job, getting along, finding dinner.

The coat, the boot, the fingers splayed out.

"The boots are the kind I've seen Russians wearing," one of the cops said.

Hans took a stick and pulled the edge of the dark green coat up. "And the coat Russian, too. The label's in Cyrillic. Looks like he's been dead a month or more, don't you think?" Hans asked.

"At least that long. His head's bashed in. You couldn't survive a fall like this," the shorter cop said.

The tall officer took one picture and then another, wiping the rain away from his eyes. "It'll have to do," he said. "I took a few before it got so bad." He slipped the camera into the large pocket on his jacket and snapped it shut.

They placed the body as carefully as they could into the black bag and zipped it. Hans bent and touched the ground, moved his hands around the rocks. He could almost feel the weight of the bones on the slick surface of sharp stones. It was lightly snowing now, and they strapped the body to the metal stretcher and attached it to the ropes. The two cops, more experienced climbers than Hans, moved along with the stretcher, steadying it over the jagged outcrops as their colleagues above pulled it slowly up the cliff.

Hans was alone in the gorge for a few minutes. He could hear the helicopter taking off. There were so many kinds of death. This was a solitary one. Even the birds had eaten their fill and left the remains. The tufts of dark hair curled around the man's ear. The body so easily dismembered. And it took so much energy to keep the heart churning year after year, only to have your body split apart and decay on the rocks in the ravine.

His first death on the job was a woman. The neighbors reported a smell. The whole street was full of it. A summer day. A rare week of sun. And the body festering for three days in the small apartment not far from where he lived in Oslo. The woman bloated. Her young face blown up and mottled like a balloon. She had no family in Oslo. They lived on an island off the west coast and had no idea she was dead.

That was a long time ago. He was belayed up finally. Snow thick on his hat and gloves.

The shorter cop laughed and said, "You sure you can find your way to the village?"

"I'll just follow your snowmobile tracks," Hans said.

"At least take this headlamp," the cop said. "We'll meet you there."

HANS SKIED FAST BACK to Lismavarri over the winding trail and down the hill. So dark this time of year. There was just an hour or so of light left.

Across the small birch woods, the land sloped down to the river. Tatters of bark. He'd forgotten how beautiful it was in the forest. How fresh the air was on the vidda. The softness of the light.

The snow was perfect. He was flying along. Past bristly willow thickets and clusters of birch. He never had much time off from work to ski, but it was something he should do more often. The rush of flying downhill, curving right and left on the velvet surface of the snow. No thought at all, just the motion of his body.

A buzzard swooped in a wide circle overhead, a swish of wings. Around him the whole arc of the world spread out in luminous white. It was easy to slip across the flat surface of the snow, pounded down by snowmobiles.

HE RENTED A CAR in Tana Bru. A shit box. A Soviet-import Lada that rattled and bounced on the gravel roads. The lab wouldn't find out much about the body. Too long after the death. One hand missing, the other pecked almost to the bone. Difficult to get a set of prints.

There was a good chance, though, someone in the village knew more about the person now in the morgue than they'd told the police. It seemed to make sense the death was connected to the sabotage. Someone knew too much, though it didn't seem likely anyone in Lismavarri would kill a stranger to keep him quiet.

He drove the narrow roads fast. Bent, white birch. Alder forests in shallow hollows here and there filled with snow. The office in Tana Bru put him up in a hotel not far from

Lismavarri, near the place where salmon swim over rapids on their way upriver.

Hans called Olav Elstad and told him he had a few more questions about the case. An informal interview the next day, just to get some things straight. The Alta police had transported Elstad home to Lismavarri like a criminal, but it was only for show. The driver was Elstad's second cousin.

He figured he'd give this part of the investigation two days at most and then leave. He wanted to see his mother and father near Kautokeino, so he was taking advantage of the weekend coming up.

He never slept well when he wasn't in his own bed. Twisted in the duvet stuck around his legs, he was haunted by dreams. Reading Turi's book was infecting his subconscious.

He couldn't quite remember the dream, but he was lost on the vidda in winter. Dark except for the glow of December. Men were looking for him, and his mother told him to be quiet. It was Christmas. Turi jokes about deep winter as the most dangerous time of the year for the stallo, very big monsters. Stallos were half human, half troll. They were known to eat people.

There was a lake in the woods not far from their house where there were no fish and his father told him a stallo boy was buried there. Poisoning the water.

In the morning he shook off the duvet and stumbled out of the uncomfortable bed. He went into the tiny hotel bathroom, and studied his face in the mirror. Drawn, rough with stubble. A bit like his father. He soaped up his face and picked up the plastic razor. He was shaving his neck when he scraped off a patch of skin with the dull blade. He needed to buy a new package. He couldn't remember when he'd last been into the pharmacy. Before, Astrid had always packed his travel kit.

Hans drove to the village to meet Elstad at his house. He turned off the main road and followed the little village road to Elstad's. A Saab and an old Toyota were parked along with two snowmobiles on the side of a shop. He pulled in near them, next to a large red barn. He debated whether to lock the door—a habit from living in Oslo and using one of the fleet cars from the office.

Hans opened the door to the shop and looked inside. It was a post office, along with shelves of groceries and all sorts of tools and fishing gear. Expensive rods and reels, rolls of nets, and waders. He couldn't imagine they'd get that many tourists here to support the stock of expensive gear.

A woman with short dark hair turned toward him. She was putting tubes of tomato paste on a shelf.

"His house is just across the road," she said and pointed.

As he walked toward the house, he could see cows inside the open doors of the barn, packed together. Their breath white in the cold air. All around him the fields stretched out to the riverbank. He turned to see the edge of the snow-covered fields where they dropped off. Above the village road, the forest began. There was so much space and so few people. Everything was still. Odd that the wind had stopped blowing.

The house was small, painted bright green. The kitchen tiny. Just enough space for a table and chairs. There was an old stove, compact, polished. Above the stove were racks for pots. The table was worn, scratches from knives and plates etched into the surface. One window looked out at the white fields stretching north from the farm.

Elstad's parents were in the barn. "They're too old for this, but they won't give up," he said. He poured Hans a cup of coffee and brought out salted salmon. White, dense bread.

"So you're a free man?"

"As free as I can be." Elstad smiled. He pointed to Hans's neck. "I see you've run into a villain."

"Just in my dreams," Hans said.

"Dull razor?"

"Yup."

Hans asked if he lived alone with his parents. Elstad said his brother and wife and two children lived with them now. "They're waiting for the village to give them permission to build up near the forest."

"The police told me your sister-in-law wasn't the one who found the body," Hans said.

"No, Ellen's cousin was marking his reindeer and they were camped close to the river. They found the body. He told her when he got back to the village."

"You didn't see the body?"

"No, as I said, Anders told me he came back from the forest and he and another man had spotted it on their way home. It's not something you see around here."

"So people don't come through there all that much?" he asked.

"There's not any reason unless you're on your way back to the village from the lakes north of here."

"Or you want to eliminate someone who's become inconvenient."

Elstad poured himself some coffee from the pot on the stove, his back to Hans. He turned slowly and took a sip from the cracked blue cup.

"Why is this so important to you?"

"It matters if the two incidents are linked. The fiasco at the dam site and the body in the ravine," Hans said.

"But they might only be linked by the village. By the people in the village and nothing more."

"But that's the point," Hans said. "It's too much of a coincidence." He cut another piece of the bread Elstad said his mother baked. "Weren't you afraid that staging the explosion at the bridge would jeopardize your whole family?"

"I never said I was there. And I haven't been charged with that, have I? You see, almost everyone in the village thinks the dam is a bad idea. More of our land lost, a whole village under water, the salmon runs disrupted."

"But you don't see yourself as a radical?" Hans asked.

"Ah," he said, "Not really. Let me tell you a story." He picked up the loaf of bread and took a big chunk off with his knife.

"A boy who lives in Lismavarri and his father were out fishing on the river, and they caught five salmon, and some Finnish people came and wanted to buy the salmon cheap. So they gave his father liquor, and he was very drunk and he sold them the salmon for nothing. He was so drunk he took his boat out later and sped around and around in a circle. His son was terrified and yelled from the shore to tell his father to stop, but his father wouldn't listen. And he watched his father fall out of the boat. His son ran to get his grandfather, but when they came back to where his father fell in the river, he was gone. Later they found the body washed up on the bank. So, the Finns got their salmon, but the family lost the boy's father."

"So the dam," Hans said, "is like liquor?"

"Perhaps," Elstad said.

"I can see that. A kind of trick. All the same, there's something going on. Isn't there?" he said, looking straight into Elstad's eyes. "You're not telling me the truth."

He could feel the heat moving from his neck to his face. A familiar switch clicked in his head, and he swept his dish away. It fell to the floor and cracked apart. His hands were shaking as he bent to pick up the pieces of the plate.

"You're not telling yourself the truth. You don't know who you are," Elstad said. He took the broken plate from Hans and put it on the counter. He pulled open a tiny drawer near the sink, fumbled through it for a second, and found a small bottle of epoxy. Set it next to the plate on the counter.

"Nothing dangerous is going on. The only person hurt, besides the dead man in the morgue, is Eric."

"I don't think you had anything to do with the crime, even though you put yourself in a bad position bringing Paulsen to the clinic." Hans steadied his hands on the edge of the table. Couldn't let himself fall apart. He had to concentrate on the questions he was asking. Light was coming in through the window now. Diluted, milky.

"And what makes you think I'd be incapable of doing this?"

Hans could hear someone walking below them. The muffled cry of a baby.

"You're too responsible, too smart. You'd know it wouldn't accomplish anything. And you're also loyal to your family. So you're protecting someone. Someone passionate. Someone who makes rash choices. It's not your brother. I've checked that out, but maybe a cousin, or someone else who you care for. A lover?"

"Ah, I'm just an old bachelor. I have no lovers." He laughed. "I told you that before, but you didn't believe me."

"You've got to be a few years younger than I am."

They stood and Elstad covered the salmon, put the bread away in a wooden box.

He handed Hans his coat. “Not a practical coat, is it?”

“It works for Oslo. Sorry about the plate,” Hans said.

“I heard about your wife.”

As Hans put on his woolen coat he said, “I’m going to visit my parents for a couple of days. I hope we’ll have a chance to talk again. Thanks for the breakfast.”

“It’s nothing,” Elstad said and opened the refrigerator. He pulled out a foil package.

“Salmon for your parents.”

“They’ll be very happy.”

They shook hands and Hans walked through the living room, past pots of tiny pink roses blooming on the windowsill, into the brief dawn. The fields glowing red with the sunrise sloped down to the river.

The car door squeaked as Hans opened it and sat down. He closed the door and rested his head on the wheel. Took a deep breath. He was embarrassed about the broken plate. *Shit*; he slapped the wheel. *How did I lose it so quickly*?

Elstad wasn’t such a bad guy. Was he right? Had Hans lost all sense of who he was?

He’d known men like Elstad growing up. Fiercely loyal to their families. Even when their sons drank until they were passed out in front of someone else’s house. The snow piling up on their parkas until a neighbor came out and dragged the kid inside. He supposed his father was like that, wasn’t he? Though sometimes Hans didn’t feel like his father wasted any time defending him. He just figured Hans had made his choices and was strong enough to follow through with them. Even if they weren’t something his father thought mattered.

But maybe he was wrong about Elstad.

The steering wheel was cold against his forehead. He looked up. The sunrise quickly extinguished by the clouds.

There was a light on in the Elstads' house. A small glow in the darkness that had filtered down all around him. He grabbed his notebook off the seat and scribbled a few notes from their conversation.

He closed the small book and fastened his seatbelt and sat for a second.

For months, it was enough to wake up. Get out of bed. Pull the curtains away from the windows. Brush his teeth. He'd eat a piece of bread and an apple and walk slowly through the University gardens and down the hill to headquarters.

Some mornings there were apple blossoms in the gardens. Other mornings the apples were small hard globes. Sometimes he stepped on the rotten bodies of ripe apples, his Adidas slick with their skins. The press of the predictable city. Hills leading off to the forest. The smooth faces of the buildings. Old wooden houses with pointed roofs beyond his flat.

Sometimes he could see kids spilling from Toyen School up the street from his flat. The trees and tight flowers of the Botanical Gardens just outside his window. Fists of purple blooms. Everywhere there were people walking fast for some reason or another, striding with confidence across the cobbled stones of the central squares. In charge of their perfectly ordinary lives. Convinced they were powerful and happy.

Death was easy for the Vikings. You could send your lover away with all sorts of presents. Their favorite food, fragrant, sweet. Their dog, smelling like wet fur, just washed, their horse and grain enough for several days. Their ship to get them to the other world.

He started the car and pulled out of the gravel driveway near the shop. The car shook and rattled, and he turned the heat up as he drove back to the hotel.

Why care about the dam so much you'd lose a hand? Paulsen wasn't a reindeer owner. He was a musician. The government had been taking away people's land for years. It wasn't worth it to disrupt your life for something like this. He had friends who ruined their lives going nuts over things they couldn't control.

He'd had a fight with his brother the last time he saw him. Ugly, loud. They ended up on the floor. Mikael's faced bruised. Hand battered. His girlfriend passed out, asleep on the couch.

"I might be a drunk," his brother said, "but you're a fucking collaborator. In your expensive digs. In your fucking ugly city."

Hans couldn't admit he was guilty of some kind of betrayal, even though his family seemed to be pointing their fingers at him. They loved Astrid, though. Sometimes he was jealous they loved her so much.

Elstad said his cousin Eric saw the sabotage as part of a second rebellion against the government. Paulsen believed he was prodded into a violent act, like his family in Kautokeino generations ago.

4.

HE DROVE TO HIS parents from Lismavarri in his clunker of a rental car. So dark the lights were almost invisible on the road. He could feel the edge of the forest where it sloped down to the pavement. The wind blowing from the vidda, even with the windows tight against the cold. It had been months since he'd seen his parents.

His mother had a hard time dealing with Astrid's death. The urn. The singing. The small gathering at his apartment. "So much sadness," she said. "At such a young age."

A shadow turned into a person as Hans got closer. Hitching, his arm held at an angle, thumb stuck out. Hans was driving fast and almost went past him.

He stopped the car, rattling and slipping on the gravel. He shifted the salmon Elstad had given him to the back seat, but the man opened the back door and pulled his rucksack in beside him. The guy didn't say anything. The smell of grit and cold.

Hans was tired of being pleasant. Professional. He decided not to ask him where he was going if he wasn't talking. The silence was like those first years he was a cop. Hours sitting bored in the car, patrolling. Drinking coffee and then the call. A kind of terror before the adrenaline kicked in and he was at the scene.

The man had the hood of his dark coat pulled up. Black pants and thick shoes.

When Hans got to the road to Kautokeino he stopped the car and said, "I turn here."

The man opened the door and looked at Hans. "You're in trouble," he said. And slammed the door.

"What's it to you?" Hans shouted.

The hitchhiker's face in the dark light was almost a mirror of Hans's face. The person he'd left behind when he moved to Oslo and married Astrid. Isolated, fearful, never quite part of the little town on the river. Wanting to be somewhere else. Do other things.

THAT NIGHT BEFORE HE went to sleep, he opened Turi's book. On the long migrations from the winter camp to the summer camp sometimes the very old couldn't keep up with the reindeer and were left in the wilderness. Turi remembered that years later people would see their bones but no one mourned their deaths. They were like the bones of reindeer.

"I DON'T HAVE A cousin, do I," he asked his mother at breakfast the next day, "who looks a lot like me?"

"Of course not. Don't you think you'd know by now?"

Did he imagine the silent passenger? The rancid sour stink of his parka. The smell of fish on his hands. The man's head bent into the wind as he walked along the side of the gravel road.

His mother poured him more coffee and set out jam and honey on the table. It was lightly snowing outside. He was eager to get skiing, a break from the stress of the last few days.

His mother laughed when he told her about Turi's book. "Oh, why would you want to read that?"

"Yes, it's odd I'm reading it now after all these years," he said. "I've started to like him."

"Turi was just a show-off. Full of big ideas."

"But he did get all the old stories written down."

"Everyone knew about all that, didn't they?" she asked as she put a basket of bread on the table.

"It's a new edition. Nils sent it to me. Lots of people are interested in it."

"Your cousin wasn't happy when you moved to Oslo."

Hans laughed.

"You know, one of the women you arrested in Oslo was Merethe Paulsen. And now her son is far away from her. He blew off his hand all because the government is blind. I knew her son as a child. You probably knew him too, a little boy with golden curls."

He felt a twinge of guilt about arresting the protestors at Stortinget, women who met to drink coffee and knit with his mother, but definitely wouldn't admit it. He'd never hear the end of it.

"I've gone over that with you," he said and laughed. "There was nothing I could do. If I don't follow orders I'm out of a job."

"It doesn't make it any better," she said and left to take care of her sheep.

His parents' house was tucked off by itself in a thicket of birches, the small barn for the sheep off to the side. Not far away you could hear the river rushing through town from the mountains near Alta, through land where his family once followed reindeer.

His father built the house years before Hans was born. He wanted his mother to feel like she was home. They'd met on the train to Narvik. There were so many children in her family. She wanted to do something different. His mother couldn't see herself married to one of the boys she grew up with. One of her brothers ended up working across the border in the mine in Kiruna. Another owned many of her father's reindeer. She went to school to become a teacher, but she wanted to raise sheep, so that's what she did. His father indulged her. When Hans was small, he'd slept out with her near the ewes just about to give birth.

Now his cousin Sara, home from Tromso for a few days, was helping his mother with the sheep. When her father died, Sara was only three. Her mother moved from Sweden to Finnmark to be near Hans's mother. She wanted a new start. "But it was like moving home," his mother said. Sara was almost an adopted sister. He'd taught her to ski when she was about four. He felt closer to her than to any of the other cousins in their family.

Hans opened the door to the ski shed and pulled the string hanging from the light bulb. He liked the smell of wood and ski wax.

He pulled his Åsnes skis from the rack and wiped them down with a rag. His father's old t-shirt. They were 220s, too long for anyone else. He hadn't skied on them for years. He and Astrid hadn't gotten north very often. They'd rented skis when they wanted to ski in the woods above Oslo. The thought of Astrid unbalanced him, but then he got back to work. He clamped the skis onto the bench, poured paint thinner on another rag, and rubbed each ski from tip to tail. The skis were gooey with pine tar and old wax. He breathed in the scent of the mixture. The rhythm of the movement of his arm up and down, up and down each ski calmed him. Muscle memory.

He wasn't sure the can of grundvalla was still okay. His mother and father didn't ski much anymore. It was easier to hop on the snowmobile. But he pried the top off the can and sniffed. It looked fine. This was the part he loved, painting the skis with a small brush and then holding the torch above the wood until the grundvalla bubbled. It was the tricky part. You could set yourself, or the skis, on fire if you weren't careful.

It was probably green wax. Cold with fresh light snow. They'd be skiing up into the forest. He grabbed the small round container, popped the plastic top off, and peeled the green lead foil. He liked to wax the skis from the middle out, and he used the heel of his hand to smooth and soften the wax.

"So you want a track to the waterfall?" his father asked, sticking his head into the shed. He was wearing an absurd-looking Russian bear hat with ear flaps almost down to his shoulders. "I'm checking the willow grouse snares this morning."

"Hey, that's great," Hans said. He unclamped the skis from the vise, put them outside against the shed to cool.

"You know that whole fiddle-faddle at the construction site was nothing. Just a couple of boys and a prank that went wrong. It could have been your brother's friends. And then you'd feel wretched, wouldn't you?" He started to hook a track setter to his snowmobile to set the run.

"The department sees it as part of a bigger problem. It makes the officials uneasy."

"We have no power. They don't have to worry about anything. We're like mosquitoes, nothing more," his father said.

Hans found his mother in the barn. "Can I borrow Sara for an hour or so for some skiing?"

His mother wiped her hands on her pants.

"Yes, take her, we're finished now," she said. "I've got them all fed." His mother put the pail, empty now, down on the wooden floor. Hay was scattered over the smooth boards. "You know he's here about the boys who tried to blow up the bridge?" She nodded at Sara.

Hans shoved his left foot into the ski and heard the pins click. Sara snapped her skis on. She pushed her thick hair under her red cap. "I don't think they'll succeed in building such a big dam. Too expensive and not much support. Anyway, I have too much to worry about besides dams."

"Ah, your clever boyfriend?" his mother said and stroked Sara's cheek.

"No, exams next week. I have to know the names of all the famous paintings in the world. And why they're so famous."

His father finished attaching the track setter to the back of the snowmobile and stuffed a paper bag full of bread into his pocket. He started the machine and took off into the forest. Hans watched him disappear into the trees. The smell of gas thick for a minute and then gone, too.

His life was so cut off from his father's. Sometimes he felt as if they spoke a different language now. And even when they were talking to each other, the words didn't make any sense. He didn't know what he would do if his father died. Would he feel they had some unfinished business? He was a bit envious, maybe even resentful, of his father's love for his brother. His father thought Mikael was a young kid even though he was a grown man. Too old to be angry, unpredictable, violent. But that's what his father loved. That wildness in his brother.

Who could tell anyway what made this kind of love tick? He always came up short in his father's eyes. It was just the way things were.

They had a double ski track as wide as the snowmobile all the way to the waterfall. Sara wanted to ski past a cliff where falcons nested. She was interested in Johan Turi's life, too. "He was a revolutionary," she said. "He wanted to let everybody know how treacherous the government was then."

She scratched her nose and then pulled the straps of her poles over her mittens. "Your father's made a great track for us."

He followed her as she flew along the fresh track. He was poling as fast as he could, sweat dripping into his eyes. She was so much younger than he was. But he was happy in the forest, the taste of snow on his tongue. The metallic smell of the air. Silvery light trickled through the birches.

"Great snow," he shouted. And the rush of his body skimming the surface of the snow erased the sadness he'd been feeling almost constantly for the last several months. Moving smoothly now as he skied along the packed snow, he'd caught up to Sara.

She said she was studying Emilie Demant's paintings. Emilie helped Turi write his book, *Muitalus*, then translated it and edited it. Their patron in Kiruna, a rich mine owner, got it published.

"Emilie was the way he could get the book written," Sara said.

"I've been reading the new edition," Hans said. "He's not as crazy as my mother made me think he was."

"Not crazy at all, I bet," Sara said. "He was angry his family had to move south from Finnmark to a village near Kiruna. Not enough grazing land."

The pieces of orange tape his father used to mark his willow grouse snares fluttered in the branches along the trail.

"Emilie was a wonderful painter," Sara said. "I went to Stockholm to see her paintings. Mama thinks it's stupid I'm going to so much trouble to learn about a Danish woman who made Turi even more famous than he already was. But I feel a kind of inspiration from this woman who cooked and cleaned and encouraged our great uncle as he wrote. She's kind of an honorary ancestor."

"Very cool," he said. "But strange she came so far to cook and clean."

They followed the smooth line through the birchwood and up onto the vidda where the trees disappeared. New snow covered stunted willow bushes, the tracks of willow grouse under the branches. Their repeated indentations in the snow.

"Oh, I don't think she actually cleaned. They lived in a miner's cabin with another family for those weeks. She spent over a year with our family and then she paid Turi back by helping him write the book he always wanted to write. Aunt Inga told me she remembers Emilie."

"Christ, she's ancient," Hans said. They were just about at the waterfall. The river rumbled under the blue cascade of ice. He was warm, wishing he'd remembered he wouldn't need the second sweater.

"Old as wind, yes. But Emilie sent her beautiful letters. I've read them. Aunt Inga's thrilled I'm writing about her. Emilie kept in touch with her for years.

"Aunt Inga said Emilie was once in love with the Danish composer, Carl Nielsen, when she was young. Very young, fourteen or fifteen. They met in the summer in Selde where she grew up."

"Was Emilie making this up?" Sara was so passionate about this woman. She'd always loved stories. It made sense she was studying art history. She was ambitious and seemed inspired by Emilie.

"No, not at all. I've heard from a friend there's a manuscript with some of his letters to Emilie. He was famous in Denmark even then. But Aunt Inga told me everyone thought she'd marry Johan Turi after they spent those weeks together. And then Turi and Emilie fought about money years later for the book they wrote together."

Astrid had loved Carl Nielsen, especially the choral pieces. They were too over the top for him. Too metaphysical. He liked the symphonies better. Playful, unpredictable, but he couldn't listen to them anymore. He imagined Astrid's face lit up, off somewhere else as she listened to the Fourth Symphony. She said it was a current, a kind of life force that Nielsen wanted to compose.

Classical music wasn't his thing. He'd fallen in love with jazz when he first moved to Oslo.

His father had curved the tracks in a wide circle near the waterfall for the journey home. How many times had he repeated this trip out into the forest over the years?

"Look, you can see the nest there." Hans pointed at a narrow ledge high above the frozen pool at the bottom of the cliff. A mess of sticks balancing on the rock. He admired the falcons' choice of a place to make their nest. Remote. Uncompromising.

"They're long gone south, aren't they?" Sara said. They turned to head back through the forest.

"Weeks now."

They skied fast. Silent as they sped down the hill toward the barn. His father had banked the track perfectly and they hardly had to pole at all.

When they were almost back to the house, Sara stopped. The trees opened up and the sunset had painted the low hills beyond the barn pink. Swirls of color wound around the horizon and up into the clouds.

"It's way too beautiful. I'm pretty homesick in Tromso. Aunt Inga said Emilie was homesick, for the rest of her life."

Hans kicked his skis one after the other hard against the track to loosen the snow on the bottoms.

"Emilie was writing a memoir about Carl Nielsen. She told Aunt Inga in one of his letters he wondered if she was as timid as she was in the summer when they met. He thought she couldn't really love him. He still thought that he loved her more than she loved him."

Hans blew on his hands to warm them. Sara's cheeks were red. She wiped her nose with her glove.

"Many years after their romance, she and her husband Gudmund used to play bridge with Carl and his wife when they all lived in Copenhagen."

"What happened?" Hans asked. How could you trade one love for another? How could you play bridge with a man you once loved? Another life. A kind of physical memory but the hands unfamiliar.

"His letters stopped. Maybe he was tired of waiting. She never went to see him, and several years later he met Ann Marie. Emilie met Gudmund. She told Aunt Inga she guessed her life would have been impossibly unhappy if she'd married him. His wife put up with his affairs for the sake of her children."

The light was almost gone. "Ready?" he asked and they started skiing again on the double track.

Sara said, "Emilie's husband sent the letters she'd written to him—Gudmund—while he was away, to Aunt Inga. Emilie had written them one winter not long after the war when he was in America teaching for a semester, and she was in Denmark, too sick to travel."

Their bodies were synchronized as they skied at the same pace. Sara was just a couple of inches shorter than he was.

Breath smoky in the cold. It was comforting to hear the swish of the skis on the perfect snow.

"She was trying to figure out if she still loved Gudmund, after all that had happened during those war years," Sara said.

"Why did Gudmund send the letters to Aunt Inga?"

"I suppose it was like sending them home. Emilie loved the north so much and she and Inga were close to each other. You know, I think the letters would fill in some of the pieces Turi probably leaves out in his book."

Sara had said she was looking for clues to Emilie's paintings in her letters. Maybe the letters about those months with his family might help him understand Eric Paulsen's obsession with the dam in Alta. Why would someone risk everything for land only good for reindeer pasture?

THAT NIGHT, AFTER HE helped his mother with the dishes, he had to get outside. He was fed up with her persistent questions and disapproval. She liked to talk about Astrid, how pretty her brown hair was. How smart she was. How she made him so happy. Did he think he'd ever meet anyone again as nice as Astrid?

He lifted his ratty old parka, patched with black electrical tape, off the peg by the door, pulled it on and walked to the edge of the birchwood. It was absolutely clear. The stars scattered over the sky stretching across the universe. Something he could never understand even if he'd studied physics. The kind of sky he missed in Oslo. Shimmering bursts of light. It smelled like snow and birchwood, the smoke from his parents' chimney.

He lay down on his back in the frozen snow, windblown near the barn. Stretched his arms out. He closed his eyes. The cold seeping up through his jacket. The ghostly birches bent and rattling in the slight wind. It felt good to be this close to the earth's heart.

He opened his eyes again. Turi wrote that when there are many stars there will be snow. He wanted to study the sky until dawn. Tracing the constellations Turi had drawn in his book. *Fávnnadávgi*, Fávtna's Bowl, or the Big Dipper; *Lodderáidaras*, the Trail of the Birds, the Milky Way; the Morning Star, *Guovssu-násti*. Castor and Pollux, *Cuoiggaheaddjt*, the Skiing Hunters.

But he was too practical. His mother would worry. Soon she'd be calling to him. You've got an early flight. Come in and go to bed.

5.

THE NEXT DAY AFTER breakfast Sara handed him the packet of Emilie's letters to Gudmund before Hans drove to the plane at Lakselv. "Here you go. They could be more historical evidence for your case." She chuckled and then patted his arm. "I've finished reading them. Just get them back to my mother at some point. I know you'll be careful."

He held the letters for a minute, not sure if he should take them. After all, they were private. Not anything to do with him, but he was curious about what this woman had to say about his family's life. And he wanted to know about Gudmund. Why send them to Aunt Inga? Cherished letters from Emilie. Gudmund had her voice in those letters.

Hans opened his duffle and slipped the letters into the pocket. He ought to give them back to Sara. He didn't need a detour away from the case he was working on.

BEFORE HE LEFT, HIS mother handed him a photo. "Here, it's one of Uncle Johan."

Outside it was snowing. His father's desk filled with stacks of papers and postcards he collected. His mother's knitting tucked into a basket by the side of the desk, near the chair where she could look out at the birch woods. Bright hanks of yarn rolled into balls. Her spinning wheel took up a good part of the room.

"I found it when I was looking through some pictures from my mother," she said. I'd put them away with some other things she'd given me. You know how things get forgotten. You look a little like him, but you're much taller, I think."

She touched his face gently. "But you have your father's brown eyes."

The photo had a scene of forest and mountains. Turi was gone most of the winter hunting and killing wolves. The photographer set the stage with snow piled in front of a backdrop.

He was wearing his winter skin *peska* and leggings and mitts. The collar of his tunic touched his cheek. One foot rested on a log. His dog looked right at the camera, tied to the pulk in the foreground. Turi's skis were almost hidden in the snow. Large metal wolf traps sat on the edge of the wooden sledge. A wolf skin and a woolen tunic spilled out of the pulk. In front, his iron coffee pot. His face turned to look at the camera. His mustache luxurious and trimmed.

The world was so different then. Colder, more remote. You could get lost for years. No one would find you. You could walk off into the snow and your neighbors would pretend you were dead. Finnmark was the end of the world. The roads still new. Electricity unfamiliar. There was something wonderful about going off into the forest with no attachments. Shedding your whole life, if you wanted.

"I'll tell you a story about Amund Hansen's wife," his father had said one day when Hans was visiting years ago. "Since you like mysteries. Her uncle was a rich reindeer owner and her father a farmer. Her father was dead and her cousins had lost half of the uncle's reindeer.

"She had a lover and her daughter had the same lover. And then she married Hansen and threw the lover out. The lover went off into the forest. It was autumn. Snow covering the paths. The river Lavesjokka was frozen except in one place. And the man walked to that place and then followed his own footsteps back.

"And he was in the forest for a week or more, perhaps even longer. I don't know. When they came to the forest to find him—his brother, the shopkeeper, and the others— they found only footprints going into the cold river. And then the man moved to south Norway near Stavanger, and after fifteen years married a girl seventeen years old."

"So, everyone thought he was dead?" Hans asked.

"Of course. But then they found out he was still alive."

On the way home Hans flew over the turquoise water of the ocean around the Lofoten islands. It looked tropical. He pulled Turi's book from his duffle and opened it to the page where he had stuck the photo.

He turned it over and looked at the tiny handwriting on the back. His eyes were getting so bad, he couldn't read it. Wasn't he too young to be having problems with his eyes? Malin said it was stress. "It does lots of weird things to you."

6.

THE FLIGHT FROM LAKSELV to Oslo had landed at about midnight. He'd slept just a couple of hours once he got into bed. He was walking to the University Gardens, bare in November, on his way to police headquarters. An ordinary Monday. It was still dark. Dawn an hour away. The smell of snow in the air.

He hardly felt it at all when someone came out of the shadows and hit him on the side of the head. So quick. The sidewalk damp against his skin. His neck and the back of his head hurt like hell. His left arm throbbing. So simple to just give up. Let the rush of the city pour down around him.

"He's drunk," someone said. Hans saw feet, the hem of a black coat, a copper-tipped cane. The wheels of a stroller. Rubber boots, polished black shoes.

"A bender?" A man asked. "Maybe he's had a seizure or something."

"Maybe it's his heart," a young voice whispered.

"We called for assistance," a woman with beautiful eyes said. She pressed her face close to his. He could smell her perfume, like cloves. "The ambulance should be here soon. You probably shouldn't move."

"I'm okay. Not dead yet," he said and shifted his weight onto his right hand. Propped himself up. His arm ached. He felt his head, oily blood on his fingers. A rough board beside him. A small crowd was gathered around him. Kids in down parkas shuffled by, carrying their rucksacks on the way to school.

"Here, take this," a man holding an ironed handkerchief said. "Press it against the wound."

Two cops showed up before the ambulance, and Hans pulled out his identification card wedged into his coat pocket. "You'll want to take the weapon as evidence," he said. It was so arbitrary, as if his attacker had picked the piece of wood up a block away.

They laughed. "Not a very clever villain, eh? A brick would have worked better." The older officer patted his shoulder and winked. "Ah Hans, I heard you'd gone north to Alta. Stupid of them to think they could stop such a big dam in Finnmark."

When the medics arrived, the crowd disappeared. "Take care of him," the older cop said. At the hospital, an aide pushed him into the emergency room on a stretcher, past a boy vomiting into a metal basin. The ER was full of patients. An intern in a spattered white coat leaned against his stretcher. The doctor had ordered an X-ray of his head and shoulder.

Hans pulled out his badge and asked her if she could call his supervisor. A toddler was screaming, her mother holding her tightly on her lap.

Sometimes he couldn't feel at all. The IV attached to Astrid's hand pumping one thing or another into her veins. He'd been in and out of hospitals now and then, before she got sick. Work related. It always unsettled him. It had been almost a year since he'd spent those days with Astrid.

A doctor who looked like a kid examined Hans in a tiny cubicle, a gray curtain pulled across the space. The doctor's dark hair was pulled into a ponytail. His lab coat rumpled.

"You seem like you're in pretty good shape," he said, "though you'll be sore for a few days. How old are you?"

"Thirty-eight."

"You've sprained your wrist and have a pretty serious concussion. I will give you a prescription for the pain," he said. He picked up a pad and pulled a pen out of his pocket.

"No, I'll just take a couple of aspirins," Hans said.

"It's not a contest to see how tough you are." The doctor laughed. "It might be a good idea for you to have some company. A friend to check on you during the night."

He couldn't think of anyone who might stop by to make sure he hadn't passed out. His mouth tasted like metal. Everything ached. He'd been so much more likable when he was with Astrid. Someone people wanted to have over for dinner or meet for coffee.

"Don't walk," the doctor said. "Take a cab."

Everything felt off balance as he left the hospital. The revolving door spitting him out onto the sidewalk. Tilting pavement, dull sky. The roar of trucks and cars passing him. Grit under his feet.

He wondered if it was a random attack. Someone had frightened the bastard and he ran off. How could he know Hans was a police officer? Astrid had told him when they first met, with his long dark wool coat and sneakers, he looked more like he was on his way to an ad agency than a cop.

Odd it had happened the first morning he was back in Oslo. It was too much of a coincidence. It had to be someone who knew him. Knew he walked to work every morning. Knew what time. Someone who knew he was looking into the sabotage at the Alta dam site, or the body in the ravine near Lismavarri.

7.

Later that morning, Hans struggled to open the glass door at headquarters. His head was bandaged, and his arm in the sling a nurse had given him. He'd wrenched his elbow. The desk sergeant laughed when she saw him. "Train wreck, huh?"

"You look pitiful. You should go home," Malin said, when he walked into the large open office on the second floor. The lights were on, hanging in frosty globes above the desks. Her long silver hair was pulled up in a twist on her head. He admired Malin Lund more than anyone in Oslo. He liked the way his boss was convinced she knew all the answers. It gave her a kind of polished swagger he thought endearing. She'd worked hard at the police academy to get where she was. Malin could drive other people crazy.

She set the coffee she was sipping down on her clean desk: the picture of Malin in her dress uniform was new, Chief Inspector Lund printed in gold at the bottom of the photo. "I'll send someone to check on you during the night. You shouldn't be alone. They told you that, didn't they, at the hospital?"

"Forget it," he said. "I'll be fine."

"Don't worry. I'll send Lars. He's up all night anyway. Insomnia." She looked over at Lars standing nearby, sorting through his mail. Other officers were typing at their desks or talking on their phones. There was a low buzz in the room. Someone had turned on the fluorescent lights.

"I don't mind being your nurse, big guy." Lars Dokken looked up. "You look awful. Did someone put a herring up your nose?"

"Thanks," Hans said. "But you can come up with something better than herring, can't you?"

Hans knew almost nothing about Lars, except for a few basic facts, even though he was a good colleague. Trustworthy, compassionate. A bit cocky. He played golf sometimes. Now he was dressed in a checkered shirt and pile jacket. His short brown hair brushed straight up. Too young for the lines etched on his forehead.

"We'll see if we can get any prints off the board the perp used, though the wood makes it tricky," Malin said. "A strange way to rob a man. It might be that someone wanted to seriously hurt you. Get you out of the way, and they sent an imbecile. Do you think it has anything to do with the case?"

"I'd like to think it doesn't. It could just be bad luck. It's odd, though, whoever it was didn't steal my wallet once I was down."

There was a good chance the person who had attacked him was someone he knew. Angry that he was a cop. He decided not to tell Malin about this right away. The deception made no sense, except that it might be a friend of his brother's. He didn't want to find out just how much Mikael hated him. Fallout from Hans's years away from Kautokenio. But it didn't make sense someone was getting back at him now.

"Lars will drive you home later. You can finish your report on the sabotage in Finnmark tomorrow. It's interesting the body was discovered quite near the village where the two saboteurs live." She picked up a file from her desk and flipped it open.

"Messy business."

"Your life or the sabotage at the bridge?"

He took the slim file from her hand.

"The Interior Minister's suspicious this bomb is the start of something much bigger," Malin said. "He's afraid it's a sign the Sami nationalist coalition has some power. The body in the forest above Lismavarri's a gift for him."

Hans opened the file. "It's a plausible reason for us to keep looking into the case."

"The minister's concerned there might be more attacks. And the next attack could hurt more people. He was turned off by how bad the protests looked on TV. All those protestors chained together in the cold. Bulldozers parked close to their heads. Hundreds of cops loading them onto trucks."

"I don't think there's a coalition. I think this is it. The protests were sexy, all those exotic tunics and big knives and odd folksongs, but this is just a joke. My father thinks it was a prank." Hans laughed.

He looked out the large windows to the harbor. The water was metallic gray under the cloudy sky. Fishing boats were lined up on the horizon.

"I still think the Ministry's afraid of more of the same," Malin said. "The government wants to take a strong position. I know the energy commission has more projects up their sleeve. They see the land in Finnmark as up for grabs. The commission doesn't want this protest to set a precedent and discourage development. How could anyone have such a violent love for those frozen miles of landscape?"

"You're an Oslo girl." Hans laughed. "You need your luxuries, don't you?"

"Of, course. There's nothing wrong with that," she said and lined up the sharpened pencils on her desk.

"Anything that stands out now for you about the case?"

He pulled a chair close to her and sat down. "Yes, I suppose. Olav Elstad, the suspect in custody, lied to me. He said he wasn't involved with an American girl who worked on their farm last summer. Kathryn Cole."

"Oh?" she asked, arching her dark brows. "In the interview?"

"At the jail. And then I asked him a second time at his house, and he denied it again."

Lars had finished sorting his mail and turned to face them. "And how do you know it's true? From the police report it looks like it was just some village gossip. She was there through an international work program along with a German kid who came later in the summer. Gunter Schmidt. Both in their early twenties."

"Just a hunch," Hans said.

"I suppose it says something about Elstad," Malin said, tapping a pencil against her palm.

"Yes, but it's not clear what," Hans said. "He might want to protect the girl, or it could be there was nothing between them. It doesn't seem like a good idea, getting involved with someone so young who came from so far away."

"I agree," Malin nodded her head. "And what drove Kathryn Cole to spend months in Finnmark working on a farm? Is Elstad lying because he feels guilty somehow, or is he lying because he feels like it's no one's business? Lars, you can dig into Elstad and Paulsen's lives. There must be someone in the village who wants to talk about why the saboteurs decided to do such a useless thing."

"The town I came from was full of gossips," Lars said, "especially my aunt. A windbag with a terrible mouth."

Hans stood and stretched. His shoulder was throbbing. He was worried about Mikael, so bitter that Hans had moved south away from his family. There was an older cousin he never saw who'd moved to Oslo twenty years ago. Was he someone who might hold a grudge against him?

"You haven't even asked about Matisse," Malin said.

"That dog loves you. He probably doesn't miss me at all."

"I don't know about that. How about I drop him off later today. After I'm finished here."

RAIN SPATTERED THE WINDOWS of the car as Lars drove down Toyengata to Hans's flat. He'd been home for less than a day and already the north was receding. Being erased by the pain in his head.

It was still early in the afternoon, but the light was just about gone. The tires hissed on the wet road.

"Want help getting settled?" Lars asked, as he pulled the rusted green Saab carefully into a parking place near the flat.

"I'm not a baby, but thanks," he said, knocking Lars on the arm. "What the hell, come on up and I'll give you the other key, so you can check on me tonight. Make Malin happy."

"Perfecto."

They crossed the street to the apricot-colored building. Four stories, square, stone, like many of the places on the curving street. "Insomnia?" Hans asked as they climbed the stairs to the third floor.

"For about five months now," Lars said. "The stress of having a kid. You can never be ready. Then you worry for the rest of your life, my father tells me. He's not happy I'm a cop."

"My parents are proud but suspicious," Hans said. "They think it's dangerous. Not very lucrative. I suppose they're right."

As they came around the first landing, he thought, now's the time for someone to jump me on the stairs. But there was no one. No one hiding in the winding hallway. No one in the apartment. It was clean and almost empty. A 1960s rehab with a kitchen at one end and the living room across the front of the building. The bedroom and the bathroom tucked in the corner. He'd sold the futon and the big table where Astrid had worked, swept away the jars full of shells. "Here's the key."

"Take care of yourself," Lars said. "I'll check on you at about eleven tonight."

Hans patted him on the shoulder and said, "I'm so glad you're my friend. You've got enough to do." And he was relieved that he could say this. He was not as alone as he'd thought.

"I'll see you later."

HANS MADE A CUP of strong black tea. Sometimes he had to remind himself to do ordinary things. Buy the paper. Put milk in his tea. Lace his shoes. Touch the arm of someone near him. Laugh now and then. A kind of mechanical checklist.

He pulled a bottle of milk from the refrigerator and sniffed it. Couldn't remember the last time he went to the store. He picked up a pad off a stack of books on the floor and placed it on the new wooden table in the kitchen. No marks on the surface. He hadn't touched a pile of crossword puzzles torn out of the Sunday magazine section of the *New York Times* for months. He'd asked a neighbor in the building, a pilot for SAS on the Oslo to New York run, to snag them for him when he was in New York. His neighbor delivered them once a week, slipped under Hans's door.

He sat down and started to write. His hand wasn't working. He could see the words on the page but couldn't grip the pen. Sweat trickled down the sides of his face. Don't panic, he said to himself. Must be something to do with the concussion.

A body in the ravine miles away from Alta. Desiccated. Torn apart. Head bashed in. A bomb at the dam site. The two foreign workers at the farm in Lismavarri, gone now for weeks. No obvious connection to the Alta case. One German boy. One American girl who got herself tangled up with a saboteur. Or so he thought the story went.

The hour in the ravine near Lismavarri had stayed with him. The texture of the rocks on his hands. The smell of the water. Snow on his eyebrows and down his collar. The way the body looked like it had broken apart on the stones. How far away from everything the man had been when he died. He must have been escaping something or someone. It wasn't the kind of place you'd want to end up in. Remote, empty. It was hard to find food unless you knew what you were doing.

Hans had no idea who could have killed him. Eric Paulsen might be the key to that mystery but there was no way to track him down. There were very few murders in Finnmark. One or two outside a bar in a town like Vadso. Knife fights, but nothing like this.

During the protests at *Stortinget* against the dam in the north, he'd gotten calls. Anonymous. Threatening. He hadn't told anyone about them, thought it didn't matter. Someone's cousin or brother must have heard he was there, defending the parliament building. On the wrong side of the dispute. Looking official. Giving orders to his colleagues in their blue uniforms.

"They're idiots," Astrid had said, "*yoiking* in public. Just one more reason to call us stupid Lapps."

"It's a secret code, isn't it? I saw a few people come up and tell them they were Sami."

"Maybe I'm jealous," she said and put her pencil down on the table. She took her glasses off and poked his arm. "You understand what they're singing. I don't."

She couldn't decide whether she was happy or sad she was Sami. Her mother had hidden her past so well when she moved her family south to Oslo. She didn't want the nurses she worked with to know she was Sami. But Astrid liked her aunt and uncle and the little village on the sea north of Bodo where they lived. When her mother finally told her the truth, she visited them and asked if they were Sami. Her aunt laughed and laughed. "Of course. But there are lots of people in the town who would tell you they aren't."

"You're too sympathetic. You want to be tough, but you're not." Astrid told him this years ago when they first met.

After her death, Hans wanted to smash someone's face in. It didn't matter who. The butcher. The desk sergeant. He wanted to beat someone to a pulp until his hand was broken and the guy's face was nothing but soft, pounded flesh.

Malin insisted he go to a support group. "I'll put you on indefinite leave if you don't," she warned him.

She'd found a group for him in the basement of the school near his flat. The room was damp, dark. They sat on metal folding chairs in a circle. He was like an alien. All the other young widows and widowers had kids who drove them nuts. The leader was an efficient woman in a purple suit who married someone four months after her husband's death. It was a slap in the face for the rest of the group.

And he couldn't stand her voice. Thin, whining, doling out advice. He made it through three meetings and then he found the nesting falcons in the Botanical Garden. And that was enough to tamp his anger down.

He pushed the stack of letters from Emilie Demant Hatt, curled at the edges, to the side of the table. He'd unpacked quickly the night before and wasn't sure where to stash them.

The letters were the pieces of a story he wasn't sure he wanted to investigate right now. His hand was unsteady as he picked up one of them, unfolded it, and held it near his eyes.

Kauslunde
January 6, 1949

Dearest one,

I'm happy this morning. Spent all yesterday and today painting the two turf huts where Juona and Anne and their cousins lived during the summer. It's late summer and the fires are lit. Anne's dog is looking very large beside the hut, his ears pricked up. No one is about. We're all sleeping. It's dawn, the brush of daylight coming up in the east. The reindeer are eating the sweet grasses of Norway. Soon they'll start their trek back to Sweden. Two dark water birds are flying north. The little windows in the conical huts reflect the light. The doors are shut. Around the houses the grasses and moss and little flowers are growing burnished. The rising sun lighting the flames from the nearest hut, but the light is pure and silver. I can almost smell the cold fragrant air as I paint. What would my life be like without those years in the north? I think it opened me up to the beauty of the world. I was such a stupid girl, so bound into myself even though I thought I was an artist. And I loved the harsh music of the language. Even now I can hear the conversations as we sewed or took care of the babies or stirred the stew in those battered black pots.

More later, I promise.
Love,
Emilie

Hans laid the letter back on the table and went to the bookcase in the living room. "The harsh music of the language," the Danish painter called the conversations on the vidda.

He turned on the radio and fiddled with the dial until he found the jazz program he liked. Jerry Mulligan was playing. He loved the throaty roar of the baritone sax.

Those months just after Astrid's death he couldn't listen to music. She'd been starting to get into jazz. It had taken her years, but she became obsessed after they saw Chick Corea and Gary Burton play in an Oslo club one summer. She bought *Crystal Silence* and blasted it whenever she needed a lift. The delicate pop of sound and then the staccato chords as Burton played the vibes in a duet with Corea on the piano. At the concert, light reflected off the vibes' metal bars and ricocheted around the stage.

"Wow, magical," she'd said.

He'd been so muddled for months about who he was after her death. She'd given him clues all the time.

"You're too soft, soft as butter. The police in Norway are wimps," Astrid told him. "No guns, no swagger, all politeness."

It had been a circus in Oslo during the hunger strike. A concert. Kids in bright clothes in a tent. Lounging on the ground and refusing to eat. And then the group of mothers. Supporting their sons protesting the dam. People stood in their dark coats around the *lavuu* and watched.

He was just doing his job when he arrested the women at *Stortinget*. Just doing his job investigating the sabotage at the dam site. Feeling nothing about the loss of so much land in Finnmark. Not enough time to care about anything. Except his own loss.

What was it like to walk into the forest to the frozen river and then just simply disappear, like the man his father told him about? How could you find the one spot clear of ice and almost jump, only to retrace your footsteps in the snow and head south. Could you shake off the pain of one life with the trappings of another somewhere else?

(SPRING)

KATHRYN

8.

At first Kathryn thought Lismavarri was ugly. She'd taken a slow bus from a town hours away on the coast and she was tired and her head hurt. The jagged mountains ended abruptly in the water. She rubbed her fingers on the smeared window. Dark birds with narrow wings flew above the rough waves.

Even though it was May, there was still snow on the low hills. Once the bus turned inland, they left the mountains and went past small forests of stunted trees, gnarled, bent toward each other. Everything was gray or white. The low hills with patches of snow. The bare trees. It wasn't what she'd expected when she signed up to work on a farm in Norway for several months. She'd picked the most northern farm she could find. It was beyond the Arctic Circle. Almost at the top of the globe.

When the bus driver pulled into the turnaround on her way to the village that first long day, Olav Elstad was waiting at a bend in the main road. He was leaning against the side of a dark blue Toyota and waved as she stepped off the bus. He looked like he'd been in the middle of doing chores on the farm. His parka was dirty. His boots were covered with dried mud. There was something about him that surprised her. Put her off balance. He wore a blue and white striped ski hat pulled low on his forehead.

He opened the trunk, and she pulled her pack off and wedged it in. Her climbing helmet was strapped to the back. "There are no mountains to climb here." He laughed.

So she'd gotten that wrong. She was sure she'd seen pictures in National Geographic years ago of cliffs in Norway with climbers roped up.

She was almost too tired to talk. "You speak English," she said.

"Of course."

She hadn't spoken to anyone in days and it felt strange to hear her voice again. He pulled his hat off and threw it on the back seat. His hair was light brown, clipped close to his head.

They were silent most of the way to Lismavarri. He pointed out the village on a dirt lane below the main road as they came around the last curve.

"There you can see our house," Olav said, waving his hand at a little house on the edge of a brown field. He drove slowly past wooden houses and empty fields and parked near an old barn. Next to the barn sat a narrow house with a couple of cars parked in the yard. "That's our shop."

She'd traveled through villages with white and yellow wooden houses, and farms perched above the village on steep slopes. In Tromso the houses had windows filled with geraniums pressed against the glass. She sat in cafés sipping hot chocolate as thick as pudding, wondering about her life. The sandwiches were heart-shaped and sweet.

Everywhere she went she pulled her sketch book out of her backpack and drew the peeling houses and the steep pastures and the women talking to one another in the cafés, pushing their hair away from their foreheads.

What did people see when they looked at her? A small woman with a large pack, her brown hair pulled into a thick braid at her neck. Her narrow face polished with cold. The chatter of people was all around her, but she couldn't understand what they were talking about. The clatter of their cups on saucers. The scrape of chairs on wooden floors. There was something electric about the idea of being somewhere completely different. No one was talking about Carter and the Iranians. Or the long lines of cars at the gas pumps. Or the homeless in New York gathered around burning oil drums.

On her way north, a woman on the train to Bodo told her that people were good to each other in the north. The woman was dressed in an expensive suit. She wore a heavy amber necklace and fiddled with the beads as she spoke. But, she said, the Lapps were bad and they drank and killed each other with knives. She told Kathryn people didn't like Americans in the north because of Vietnam.

Lismavarri was built on a bluff above the Tana, a wide shallow river that flowed to the Arctic Ocean. She liked the idea that she could dip her toes into water that rushed north and emptied at the top of the world. The people along the river in the far north still talked about the shopkeeper who gave chocolate to the Germans and the woman who had four lovers one after the other on one afternoon, and now was old and fat.

The Elstads' house was so ordinary. A small green house with a large door and a picture window that looked out on the village road. Olav lived with his father and mother. His brother Jorgen and his wife Ellen lived there too. They had a new baby hidden in her bassinet. Their little girl, Maren, was two years old. Kathryn's room was next to his parents' bedroom. A hot room like a cell with a window as small as her face that looked out on the field near the river. Someone had sent her novels with the covers ripped off. Mysteries with bloody endings she read one after another, curled on the narrow bed. At night Olav's parents snored on the other side of the wall.

Olav's father was barely as tall as she was, bent from his work, and his mother was shorter. She wrapped her curly gray hair up in a striped scarf when she went to the barn. They reminded her of her grandparents. It seemed like they were always arguing. Later, she'd learn it was just the way they talked to each other.

One of Kathryn's first mornings in Lismavarri, Olav and his father got up from the table after their coffee to load the tractor with fertilizer.

She put on her hiking boots and ran outside to help, but Olav said, "Ah, you do not help with this." His father took the weight of the bag on his back and slid it to the ground from the truck and then onto the tractor's wagon. The bag thumped against the wooden slats. His hands were gnarled and bent. His face was grooved with lines.

The wind blew across the low hills, bare birch trees bent from years of wind. There was no sign of spring. This far north it was still winter.

Those first hours she wanted to walk across the low barren hills out of the life on the farm. She thought she'd made a mistake. Loneliness crept up on her, even though most of the time she liked being alone.

When she heard about a job in Norway it seemed like the answer to those months when nothing had turned out the way she thought it would. She wanted to go to the far north. As far away from the life she knew as possible. Finnmark.

A place that sounded like a fairy tale.

Everything Kathryn read seemed to be telling her she needed to simplify her life. Strip it down. If she wanted to be an artist, she needed to see clearly. And then she was afraid she might be crazy. She was so different from everyone in her family.

It seemed like going north as far as she could was the solution to the unease she felt off and on, especially back on the East Coast where everyone her age was married. She was bad at picking the men she thought she loved. She hadn't met anyone she could imagine marrying. She wanted to be swept clean by the wind and have no attachments at all.

9.

That first afternoon, Olav took her out to the forest and showed her the tracks people used to pick berries later in the summer and the place where the reindeer herders corralled the reindeer in the fall. There were glinting ponds and two buzzard nests.

"Look, moose tracks. And the tracks of a hare," he said, leaning down to touch the wet ground. He knew each rock and curve in the landscape, a map of this world tucked in his brain. It was comforting to know he could walk for days in the forest and on the treeless vidda and still know exactly where he was.

Olav's mother and father were worried she ate so little. The second day she ate cloudberries and cream and thought it was the most wonderful thing she'd ever tasted. The berries were sweet but smelled like cinnamon and burst on her tongue, tangy and unlike any other fruit she'd eaten. All day on the second day she was there, it snowed.

Olav had a workout room in the basement near his office. He showed her a discus and a long pole to use with a high jump he'd made near the house.

"Here, you can wear this pair of mother's rubber boots in the barn," he said and handed her the green boots.

Mr. Elstad woke her up each morning to work in the barn, rapping on her door. Sometimes Olav's mother slept late in her little bed, and she was alone with his father.

In the barn they were all silent. Just the rustle of grass as Olav's father forked the fragrant hay down from the loft. His mother attached the milking machines to the cows' slack, hairy udders as they shifted in their stalls.

The smell of the cow manure made Kathryn gag some mornings as she moved the rubber rake like a large spatula and swept the concrete floor clean, pushing the slimy brown clods into the gutters. She worked as quickly as she could, shoveling the manure into the hole in the floor, keeping her feet planted wide so she wouldn't slip in.

In the field near the house were newborn lambs, tiny white animals nuzzling their warm mouths against her hand. The lambs called for their mothers all night. Soon there was no night at all.

She wanted to stop trying to figure out why she carried a kind of persistent sadness around with her. What good was it, except to keep her from getting tied to anyone. In the forest she was close to feeling completely happy. So wilderness could be this place where the wind blew constantly and people followed reindeer. It didn't have to be high mountains, like the ones she'd first fled to in the West.

It was this place where she sat on a rock Olav told her was sacred. Where her heart was wiped clean.

For breakfast, she ate hunks of smoked salmon with silver skin on thick bread. When Maren had breakfast with her, she helped the toddler eat cloudberries in a little bowl. Later, she gave Maren her bath in a large plastic tub and dried her soft hair.

She knew how to milk a cow now, the teat soft and warm in her hand. Olav's mother had showed her how to hook the cows to the milking machines. They were patient cows and chewed hay as the machines worked. As she swept the stalls clean with the rubber rake, the acid sting of the cow manure burned her nose, the slop splashing up on her boots. She smelled like the barn all week until her bath on Saturday.

She pitched the hay quickly from the loft, a rush of dried grass down the hole, warm sweet cow smell coming up. She loved the little calves who licked her hands with their rough tongues. She coaxed them to eat handfuls of hay, and they bit her arms with their lips and licked her shoulder. Sometimes they nipped at her legs.

Olav's father brought out his fishing net from the shed and repaired it on the grass. It was beautiful suddenly, colors like bird feathers, iridescent and soft. She could feel herself slowing down, pushing brooms and rakes, implements with hand-turned wooden parts.

There was the smell of the forest, berries and moss and lichen. Salmon in a bucket. Milk in silver containers, cool clean water butting up against them in the dairy. She could almost feel the shape of an hour.

The days were warming by inches. Pussy willows appeared suddenly.

She was learning how to make the loaves of bread they ate each day. She liked pushing and pulling the dough, soft and alive under her fingers. The pop as she folded and turned the dough. Her hands white, covered with flour. It was quiet in the small kitchen. She could hear her heart beat if she stopped for a minute. Later she'd punch the dough down and let it rise again, yeasty smelling and warm on her fist. The pans old and battered.

Some mornings, she raked the yard near the old house with a tall man Olav told her used to be something once. He'd had a job, lived in another town, but now he was happy to do small things like rake grass on an early spring day. "I was crazy once," he said. "And now I'm not."

"Can you grow vegetables here?" she asked him as she pulled the dead grass off the curved tines of the rake.

"There's a man up the river near the coast who grows them under glass. Carrots, cabbages."

They raked the yard by the woodpile and the second shed, clearing dead grasses and slivers of wood from green shoots. She piled up split wood and chips in the sauna near the stove. Latched the door when she left. As she was raking, she noticed dandelion leaves near the house. One night she made a salad of greens for Olav's mother.

"Achhh," his mother said and made a face and then laughed and laughed, her body rocking back and forth.

At lunch sometimes when they were eating reindeer stew, Olav and his father cracked reindeer bones on the kitchen floor with a hammer and then sucked the marrow out. His father was strong enough to crack some of the bones with his knuckles, but Olav took the hammer and came down hard on the bone. Then there was the deep red marrow exposed. "Delicious," he said. "You should try some, Kathryn." But she didn't.

Her grandmother used to suck the soft bodies of steamed clams out of their shells. She could smell the wet brown paper bag bursting with clams that her grandfather brought from the wharf, and the salt, the butter on the stove. Steamers, her grandmother's favorite, but her grandfather was dead now and her grandmother lived alone.

Once she asked her grandmother, "How did you know you loved Grandpa?"

"Oh, that's easy. I was young, he was handsome. You've seen the pictures. He had a good job. He made quite a bit of money driving trucks. He was good at it. I wanted to get away from my sister. She was married. She didn't have room for me anymore."

She'd been to the town where her grandmother grew up, little square wooden houses and white fences. A leafy street through the center of town. Aunt Colette's children sitting on the steps of her house. Old men at the kitchen table inside. Someone smoking and watching television. Uncle Claude.

In her wedding picture, her grandmother looked like she knew she'd landed a catch. Her head cocked. Her shoes pointed and white. She held a small bouquet.

She was unsmiling.

Now something was happening besides what Kathryn felt all through her sitting on the steps near Olav while pulling on her crusty boots to go to the barn. She wanted to touch his face as he bent to pull his boots over his worn pants. Now the adventure starts, she thought, as she walked from the house to the dairy to scoop the cold milk into the white jug. She wanted to escape the body she knew. Become someone else.

10.

ONE WARM DAY THEY walked up to the forest to meet Olav's uncle and his daughter where they were camped to watch the reindeer and wait for the cows to calve. Olav told her in the past the Sami would spend their time repairing the sledges and tarring the bottoms. There was a danger the cows might lose their calves if they were frightened or the dogs chased them too hard. They were midwives for the cows.

"It's called slipping," Olav said as they sat near his uncle, poking the fire under the coffeepot.

"A kind of birthing for the reindeer. If there are complications, the midwife delivers the calf. Sometimes the cows won't nurse their calves." He held his cup for his uncle to fill.

"But they're so quiet now," Kathryn said, watching the cluster of reindeer pulling at tufts of grass.

"A bit too early for that yet. But in the next few days there should be several new calves. The cows run like they're crazy before they deliver. The calves kicking inside, the cows running from one side to the other. Everyone keeps watch so the cows won't run away to a wild place where they would be alone and in danger. They might run for two or three days and then calve."

The wind was blowing slightly. The narrow leaves of the willow brush moving in the wind. The wet smell of the moss all around her. Almost June. But not like any June she'd known before. The fire under the coffeepot flickering and cracking.

Running for two or three days with a calf kicking inside seemed painful for the cows, but it was better, maybe, than waiting on white sheets in the hospital. She knew it was difficult to be an artist if you wanted to have a child. So many people were working against you if you tried to do something out of the ordinary.

OLAV'S MOTHER GAVE HER orders. "*Vaske*," pointing to the windows in the house, or "*Du, kom hit*," handing her a basket of heavy clothes to hang on the line. Kathryn liked pulling the wet sheets out of the wicker basket and pinning them on the line. The clean smell of the sheet, the snap against her face as the wind blew. When she was younger she hated hanging clothes on the line in her backyard. Maybe because it was something her mother expected her to do.

One afternoon when she was sitting in her bedroom drawing, all the dishes washed, Maren in bed, clothes folded and put away, Olav's mother tapped on the door. It was open and Kathryn looked up and smiled. She was holding an atlas. A big book she cradled in her arms. She sat down next to Kathryn on the narrow bed.

"Where are you from? What's your home?" she asked Kathryn in Norwegian and opened the atlas to America. Kathryn pointed to New Hampshire. "Home." A place so far away from her at that moment it seemed like the end of the earth. She wondered what Olav had told his mother. Why was she interested in this suddenly? It didn't seem like she was thrilled that Kathryn was living on the farm. It was more like she put up with her. Maybe it was just the way she was. Protective of her family.

"Very far away," his mother said, smoothing the duvet. And then she put her hand on Kathryn's arm. She was looking into her eyes as if she knew there was an answer to why Kathryn had come from so far away to work on the farm when she probably had a perfectly good life in her own country.

The only piece of land Kathryn loved was a patch of woods and field. Her house sat on the very edge. At the lip of a cliff. When she was walking in the woods one day, she discovered at least ten of the old pines had been cut and dragged away. She could see where they'd been hitched to the skidder. It wasn't her land. She couldn't do anything about who chopped down trees. She sat on the thick wet moss at the base of the stump of one of the pines and cried for a long time. It wasn't worth it to care so much about something you didn't own, but she couldn't do anything about that either.

Olav pulled his car up beside her as she beat the rugs hanging on the line with a stick. She'd been cleaning with his mother. Dust covered her hands and her face. He laughed and wiped the sweat and grit off her nose and cheeks as she leaned toward him.

"Come, I'll take you up to where we can see the bend in the river." She hopped into the car, gripping the narrow stick in her hand.

Her heart was beating hard as Olav said, "There you can see Ottar in the boat with the schoolmaster's girl. And there's father putting nets out for the salmon." He pointed to a narrow black boat.

Olav maneuvered the car into a small space by the side of the road near a path that climbed a low hill near the river. When they got out of the car the wind was blowing against Kathryn's face. She was close to Olav. He was in his training clothes. Dark blue sweatpants and a tight jacket. He'd been running and she could smell his sweat. They ran up the narrow path to the top of the hill.

"In Finland on the other side of the river is the place where Sami couples would live out their first year together alone—away from their family. Near that big stone, there. You see it? It was halfway between summer camp on the coast and winter in Finland. There were earth huts there."

"Wasn't that hard?"

"No, you see, it was good. They had time to know one another."

Who did anyone know, she thought, as she looked at the wide river flowing north. People lived together for so long and weren't in love. She didn't want to end up like that, drawn into something that ended. Just fizzled out.

"Is Ottar in love with the schoolmaster's girl?"

"Ah, no, she is just one of his lovers."

"Does she know this?"

"Of course, everyone knows about Ottar."

KATHRYN SAT UP IN the loft of the barn, smelling the dry hay, the door open to the river sloping down to the field just plowed. Large black birds croaked as they flew over the barn, headed up to the forest. It was a refuge. The cows in their stalls. The warmth from their breath. She was competent, strong, she could take care of them. She tucked the loose hair around her face behind her ears.

The shop in the old house was not far from the barn. She'd only been there once or twice. There was a post office where she bought stamps. It was like a general store in New Hampshire. Groceries and tools and fishing equipment. Anything you might need for repairing a car or a snowmobile or a small motor. Olav kept track of the books and his brother Jorgen managed the store. Often there were workers at lunch in the little kitchen in the Elstads' house. A fish soup or a reindeer stew cooking in a big pot on the stove.

She was pulled more and more toward Olav. But wasn't he too old? Too different from anyone she'd ever met?

At night sometimes she could hear someone laughing in the barn. Kathryn wondered who was in the loft so late at night. Could it be Olav and some lover she knew nothing about?

"Who's in the barn sometimes late at night?" she'd asked Olav one day as they opened the door to the dairy, and then regretted saying anything.

"No one." He scooped the cold milk up from the bucket, wiping the jug with a cloth he folded and hung on a hook. How much was he hiding from her? Were there other things she couldn't imagine that happened every day on the farm?

Things were gathering, she could feel it. That night she stood on the bank of the river and watched a man poling his narrow black boat through the glittering water. It was almost as bright as noon. He was singing. The sound of his voice carried through the night all over the river like ripples on the surface.

"It's his *yoik*," Olav told her later. "It's like a fingerprint."

"He's singing about his family's history?"

"Almost. It's very personal."

Her parents called and she couldn't remember their voices. They were calling from another planet where she used to live.

11.

The next day they left for the hike they'd planned. She had three days off from her chores. They walked up to the forest from the village along a stream flowing through the moss on the way to the reindeer owner's cabin.

Olav climbed a tree, impossibly slim and rotten, and peered over the top of a bird's nest. "Four tiny ones."

He told her they'd reach a large waterfall on the second day. They passed by Eldor's hut, a small dirt hut with three windows. She pressed her nose against one of the windows and saw benches on the wall, a little rusty stove, wood neatly stacked on the floor. It seemed like the kind of place where she could live for weeks. Alone by the edge of the small lake.

Their supper was roasted meat on a stick over the fire he built carefully near the reindeer owner's cabin. Willow grouse were buzzing and squeaking in the brush. Olav put the teakettle on the smoking birch sticks. The cold wind of the north swirled around them.

"You are like a nun," Olav said in the morning. They were sitting on the cold ground, spongy with moss. Against their backs, the long wooden shed where they'd spent the night. A row of windows looked out toward the hills of the forest and the place where the forest stopped and the low bushes of the Arctic took over. Kathryn had slept curled in her sleeping bag on a bench along the windows. The wind pushing against the glass all night, rattling the panes.

The musty smell of heavy reindeer skins filled the room. Olav had slept on the floor near her. She'd woken once during the night and watched him for a few minutes. He was completely relaxed. She could barely hear his breath.

She thought he was trying to get her to sleep with him, but she wasn't sure. She kept saying no when he asked, laughing. He'd said to her one evening, "You know the girl last summer who came to help on the farm, she was thinking all Norwegian men wanted to go to bed with all girls, but it is only like that in Sweden."

She didn't want to feel stupid if he was teasing her. He'd done nothing to show he felt anything for her. Not anything at all. What would happen if she let herself fall in love with him?

She thought Olav was brilliant. He knew seven languages and was a champion skier. Books covered the walls of his bedroom. She didn't understand what she felt about him. When he came back from the wide, shallow river at night after checking the nets with his father, he smelled like fish.

THE SECOND NIGHT, THEY slept on a ledge above the wide waterfall cascading over a series of rough boulders. It was the wildest place she'd ever been. Still cold in June, but the night was as bright as afternoon.

The falls were glowing with the low sun of midnight. All around her the waterfall thundered. Buzzards nested in the reddish rocks at the ravine. Olav counted four fledglings.

"Did you throw eggs off the cliff too?" she asked him when he told her that boys from the village steal the eggs and bash them below on the rocks.

"Of course," he said.

She couldn't know that a man would fall off the ledge just weeks later. And a detective in a long dark coat would ask Olav question after question. And the body would be unrecognizable except for the clothes.

In the morning, on their route back to the village, they stopped to fish at a pond surrounded by dwarf willows just leafing out. They netted six fish, pink-fleshed and shining as they pulled the char out of the water. It was cold as it splashed on her arms and legs. She'd caught the fifth fish but lost it in a deep pool. Olav spent a long time heaving out slippery rocks from the pool, pushing aside hollow reeds to find it.

"Why'd you spend so much time looking for the fish?" she asked him as he placed the char in his creel. He cut a rectangle of moss and covered the fish.

"Once somebody touches the scales, the fish suffers," he said, and then strapped the creel to his pack.

Olav was looking at her and she could feel it all through her body as she pulled on her pack and tugged the belt tight. She followed close to him, her hands cold. So cold they were stiff.

He said, "All the land is much the same in Finnmark."

She was out of breath. The whole silent forest was spreading out below her. The shimmering top of the globe. The rest of her life was disappearing as the sun made its circle around the sky and never set. Who was she? Someone who was walking on the top of the earth. Someone who was half in love. Someone following a man with secrets.

The narrow leaves of a low bush brushed against her fingers. She touched the ground. "It's warm!"

"From a willow grouse." Olav pointed at the bush. "You can make a tea of that. It's called Finnmark rose."

They jumped over small streams cut into the taiga, flowers just starting to bud on the edge of the spongy moss. Her pack slammed against her back as she landed on the mounds of stiff bushes. She was afraid of what she felt for him. It didn't make any sense to her. They had nothing in common, did they? Her mind wanted one thing. Her body wanted another.

He took her cold hand in his. "Come, we're almost home now."

12.

All the bonfires were burning across the river in Finland. Embers in the light that glowed even at midnight. How could she have known the north would be so charged with light? Kathryn was lit with the constant light. A strange tug as she cleaned the stalls in the barn, or filled the white pitcher with milk, or pulled her boots off at night. She thought she should leave, go away. Travel south. Break this longing.

Already her body was marked by her days in Lismavarri, June in the north, the hours pressed around her like leaves. The bright birches growing near Olav's uncle's house, and the smell of the riverbank. Salmon as big as small children. The gnarled hands of Olav's father, and his mother, her head wrapped in her bright scarf. The rutted track through the mossy forest, little streams cutting through the taiga. Thundering waterfalls on the edge of the vidda. The esker where the fox lived. Cloudberries ripening on their slender stems. The rough tongues of the calves against her hand. Swimming in the ice cold river.

A beautiful woman with long, very dark hair sat in the Elstads' living room nodding her head and smiling. She was talking to Olav, who leaned against the doorway into the kitchen and listened carefully. He was studying her face. Kathryn walked past them. The woman seemed to be explaining something important to Olav.

Olav's sister-in-law Ellen cut a little puff pastry and scooped cream into the middle before she replaced the pointed top of the pastry. Her hands were delicate and small. Her dark hair curled around her face. She was quiet, calm. Gentle with her children. Reserved with Jorgen, her husband.

Kathryn set the good cups out for coffee on the table in the living room and lined up pickles and pieces of salted salmon. Olav's mother watched and muttered something Kathryn didn't understand. She was learning Sami slowly.

The woman ate a cream puff and licked her lips. It was almost ten at night, but Ellen filled the plates with thin slices of salmon and little boiled potatoes and waffles.

"My old lover," Olav told her later. "She and her sister have put up a tent in the field near Uncle's house. She sings with my cousin Eric Paulsen's band."

Were they still lovers, the woman and Olav? Was that who was in the barn laughing at night?

Later, she went to the midsummer night celebration in Lismavarri on the bank of the river where Eric's band was playing. People were dancing and singing. Someone was drumming in the field. She wore the only dress she had with her. Thin cotton. Pink. A woven sash around her waist.

The band played on a wooden platform at the edge of the field, the river like glass below. Tents, white in the glowing light, lined the riverbank. Olav's parents were fast asleep in their narrow bed at home.

Olav talked to the woman. Her name was Ingrid. She was wearing a shimmery blouse, transparent. A long white skirt. Below them the river stretched out, rippled with sun at midnight. Olav moved his lips and clenched his hands.

Kathryn wanted to touch his hands, calloused on the fingers, and bring them to her lips, but she walked across the field, the grass high and wet.

Ingrid left Olav and stepped up on the platform. Eric was strumming his guitar. Plaintive chords rippling into the air. Ingrid began to sing a song that cut in and out of Eric's melody, her face lit by the fire. Her hands moved in an arc around her body. Now she was twirling, her long hair brushing her face as she danced.

"She's singing about the reindeer, the beautiful reindeer. And a wedding and the bride who fell from the sledge in a thick snow-smoke and her husband looking for her," Olav said. His lips close to her ear.

13.

Olav told her the hay wouldn't be ready to cut until August. It was a cold summer. The farmer up the road came by every day, taking his cows to pasture. There was no hay left in his barn. When the hay was all gone from the loft, Olav's father shoveled it out of the silo, smelling moldy and wet.

They let the calves out in the field and the three oldest wandered off into the forest. The little ones were still learning how to walk, unsteady, swinging their heads like pendulums.

A boy arrived one day. He'd traveled from Germany to work for a few weeks on the farm. Tall, laughing. Putting his feet up on the chairs in the kitchen. Gunter was an interruption with his striped t-shirt and ragged jeans.

Kathryn was afraid he'd break the spell somehow of the north. A kind of intoxication she didn't understand. He was a year younger than she and slept in the old house above the shop.

They were drinking coffee from little white cups at the kitchen table. The coffee was bitter and dark, cooked in a chrome pot on the stove. The sun on the edge of the horizon. They'd finished their evening meal hours ago. Delicate waffles pressed into hearts in a machine that Ellen brought with her when she married Jorgen.

Gunter told her he'd hitched the last part of the way from the coast to the village. "I stayed, you know, with the coolest guys. A cook and a pastry chef from Paris. One was thin as he could be and the other very fat. They had wine and rice and I had bread and cheese. We made a feast. It was really awesome. I saw a herd of reindeer near Hammerfest swimming across the harbor, hundreds of animals in the water, very rough. The most amazing thing."

"I met a boy in Hammerfest who wanted to show me the fish factory before I caught the bus to meet Olav." Kathryn fiddled with the shiny spoon sitting near her cup.

"Was it cool?" Gunter asked.

"I was tired and hungry. It was smelly but kind of amazing with women bent over their fish and knives. They were carving the huge fish up. I was afraid the boy wanted me to give him some money. He told me the town was beautiful once with wooden houses and big gardens. The whole town was burned in the war."

"Did he tell you the Germans burned it?"

"Yes, but that was a long time ago, wasn't it?"

"Not that long ago." Gunter scratched his head. His light hair fell into his eyes and he pushed it away from his forehead.

Olav had told her much of the land was burned in the war. On the edge of the village the Germans were going to build a railroad through Finnmark. They'd cut all the trees down in a line above the river.

What was it like to be occupied? One of Olav's uncles was forced to guide German soldiers in the forest and through the mountains. They slaughtered reindeer for food on those long treks.

"You know, my parents don't talk much about the war. I don't know what my grandfather did. The story is that he was just a driver for a general in Norway. That he wasn't involved." Gunter pushed himself up from his chair and picked up the coffeepot on the stove.

"Then he could have been here?" Kathryn asked as he poured coffee into her cup.

"Yeah, I suppose. In Hammerfest, yes."

"When I arrived here I felt so silly walking around the town waiting for the bus," Kathryn said. "I was carrying my climbing helmet strapped to my pack. I must have looked like an idiot."

"You could have climbed near the coast. They taught us wall climbing when I was in the army. It was fun."

"I can't believe you were in the army."

"Two years. Things were easy in the army. I always knew what I had to do, where I had to be, what I was supposed to eat."

"Did they teach you how to kill someone?"

"And what do you think?"

Olav came into the kitchen and sat down next to Gunter, his legs hitting the table. "Such a small table." He laughed.

"I'd like to learn Sami," Kathryn said. "I'm tired of hearing you talk and having no idea what anyone's saying. I'm always afraid you're talking about me."

"Kathryn, Sami is impossible to learn. It's very different from English. You won't be able to learn it in a summer." Olav wiped coffee off the table. Rubbed the surface with his thumb.

She sat on the edge of the wooden chair and leaned forward. "I'm already learning Norwegian."

"Ah, you can barely say anything," Olav said, laughing. "Americans are so bad at languages."

"Why does your mother speak Norwegian with me?" she asked.

Olav leaned forward, touched her wrist. She could feel her pulse throbbing. When she looked at Gunter, he smiled.

Did Gunter think there was something going on between them? Did he see it as more than what it might be?

"She thinks, perhaps, that you can understand it better than Sami. Mother could only speak Norwegian in school. The government sent all the children away when they were seven. Her father was a reindeer herder, but Father's parents kept cows. His family were river Sami and they had cows for two hundred years. The government paid them to build barns along the river. It was a way to coax them into settling down."

He got up from the table and nodded to Gunter. "We'll go now. I'll show you the tractor. I want you both to learn how to drive it."

OLAV'S UNCLE VISITED THEM a few nights later, along with Eric Paulsen, and served them little glasses of brandy made from blueberries. Kathryn liked Olav's uncle. He was much more friendly than Olav's father. Ingrid, the singer, was camping with her sister again in the thicket of birches near his uncle's house, and she followed the two men into the living room. Wasn't it suspicious she was hanging around so much? She was taller than Kathryn and was much more sure of herself.

Gunter perched on the chair in the living room, his long hands cupped around the tiny glass. He was harmless; she liked him quite a bit.

They were talking about a dam the government was building on a river not far from the village where Eric Paulsen grew up.

"No one owns land, or you didn't in the past. Everyone had grazing rights." Eric said. "It will flood a large part of the vidda. We've been fighting it for years. It's about sovereignty, who gets what in the north. It will ruin several families. They won't be able to graze their reindeer. A whole town will disappear under water. They wouldn't do this in the south. It's political."

"I've got kind of a strange history," Gunter said. "One grandfather who drove for a general here, and the other who died in the death camp at Dachau."

"Part of the Catholic protests?"

"Yes."

Gunter had told Kathryn he was haunted by his ancestors. The Nazis burned so much of the land, sent so many people into hiding in the forest in Finnmark. "But my own grandfather, my father's father," he said, "worked to death for his resistance."

"We never thought all Germans were bad, you know, Gunter." Eric held his tiny glass up so Olav's uncle could top it off.

"It's only the old people who might think that. I'll tell you this, the protests at the dam site are like what your grandfather did. We never stood up for much, just paid the taxes, got pushed farther and farther away, some people as far as Sweden. The settlers building their farms and chasing reindeer owners off little fields with sloppy haystacks."

Ingrid said, "I used to think we should just disappear. Not worry about any of this. But that doesn't make sense." Olav watched her as she spoke. He looked away when she turned toward him.

"Perfect." Ingrid smiled as Olav's uncle poured the deep blue liquid into her glass.

Kathryn took her glass, empty now, and carried it into the kitchen.

"I don't like it," Ellen said as she washed the dishes. "All this talk about another demonstration against the dam. It's been one thing after another for years. There were thousands of people at the river, and the police swept them up, arrested Eric and all the rest. It was brutal. Very cold. Eric knows this place well."

"Ah, yes, it almost ruined my marriage," Eric said as he dipped under the door frame and walked into the kitchen.

"Why do you want to go through that again?" Ellen asked as she handed him a worn dishcloth.

"It will be quick. Something like street theater. Not very many people involved."

"Nothing is ever quick."

"I spent almost a year protesting the dam," he said to Kathryn, drying a dish from the rack.

"Nothing worked. For months we lived at the site. It all came to nothing. The courts said the construction could start. I want to rile things up again. I don't want to give up so easily. We've done that so many times. I feel like so much is bound up in that stretch of land. So much already lost."

Ellen said, "Eric was one of the hunger strikers in Oslo last year."

"One of the protestors told our mothers to cry so the police would feel sorry for us. Of course, it didn't work." He chuckled.

"And it was the strangest thing, I saw the brother of Mikael, one of my friends, at the last minute before they dragged us all off. Hans Sorensen, a detective with the Oslo police."

Kathryn took the clean plates from Eric as he dried them and placed them in the cabinet above the stove.

Ellen said, "It's always dangerous to do something like this. Jorgen thinks it's foolish. We can't do anything about it. Even the women's tears couldn't move the Prime Minister. Jorgen is not like Eric." She put her wet hand on his arm. "He likes the modern world. His motorcycles and snowmobiles.

Our house will be very new." She scooped the last cup out of the sudsy water and rinsed it.

"Oh yes, I'm a throwback. A romantic. A balladeer." He winked at Ellen.

"There's always something to do. I will be happy when we can build our house."

"You don't have any privacy," Kathryn said.

"No, not any privacy." Ellen shrugged.

Kathryn knew what it was like to get caught up in something you thought seemed like a good cause. She and three friends had joined more than a thousand protesters at the construction site of the Seabrook Nuclear Power plant. Everyone was yelling, "Stop Nuclear Power." Climbing up the big fence around the site.

When she got back to her house in the woods, she'd felt unbalanced. She'd been arrested and herded into the armory in Manchester. And lived in a completely different world in one room with hundreds of other people with all kinds of workshops and crazy dances. And all the while the press covered this, spotlighting the dangers of nuclear power, which is just what they thought they'd wanted.

After more than a week there, she bailed out; she would have lost her job if she hadn't. She'd missed the leaves coming out that week and the violets blooming just outside her door. Most of the charges against the protesters were dropped. She believed passionately nuclear power was a bad thing and had been arguing with her father about it for months.

This passion against the dam was something else. It was much more personal.

HER ROOM WAS JUST big enough for her bed and a night table and a little cupboard for her clothes. She could hear

Olav's mother and father getting ready for bed in the other room. Someone was in the living room watching TV. Suddenly there was silence and footsteps down the stairs.

She put down the heavy book she'd been reading. She was thinking about Tolstoy. Was it unusual to be reading *Anna Karenina* in a tiny room in the far north? Gunter didn't think so. He seemed to have read all the books she hadn't yet. Were schools that much better in Germany?

She pulled on her sneakers and crept from her room. The floor creaked as she reached the stairs and opened the door to the night.

Someone was in the sauna. Smoke puffed up from the chimney and she could hear laughter. It sounded like Eric and Gunter. She passed the little red building and crossed the field to the riverbank. Below, the Tana was shining. At the bottom of the bank the boats were pulled up on the sand. It would be so easy to climb down the path and wade into the silky water.

14.

THE NEXT MORNING WHEN the wind was blowing hard and there were high puffy clouds scattered on the sky, Olav went away.

"I will be away for two days, perhaps three," he said, as she pulled her boots on to go to the barn.

"Have fun," she said trying not to show him that she was upset, adjusting the boots caked with dried manure.

"It is not for pleasure, but something I must do south of here."

"Oh." She wanted to ask what he was doing but thought he wouldn't like it. It was hard to tell him what she was thinking. Or what she wanted. It was easier to go up to the forest with her sketchbook and spend hours drawing the birch woods leafing out, or tiny insects waking up from the long winter.

She had a whole theory about how people from different cultures see things in completely different ways. An essential split. How they could never actually talk to each other, since they don't have the same words. How she wasn't really out of control as far as he was concerned. She had everything under control, didn't she? She hadn't kissed him yet. They'd hardly touched. She didn't feel anything at all for him.

Olav had given her a children's book and she was practicing Sami with him. *Rieban*, fox. *Gintal*, light.

She stood outside the barn and watched him leave.

He got into his dark blue Toyota and drove south through the village. When he came to his uncle's house he stopped the car. Ingrid appeared, a bag slung over her shoulder. She opened the door and pushed her bag into the back and then hopped in beside Olav. The sound of the tires on the gravel carried all the way to where Kathryn stood in the doorway of the barn. She could see his car as he stopped for a minute and then pulled up on the paved road.

Her stomach was hollow, though she'd eaten cheese and bread for breakfast. The little calves licking her hand in the barn with their rough tongues couldn't calm her.

He must be giving Ingrid a ride to the bus or to the airport. That had to be what he was doing.

Olav's mother yelled to her as she left the barn and started to walk across the road, "Du, hit." She pointed to the four little caravans of the circus moving through the village, painted with animals from a much warmer place. She was laughing. Her whole body bouncing with each laugh.

Kathryn was tired and felt as if she didn't know who she was suddenly, or why she was standing on the tilted edge of the world so far away from everyone she knew. Even her name sounded strange.

It was what she wanted, wasn't it? She could feel her heart beating in the hollow below her neck. What's happening to me, she wondered.

Gunter was splitting wood near the sauna. Pulling his arms up and then bringing the maul down hard on the log, flat on the chopping block. The clean crack of the pieces of the log as they split echoed across the yard. Chips of wood falling on the grass near his feet.

Sometimes things were so strange on the farm. Olav and his father sucking marrow out of reindeer bones they split on the kitchen floor. The spattered light in the barn. The sun that never set, just wound around the horizon, burning under the tiny leaves in the forest. The smell of the silage, sour, wet. The piles of beer bottles outside the sauna on Sunday morning. The way Olav's mother looked at her. The wind some days on the vidda, so cold, so fierce. Strong enough to sweep her off the little tracks she followed.

The second day Olav was missing, Kathryn took out a little flowered pillbox that her mother had filled with everything she might need for the journey.

She'd milked the cows twice, washed dishes, fed Maren. It was warm enough for Maren to splash in her plastic tub on the grass near the house. There was nothing else to do. She sat on the narrow bed in her room. The sun burning against the glass of the window, open to the air. Several valiums nestled in one of the sections of the square box. She plucked them out and put them on the palm of her left hand. She took one and placed it on her tongue, and then another and another, until there were none left.

How many would it take to let her sleep until Olav came back? She thought she couldn't stand another day, even though she'd spent days in the mountains on her own barely a year before. Was it just sleep she wanted or something else?

She wasn't sure why she did this and knew it was a stupid thing to do. Except she hid the fear she had that she wouldn't make it—she wouldn't become anything. Her father had started out with nothing. A widowed mother who lived in a wooden house, the backyard filled with weeds, the porch not safe to walk on.

Friends were always complaining about Kathryn's letters, how she said nothing, she didn't say anything about what she was feeling, she said she'd be there and she wasn't. She said she'd meet them and she didn't. It was a kind of power, she thought, though she hadn't known it at the time. Vanishing and then leaving it up to her friends to figure out where she was and what she was thinking. It was easier to escape, drive across the country, not show up at the art show, skip all the classes she could, stay silent when she wasn't sure people would like what she had to say.

The problem was, they didn't know she cared about anything at all except skiing and drawing. They couldn't know she cared too much, too much about everything. It all stung and sometimes the rush of sorrow was so strong it washed over her like a cold glittering wave.

Sometimes things felt too short to her. Intense moments that disappeared, evaporated. It was different in Lismavarri. The endless days were proof of that. She knew she was looking for something she couldn't explain.

Her heart started beating erratically, thump, thump, thump and then a pause. The land stretched out in all directions into a place she knew was frozen all winter and dark, very dark. Only the glow of the moon or the lights from the houses in the village. You could be crazed with light just like the dark could make you crazy.

15.

THE LIGHT STREAMED ONTO Kathryn's bed from the tiny window. She touched the folds of the rough cotton coverlet. Little nubs of thread on her fingers. The air was warm blowing in through the window. The smell of cut grass. The big black birds were cawing, rustling their wings as they flew past the window.

She was happy she was still alive, her heart settled once more into a normal rhythm in her chest. What a jerk to be so tied to a man who knew nothing about her.

THE THIRD DAY OLAV was gone, Kathryn went with his mother to the circus in Shipagurra. The tent was shaped like an upside-down tulip and filled with women and children. Olav's mother held her hand.

They sat near the top of the bleachers, and she watched the children's faces, scrubbed and bright. It was odd watching the elephants, decorated with bells and ribbons, lifting their heavy legs up one by one.

Olav's mother turned to look at her. She touched Kathryn's gold necklace and gently held the delicate chain near her throat. "*Gull*?" she asked. So many of the Norwegian words were close to English.

"Yes," Kathryn said.

And then she touched Kathryn's earrings, first one ear and then the other.

"*Gull*?"

"Yes."

Kathryn thought about Maren, her small hands, the way Maren sat on her lap as Kathryn fed her sweet cream and berries. Maren liked another necklace Kathryn wore sometimes. Intricate carved beads, red and white with little dangling elephants. Her great aunt Margaret had brought it back from some exotic place. Her aunt was a nurse and traveled.

Kathryn's father said Aunt Margaret was crazy after her father's death, but Kathryn just knew her as a very thin woman with cancer. They drank warm fizzy ginger ale when she visited her aunt in her dark tiny house.

Often, Maren would reach up and pat Kathryn's cheek. "Ah, I know you like the elephants, Maren, but you're too little. You might chew them. I'll send the necklace to you, sweetheart, when you're older."

"*Hvor er min sonn*?" Olav's mother asked her.

"I don't know," Kathryn said. Just then she saw Olav at the edge of the tent. He was looking up at the rows of people clapping. He wasn't smiling. He couldn't see her and he couldn't see his mother. He was wearing a brown corduroy jacket with a patched wrist. His mother had mended it for him.

Who had Olav met? What did he do when he was gone? Were his days spent with Ingrid?

"*Ah, han er der*," Olav's mother said, and pointed to her son leaning against the tent pole.

THAT NIGHT, SHE COULDN'T sleep, so she got up. No one was awake in the little house. Not Ellen or Jorgen or their baby. Not Olav or his parents. Maren slept, too, curled in her crib. The large black birds were sleeping somewhere and even the salmon must be dozing in the river. She began making hot chocolate to help her sleep. She was cold all through her bones.

She poured some milk into a little pan and turned the stove on. She fiddled around in the cupboard as quietly as she could to find the tin of cocoa.

Soon she was sipping very hot liquid in a blue cup and Olav appeared at the door of the tiny kitchen.

"I couldn't sleep," she said.

"Ah yes," he said and held his hand out to her. It took her a few seconds to rise from the chair, but she did and soon she was in his room and things got more complicated once they kissed.

(NOVEMBER)

HANS

16.

GRAY. COLD. OSLO WAS so oppressive after those days in the north. And was it just bad luck that someone hit him with a board the first day he was back?

Hans felt trapped in the apartment. Late afternoon, November light gone by 4:30. The white walls pressing in around him. The large black and white photos on the living room wall behind the couch seemed like they were from another universe. Stripes of rippled water in a summer river.

He was sorry he hadn't taken the doctor up on his offer of a stronger analgesic at the hospital that morning. He still had a dull ache in the back of his head. Had he imagined the face of the hitchhiker near Lismavarri? He didn't believe in ghosts. It must have been the dim light in the car. The days of travel. The photo of the hand on ice at the morgue.

"Relax," Malin said when she arrived at his door at six that night. "We can catch up on the rest of the details of the case tomorrow." She handed him Matisse, wiggling in her arms.

He scooped up the small white dog and patted him, scratched his chin. "You've missed me, haven't you? Admit it," he said to the dog.

"I don't think so. You're right. Matisse is quite happy with me when you're gone. I thought you could use some company, so I left the office a little early to pick him up."

Matisse jumped out of his arms and scrambled around the apartment. He was such an optimistic fellow. He kept thinking Astrid would come back. She was just away on one of her trips. And when he couldn't find her, didn't hear her voice, he thought it was just a very long trip.

HANS SAT AT THE table and picked up the pile of Emilie's letters. Sleet hit the windows as he arranged the letters by date. He knew it was an obsessive thing to do. Matisse jumped up on his lap and barked.

"So you're hungry? Malin didn't feed you enough? I don't have any treats," he said. "It'll have to be kibbles." Matisse jumped to the floor and trotted over to his bowl. The little fellow crunched his food happily and then curled up in a ball on the new orange couch. Astrid wouldn't have liked the color, but it cheered Hans.

The trees in the garden were twisting with wind. For years he'd watched children, bent under their rucksacks, racing up the hill to Toyen School, and then running in the afternoon darkness back down the hill home.

Not long ago a woman he'd met at an outdoor club meeting told him if he spoke to Astrid she'd answer. He could ask her for things. "Like a guardian angel?" Hans had laughed.

The woman said no. "She has powers you don't. She can get things done where she is." They were walking in the forest, and no one had brought water. It was something Hans thought he should do, get involved with a group, but it was a mistake.

Sometimes he thought things were different in the kitchen. A cup in the sink. Crumbs on the counter. Red lentils spilled on a shelf.

The memory of Astrid's laughter kept him awake some nights, longing for her laughter. He felt her everywhere, then didn't feel her at all. He could see her hands or her lips and then not see them.

Hans spread the letters out on the table under the window. The long view into the garden. He'd been comforted by that view the months since Astrid's death. The repetition of trees. The empty garden beds in an orderly pattern along the paths. Even in the dark the silhouettes of the trees spoke to him, though he didn't think of himself as sentimental about landscape. You couldn't be if you grew up in Finnmark.

It was interesting to see how Emilie recorded the small gestures of her life, the memory of those years so long ago with his family before she met Gudmund. Days alone once again after being married to Gudmund for so many years. Their life together on research trips in the north, along with the ordinary habits of their lives before the war disrupted their happiness.

All those things that disappear once someone's gone. The time they ate night after night. The way they liked their coffee. The way they pulled on their boots. The way they washed the dishes or combed their hair or ate their cereal. The way they called to the dog when he'd run too far out in the field where they let him go wild. The way they curled against each other when the sheets were cold. The way they fit perfectly when they made love.

Suddenly the room was spinning, and he felt like he was falling off the chair. He moved to the floor and curled up, his face against the wool rug. He could see Matisse on the orange couch, but the room was still spinning, and he closed his eyes. They'd taken forever to pick out the rug. Must have gone back to the store ten times. But Astrid was like that. The wool was scratchy and flat. Woven blue and white threads. Matisse curled up on his feet. Sleet spattered against the windows.

He didn't know any more what he was doing. Where he was going. He didn't know why he was wasting time reading these blasted letters. Christ, he should be doing anything else. It was crazy to be sucked down into his family again. It had taken years to find a place where family didn't matter. The bitter coffee on the stove. Everyone with their own story about someone he hadn't seen in years. The cousins who thought they were better than he was. Their lassos draped on their shoulders. Their grubby cabins in the forest or up on the vidda.

Matisse scrambled up and started to lick his face gently. Hans gave him a pat and stood slowly. He went into the bathroom and dabbed his face with water. Picked up a towel and dried his hands. "I'm fine," he said to Matisse. "Just a little weak." It had been such a long day.

He leaned his head against the bathroom door for a minute. He'd been knocked around those first few years when he was in uniform, but something like this hadn't happened in a long time. It made him feel old all of a sudden. Out of control. He was uneasy about his conversations with Olav Elstad. He wanted to be impersonal and smart. Not attached to his past.

But that was it, wasn't it? A kind of history with the land. Elstad and Paulsen couldn't give up this attachment. Hans shook his head. It was impractical, a waste of time, this obsession with the past. Did the stranger who died in the ravine threaten that obsession somehow?

He sat back down at the table and unfolded a letter.

Kauslunde
January 14, 1949

Dear One,

You wanted to know what I remember about that year I spent as a nomad. It was probably what I'd been waiting my whole life to do. No thread to the present world, just there—on the top of the globe. Not even an attachment to the language of my past. I was speaking Sami and felt sometimes my other life was a dream.

Hans smoothed the paper. He worried, sometimes, he was thinking more and more in Norwegian. It slipped in and he corrected himself mid-thought and rejected one word for another. It had been years since he'd lived in a place where most people spoke Sami. Had he replaced who he was with someone utterly different?

Matisse settled under the table, gnawing a chew stick he'd found behind the couch.

I've been thinking of the Christmas I spent with Turi's family, all holy glitter, though there was no celebration, just quiet, even for the children. I went out on my skis to the top of the little hill near our tent and everything rang from the stillness. I couldn't breathe for a minute, the whole frozen world arrayed around me, the still point of the globe. I didn't know that not far from where I was, wolves were killing Risten's best reindeer cow, and that Nila would flay the reindeer in the tent, and we would eat her in a stew later as our Christmas dinner, or that the tent would be silent too, the children gone off to a merrier tent for the day. Turi split a good pile of wood to keep the fires burning. The tents were full of frost in such cold and it was hard to see each other. It's not good to make noise near Christmas. The evil one is out. He snatches the sinners.

Turi split a good pile of wood. It was such a simple statement. Emilie had watched Turi splitting wood. There was something very strange about this fact. They were in a world so different from his.

He couldn't remember the last time he made a fire. It must have been when they were skiing and stayed in a cabin before Astrid got sick.

It was a relief: someone else's life. He took a deep breath. Matisse shifted and shook himself.

"A little cramped there?"

The dog leapt up onto the woolen couch and curled into a ball.

He admired how easy it was for Matisse to make himself happy. Hans laughed and kicked the chew stick out from under the table. It was just a nub of rawhide now.

Emilie tried to make Gudmund happy. Her handwriting was small, but legible. Hans could almost hear her speaking. He could see why Turi had been drawn to her on a train to Kiruna when they'd met so long ago.

17.

MATISSE COCKED HIS HEAD and sneezed.

"I'm okay. Take a walk? I promise I won't keel over again."

Matisse barked and trotted over to the door, pulling his leash from the doorknob.

It was just a short walk to Zorba's, a café on Breigata near his flat. It opened early and closed late.

He refolded a few of Emilie's letters and slipped them into his parka pocket.

"INSPECTOR HANS," THE TALL waiter said, as he sat down. Holding his arms wide. "What happened?

"A small accident."

"Doesn't look too small to me," Fausto said. "And why weren't you there to protect your friend?" He wagged his finger at Matisse.

"I bet you were used to a lot worse when you were bike racing."

"Maybe." He pointed to the chalkboard listing specials. "Spanakopita sounds good."

"And a Hansa?"

"No, I don't think so."

"I remember one bad fall, yes, in France. I went right off the edge of a mountain. Bike demolished. I broke a few ribs."

"You see," Hans said laughing. "This is nothing."

"Still," he said. And vanished into the kitchen.

Hans liked sitting in the almost empty café. Candles burned in glass jars on the bar. The owner was a Greek who'd heard he could make more money in Oslo. He came from a tiny island, fought with his family who lived in a stone house, had a couple of goats and a small olive grove. He was happy to give up the sun for a different life.

Hans spent a week on an island once off the coast of Jutland. A very tiny island. Almost untouched. Astrid loved the place. In a stone cottage a friend owned but didn't use very much. It had been early spring. Cold, but the birds had started to come north. Hundreds of Arctic terns and ducks and other birds Astrid recognized. When he went for walks along the little beach black and white ducks on a reef not far from shore made a strange murmuring.

"It's wonderful, isn't it, that hooting, like something from the afterworld," Astrid said. "Makes you feel like you're dead already, but in such a beautiful place. Almost at the beginning of the world."

They found out the ducks were common eiders, but they were magical: the music of their call on the horizon. Some fierce bird, he figured, ate the eggs he found smashed on the paths. Pale green shells, the size of his palm.

Fausto returned with a plate of spanakopita and a glass of water. A knife and fork wrapped in a napkin.

"And something for the little guy," he said, returning to set a bowl of water and a small dog biscuit down next to Matisse.

Hans ate his meal slowly before unfolding a letter from his pocket.

Darling one,

Two babies were born that summer I spent in Norway on the high fells with Turi's family. It's hard thinking of that now. Our little ones disappeared in their graves. I'm surprised I could keep going on after that. But I did, didn't I? Sorrow has a way of disintegrating. I loved watching the mothers care for their new girls. Massaging their heads and ears and nose and chin with reindeer fat. Bathing them so many times those first months. Like breathing life into their tiny bodies to last a whole lifetime. It could be so dangerous out on the fells in the early summer. The chilling rain and the frozen hummocks and little pools.

Aslak told me stories of people out with the herd who froze to death, their clothes brittle with ice. Men were found huddled against glazed rocks in the morning. Sometimes people fell into cracks in the rocks and disappeared, or they broke bones trying to pull the reindeer down from icy crags with their lassos. But we were lucky that summer. We had warm weather and the babies were beautiful and healthy and I was absolutely happy and didn't want to leave. I had found a life where the present was all that mattered.

Love for now—

SARA HAD TOLD HIM about an article in *Politiken* Emilie had written years after she'd lived with their family in 1908. She described the spring migration with everyone in their good clothes and caps, the babies secured to the sides of the draught reindeer, snug in their cradles. Driving the sledges, the deep silence. Frost and snow in July. And even with a mild summer, the rest of the year a battle with weather and terrain, fog, storms, snow and ice, darkness and biting frost. And keeping the herd away from the settlers' haystacks. The distrust of the farms where they stopped sometimes at night. How she became herself so much of a Sami that she felt inferior in relation to the settled, though they only visited poor farmers.

It's not that I'm depressed.

I think it's the weight of the war. All those years. And then the trial. How far away from you I felt. Not wanting to know what I've lost. Not wanting to look in the mirror. The years etched into my face. The curse of my heart. How love comes and goes. The memory of the body and then the body quiet like a pond. How the body comes and goes. I thought about being suspended in light on the Limfjord as a girl this morning. Floating silently on the broad blue water, Hanherred faintly visible like a thin stripe of blue land. Slowly, infinitely slowly, we rowed right past Livo where there was a remnant of the wood from the beginning of time. Nothing had changed in a thousand years. My childhood world sliding slowly from past into the present. The cold rain comes down and I can't feel it. My fire is warm, the lights burning.

When they got back to the apartment they were drenched, smelling of rain. Hans shook out his parka and retrieved the letters from the pocket. He pulled a towel from the rack in the bathroom and rubbed Matisse's fur. "There you are," he said. Matisse barked and hopped up on the couch.

"Good idea," he said as he walked into the kitchen. "But first tea."

He wondered about Turi. Could Hans believe everything he wrote? He dropped a teabag into a large cup they'd bought from a potter who had a showroom down the street and poured the boiling water in.

He sat in the armchair facing the window and picked up Turi's book, and leafed through his drawings. Maps of the stars, a church village with its rough wooden buildings. A boy with a dog racing across the pasture. Who was this man? What did Hans have to do with this great uncle long dead and buried? Turi had never married. His mother thought he'd had a child with some woman, but she wasn't sure.

All this talk about finding your own roots. His parents didn't think like that. They were practical, happy with what they had.

His mother loved her sheep. The soft eyes of the sheep. The way they had their lambs as far away as possible from the gate in the field, hidden behind a rock or in a hollow in the thicket. And his father loved his books, his orderly card catalogues.

It was a kind of betrayal that Turi had written all the secrets down early in the century. Like stealing your soul. Turi wanted to write about everything he knew. He was already a famous wolf hunter. How could Hans learn anything from a man who'd lived so long ago and had nothing to do with the kind of life he lived?

The body remembering. Astrid's fingers cool on his face tracing the long scar on his chin.

"How'd you get that?" she asked, when they first met.

"A fight with a cousin. He was seven and had a big knife. He was eating meat, spearing it with the tip of his knife. I was six. He called me a dirty farmer. I thought he was nuts. I wasn't a farmer." Hans rubbed his chin.

"You wanted to be like him. You were jealous, weren't you, that his family had reindeer?"

"Perhaps." He'd laughed.

Astrid would be amused he was reading Turi's book and getting into all this stuff about his family.

"That's just another Sami story," she'd say. "Didn't you move south to get away from all that?"

Sometimes Hans wondered what a long life with Astrid would have been like. What would happen after years and years? Their love was still new. At times rough. They fought about money and family and friends. But that was nothing, nothing at all. They always ended up laughing at how stupid they'd been.

His mother's face was creased with tiny lines now. Something new. Almost invisible. He couldn't imagine her death. She'd always seemed so energetic.

His life stretched out ahead of him. An empty road. A moonless sky. He went into the kitchen. Threw the last of his tea into the sink. He went to the couch, leaned over and patted Matisse. His rough fur comforting.

Lars found him sleeping in the chair just after eleven. "So you're okay?" Matisse barking.

Matisse hopped around his feet and Lars bent to pet him. "Are you doing your job, little buddy?"

"I'm fine," Hans said, shaking the piece of writing paper in his hand. "A letter from a woman who knew my famous great uncle, Johan Turi."

"Never heard of him."

"You wouldn't have." Hans smiled. "He was a famous wolf hunter in the early 1900s."

He opened Turi's book and pulled out the picture of Turi his mother had given him. Lars bent over the chair to take a closer look.

"Impressive. Learning anything?"

"I'm not sure. Not sure it's anything important."

Lars laughed and set the key on the table.

"Thanks again," Hans said. "Be careful driving back home."

"Sure, Dad," he said and walked to the door. "I'll be back to change your bed pan tomorrow."

Hans laughed and shut the door after him. He listened to Lars's footsteps go down the stairs.

18.

THE RUMBLE AND BANGING of the trash haulers in the alley woke him. Early morning. Tuesday. And then the phone rang. He held it between his shoulder and his ear, and picked up Emilie's letters scattered on the floor near his bed. Placed them on the nightstand.

"You're alright?" Malin asked. "Not feeling dizzy, disoriented."

"No."

"Did I wake you? You sound groggy."

"I've been asleep for too long anyway."

"You're feeling fine?"

"Yeah. Matisse's my bodyguard. He's been checking on me."

"Well, good then. You've eaten?"

"Not yet," Hans said.

"You don't eat enough. I'll bring something to the office for you. Oh, and there's something I wanted to tell you. The lab confirmed the body is male. The hip structure and length of the femur convinced them. You were right, the dead man is probably Russian. The medical examiner sent the x-rays to a local dentist in Tromso. He said the work was Eastern European, probably Soviet. Quite expensive for Russia. But the man is younger than we thought. Early twenties, probably."

"That changes things, doesn't it?" Hans rubbed his eyes. The man with his body torn apart by buzzards transformed into a boy.

"Perhaps. See you soon, then," Malin said. "I'll bring one of those huge croissants you love."

"Great," he said and hung up the phone. He pushed the handset and cradle to the edge of the nightstand and stood. His legs were stiff. His arm ached.

HE AND ASTRID HADN'T talked about her death, though they'd known it was coming. If she saw beautiful leeks for sale in the market in early spring, she bought them. He'd found them weeks later in the back of the refrigerator. Now it was spotless, empty.

"You'll get through this, Hans," Malin had told him one night when they were eating dinner at her house. Her husband was washing glasses in the kitchen, curtains pulled against the cold. A row of tiny candles flickered in the center of the table.

"Just give it time. I had a wretched couple of years after my brother died. He was such an angel. The only one in my family who liked me. But now, here I am, years later. Scars still there, but somewhat healed."

He went into the bathroom. He'd painted it white after Astrid's death. She'd never liked the bright blue walls. They reminded her of a public swimming pool. He'd never gotten around to painting it when she was alive. Matisse started to bark and then trotted into the bathroom. He cocked his head to the side and watched as Hans shook two pills into his hand. Filled a glass with water and then popped them into his mouth.

"Don't worry," he said to Matisse. "I've got your back. We'll go out now and take a walk."

He followed Matisse, pulling on his leash, up the narrow streets at the top of the hill, past the brick church and houses with geraniums pressed against the windows, little yards in the back spilling over with bikes and gardening tools. They rounded the corner near a crumbling warehouse.

"Not too far," he said. They stumbled back down the hill to the apartment. The living room light was glowing in the window. For a second he could imagine Astrid's face turned to the light and then she was gone.

THERE WAS A MESSAGE waiting for him on his desk at headquarters. Kari Finstad, the reporter from Bergen, had asked him to meet her for coffee late morning. She was in Oslo for two days. Around eleven at a café on the corner of Rosenkrantz gate near the royal palace.

Hans thought of Kari, uncomfortable. He knew almost nothing about her. She lived in Bergen. He'd never watched her show.

"You look better," Malin said. They sat at the long table by the windows looking out at the harbor and the two square towers of the town hall. The ferry was returning across the fjord. She handed him a paper bag, the tip of a croissant poking out.

He'd almost bought one of the houses on the peninsula, but it was too expensive. They were filled with families who paraded in the street on Constitution Day in their pressed suits and silk dresses, the women decked out like princesses with silver and embroidery. Later, he'd see them on the tram carrying bottles of champagne in fancy bags and cakes balanced on their laps.

Lars pulled a chair out and sat down next to Hans.

"I don't know," he said, peering into Hans's eyes, "still a little dopey." He laughed. "Hans was reading some dead chick's letters till all hours."

The thin paper in his hands. The echo of the phrases that came back to him as he'd walked to headquarters across the empty Botanical Gardens, twigs of the trees encased in ice. *Sorrow has a way of disintegrating*, Emilie wrote. The days of the trial. The trial for traitors. Gudmund might have been a traitor during the occupation.

Malin tapped Lars's shoulder. "Not like you at all, Lars. Remember your junior status. You're not an inspector. Are you?" She stood up from the table and then pulled the murder board closer. Adjusted the two pictures of the body pinned to the cork.

"Whose letters?"

"A friend of my family's. A Danish artist. And yes, dead for almost thirty years."

"That's strange, isn't it?"

"What's not strange?" Hans asked. "We're trying to figure out how a Russian kid ended up dead in a gorge above a tiny village in Finnmark."

"I just think it's interesting," Malin said. "All of a sudden you're sentimental about your family. I could care less about any of my relatives. Most of them are drunks with crummy little houses off in the forest."

"Emilie Demant Hatt loved the north. After talking to Olav Elstad it seems close to what he and Eric Paulsen feel about the destruction of the land surrounding Alta."

"But she was an outsider?"

"I don't think my family saw her like that. But their affection for her is a bit hard to understand. Though they respected her."

"Any new thoughts about the case?" Malin asked.

"Not yet," he said, and pulled his chair back, scraping the floor. He stepped next to Malin at the board. "The threads connect." He touched a string pinned from the pictures of Paulsen and Elstad to a map of the village.

They looked like they could be brothers. He supposed that wasn't surprising. Paulsen's face was more open, though. He was almost smiling. Elstad was looking away from the photographer.

"But the motive is missing," he said. "Why would one of these men kill someone in the forest? We don't think there was any money involved. No one in the village admits knowing the deceased. The village gossip about Elstad and the American girl doesn't add up to something that sounds like a great passion. Paulsen, the saboteur, is happily married. He has a daughter he loves, everyone told the officers investigating the case."

"But what if it was the stranger who was involved with the American girl," Lars said. "And Elstad killed him."

"I don't see that happening," Hans said.

"You did say, though, Hans, there's something fishy about him. Something hidden," Malin said.

"The depth of his involvement with Kathryn Cole. I think there's more to it than he'll admit. But the villagers talk. They would have told the police about another man. Someone else she was seeing. It would be difficult to miss. Everything's out in the open."

"I agree with Hans," Lars said, draining his cup of coffee. "Elstad seems to be hiding something. Very cagey. He got off pretty easy, didn't he, if he was part of the bomb plot. It was just lucky there were no witnesses. And who tries to pull off such a dumb stunt?"

"I came to like him, by the time I'd spent some time with him, but you're right, I don't trust him. Not at all," Hans said.

He wanted to believe most people were just trying to make it through their lives without hurting anyone. But many of them ended up lying for one reason or another. Often to protect the people they loved, or save face, or pull one over on you to prove they were powerful. Hans didn't have that sense about Olav Elstad. It could be the whole thing was a game to him. And Elstad wasn't ready to put all his cards on the table yet.

It was warm in the office, and he pulled off the sweater he was wearing. Old, starting to pill on the arms. Astrid would've given it away.

"Lars solved the problem of the missing saboteur. Witnesses said that it could be they were seeing two people instead of three. The color of one of the coats could be blue or black according to who was describing the scene. It could have been Olav Elstad running away or running to get help," Malin said.

Hans looked out at the street, wet with rain. In the forest near his parents' house snow would be piling up near the ski shed. The body of the boy unclaimed in the morgue in Alta.

"I'd like to drop this investigation, you know, but the Minister of the Interior sent word through the Commissioner that we're to keep looking for any connections between the death in Lismavarri and Paulsen. It seems like it should be a local thing," Malin said and grimaced.

"But the Minister wants to remain in control of anything that might be linked to the series of protests about the dam. I think he wants to paint the saboteurs as more dangerous than they seem. And I think it's best, since you feel okay, Hans, to keep you on this one. I'll use Lars on a handful of incidents we have in the air here. A murder in one of those expensive houses near the Folkemuseum."

"Bizarre case, something with costumes and spears," Lars said. "Not something you'd like."

"I've lusted over that house, all glass and views of the water," Malin said. "But not now. I'm happy in my charming mess of a house."

"You live in a paradise compared to our hovel," Lars said.

For a second or two it seemed quiet in the office. And then the rain started again, battering the window. The wind picked up and whistled against the building.

"So now we know that this person is Russian," Lars said, and flicked one of the photos of the remains in the gorge in Lismavarri. "That the fall probably didn't kill him. The medical examiner said there was a compression in his forehead consistent with someone slightly taller hitting him with a wooden tool. Something like a mallet. He found wooden splinters around the fracture."

"It puts a whole new spin on the case, doesn't it? Young, male, Russian. The kind of international spin the Minister hates," Malin said. "By the way, the lab also found a very thin gold necklace in his jacket pocket. Broken. They're sending photos. They should be here in three days."

"That's odd. Nothing but the necklace?" Hans said.

"No, there were. Three keys on a ring and a pocketknife. A Swiss chocolate bar wrapper. We'll have to wait until we can examine the photographs to get more details."

"I think you should interview Gunter Schmidt," she said and touched Hans's arm, "the other young person working on the farm. You won't be able to talk to Kathryn Cole for a week or so. She'll be in Wales then where we have a contact number for her, thanks to her parents."

He'd been to Wales once. Fallen in love with a woman he met on a train. They'd spent days walking through woods blooming with bluebells, crushed the petals under their feet. It was wet and spring and he followed her past muddy patches. Cow tracks slick with rain. Furtive cows were all waiting at the fence.

He'd never been in love like that before. It turned out she had a lot of baggage. An ex-husband and two kids. She wanted him to move to the West Indies. She worked for the government there. He was tempted. An adventure that might split his life open. But he went back to his job in Oslo and then he met Astrid.

"I think it might also be a good idea to talk to Ingrid Morland, the musician," Hans said. "She's close to Eric Paulsen."

"My sister's mad about her music. I don't see the attraction. Sounds like a lot of yelping to me. I like something a bit more soothing." Malin sat down and tapped her hand on the table.

"Let's start with Gunter Schmidt, the German kid who worked on the Elstads' farm, and then see if Lars can track down Ingrid Morland."

"I'll give Gunter Schmidt a call right now," Hans said. "I'd like to hear what he has to say. He'll have a different perspective on our suspects."

Malin walked over to her desk and shuffled some papers. She pulled out a card with a number on it. "Use the small interview room. It's noisy here right now. Difficult to hear, if the connection isn't so great."

Gunter was staying with his parents until he returned to Karlsruhe University in January. Hans moved the phone in the interview room closer to the window. He took out a small pad from his jacket pocket and placed it near the phone. He fiddled with a pencil someone had left on the desk.

"Hans Sorensen from the Oslo police," he said, when Gunter's father answered.

"You speak German."

"I was pretty good in languages in school. Pick them up quickly. I'll get to the point. I'm investigating a body reindeer herders found in the ravine near Lismavarri after Gunter left Norway. I'd like to ask him a few questions about that."

"Of course," his father said. His voice was neutral. No indication that he knew anything about this.

"He's just back now from the vineyard. Picking grapes for ice wine. A wonderful time of year here."

He could hear Gunter's father calling him and then the shuffle of the phone from one hand to another.

"Gunter?"

"Yes?"

"Hans Sorensen, Oslo police. Thanks for talking with me. I just wanted to ask you some questions about the time you spent in Lismavarri. Did you see anything at all that you can think of that was suspicious in the forest?"

Gunter took a while to answer. Hans picked up his pen. Put it down. Moved the notepad closer.

"I'm not sure how to answer you."

"Did you hear anything about a body in the ravine near the village?"

Gunter's father coughed. A dog barked. Finally Gunter said, "Yes. We saw the body. We were walking home from the vidda."

Hans wrote this new information down on his pad and underlined it. Everyone he'd spoken to in the village said no one had seen anything in the forest.

"Did you recognize the person?"

"Of course not," Gunter said, clearing his throat. Hans heard Gunter's father again in the background. The clatter of dishes.

"And you didn't feel any guilt about leaving someone in the forest?"

"It wasn't my choice," he said. "It was pretty gruesome. Wolves or something had gotten to the body. It was too steep to climb down the rocks and check it out."

"Who were you with?" Hans asked.

"But Olav must have filled you in?" Hans could sense him testing the waters, unsure how much to say.

"No." Hans waited a second and added, "It's too late now—no evidence to tie you to the crime." He wasn't sure he could trust what Gunter told him.

"Crime? We thought it was an accident. I was with Kathryn, the girl from America, and my friend Eric."

"When was this?"

"Late summer, just before I met my father in France. The first week of September. Eric was planning a protest at the big dam site in Alta and didn't want to tell the police about the body and have them nosing around in the village. He wanted the sabotage to be something the government would pay attention to. People talked about blowing things up. Why not give them something big? Use something the government would understand. His father trained with English commandos in the war. He knows how to make simple bombs from all kinds of stuff."

Hans shifted the phone to his other ear. He was scribbling on the pad.

"Are you sure you didn't recognize the body?"

"Why would I? I told you it was at the bottom of a steep cliff."

"Just trying to figure out why someone would end up deep in the ravine, so far from everything else. A body of a person no one seems to know. Was there anything that happened while you were in the north that could be connected to the body you saw?"

"No. Nothing weird happened. It was awesome. I was happier than I've been for a long time. Everything was so cool. We were outside working every day. It was the freaking Arctic."

"How did Eric and Kathryn react to finding the body? Was there anything strange about that?" Hans asked.

Gunter was silent for a few seconds. "No, I don't think so," he said. "We were all upset."

It was a long shot, but Hans had hoped he'd blurt out some detail that would lead them in the right direction.

"Is there anything else that you think might be interesting for me to know?"

"Maybe," Gunter said. "One day I took a short walk up to the forest. On the way I saw Olav's brother Jorgen pacing out the plot for his house, like Olav did with some experimental cloudberry fields. Jorgen was hammering pine stakes into the ground and using string to mark the boundaries of his house."

"Why was that out of the ordinary?" Hans kept his voice level.

"He's so driven. So determined to be important. It seemed far-out that he was doing that in the middle of the day when he could have been working."

"What kind of tools did he have with him?" Hans took a deep breath.

"Oh, I don't know—a mallet maybe to pound the stakes in."

"Was this before you saw the body or after?" Hans asked.

"Before," he said.

"It would have made things less complicated later, if you had told your story two months ago and let the police know there was a body in the ravine."

"I couldn't know that, could I? And it wasn't up to me." Gunter said. He sounded angry.

He wondered if Gunter knew about what had happened at the dam site. "Did you know Eric lost his right hand when he sabotaged the bridge in Alta?"

"His hand?"

"Yes," Hans said. "His hand."

"But where is he? In jail?"

"No, his friends got him out of the country."

Gunter was silent and then said, "That's shit. It's horrible. It wasn't supposed to be dangerous. He was all fired up about the government. How they just took and took and took and didn't care if they wiped the Sami off the map."

"One more thing," Hans said. "Did you see anyone wearing a gold necklace while you were in Lismavarri? A very thin gold chain."

Gunter was silent for a long enough time that his father said in the background, "All done?"

"No, I didn't see anything like that."

"I'll be in touch. You've been a great help," Hans said. How many times had he told someone just that and never contacted them again.

Not many people told the truth about their lives. It was a kind of compromise to hold everything together. The ordinary daily routine and then underneath a whole other story.

"Something interesting came up with the German kid," he said to Malin.

She looked up from her desk.

"We might have our mallet."

"Oh?"

"Olav's brother Jorgen was using a mallet at some time in the summer to pound stakes in on the edge of the forest around the plot for his new house."

"Pretty far-fetched that he'd clobber a kid with something like that. Let the cops in Tana Bru check it out. Ask them to talk to him. Get a warrant to take a look at the tool shed at the farm."

"Will do," he said. "The other thing is he's definitely lying about the necklace. I think it's Kathryn's."

19.

WHEN HE REACHED THE entrance to the café on Rosenkrantz gate he saw Kari Finstad running across the wide street toward him. She was carrying a large canvas bag. She looked smaller than he remembered from less than a week before, when they'd talked. The light was as bright as it would get all day. The glow that burns out quickly around four.

The café was near the park at *Stortinget*. The parliament building was so small. A round façade with the long drive curving up to the door. A succession of gardens with their pollarded trees leading to the palace. The place where Eric Paulsen and the others protested against the Alta dam. So different from the low hills of Finnmark.

"Sorry," she said. "I was feeding cats."

"It's fine," Hans said. "I just got here."

Her jeans were spattered with mud. He plucked a leaf out of her hair and opened the door.

"We had to squeeze into narrow places under porches and behind trash cans. Sometimes the cats aren't so sure about us." She sneezed as they sat down at one of the marble topped tables. "I love cats, but I'm allergic to them."

She brushed her damp hair out of her eyes. "I know I'm a mess," she said and frowned. She had to know she was attractive. All those hours in front of a camera. Her short blonde hair framed her face.

"Feral cats?"

"Yes, a friend got me into it. I know the woman who organizes the group here, so I always give her a call when I'm in Oslo. You don't seem like you'd be a cat person."

"I'm not."

"You have a dog, then?"

"A very small dog."

"That's surprising, isn't it?"

Hans laughed. "I live in a small place."

She said, "I thought you might like to know I was in Oslo. What happened to you?" She pointed to the patch of shaved hair on his head.

"Not a big deal. A knock on the head yesterday."

"That's awful. Did you catch the perpetrator?"

"Not yet," he said.

"Anything to do with the fiasco at the dam?"

"Probably not."

A man in a ski jacket with a fur collar brushed against Hans's arm as he walked across the room to the door. Hans pulled his chair in. The waitress came and took their order. She put her pad back into her pocket and cleared the table next to them.

Kari's face so close. He could see the down on her cheeks. Flecks of gold.

"Somehow I can only imagine you in a wilder place," Hans said, and she shook her head.

"I spend too much time in cities."

"Did you talk to Ingrid Moreland in Karasjok?"

"Yeah. She was friendly but didn't want to talk about the dam sabotage. I did get some juicy personal stuff. She's singing in a club not far from here. The place was packed. It seems there's a fashion now for ethnic music."

"You're hoping she'll appear on your show?"

"Yes, and no. My producer told me we don't have enough in the budget to pay her to sing, but maybe I can coax her to come and talk. Good publicity for her new album. Human interest too. Her connection to Eric Paulsen. They've known each other since they were kids."

"What kind of person do you think she is?"

"Not cruel, but distant. I don't think any man will get far with her. Olav Elstad was in love with her, she told me, but she couldn't imagine living her life with him in that little town on the river. And that's what he wanted. But most of all he wanted a child."

"So I'm another source," he said and rubbed his neck. It was steamy in the café. "Of course," she said.

"Still no idea who the third man was? Or anything about the mysterious body found in the ravine?"

"We're following some leads, but you know I can't comment."

"You can give me a few crumbs, can't you? Something like a fight in the forest. A blood bath in the sauna. A young girl from America caught up in an escapade in the far north."

Hans laughed.

The waitress delivered their coffee and put a little jug of cream on the table.

Too many disappearances. Kari touched his fingers lightly. "You're troubled about all this."

"Yes."

"You're too invested in it."

"Probably."

Cars curved fast around the side of the café and children crossed the street holding hands. Their teacher walked backwards as he pointed and shouted to the kids. They were in uniforms, blue and white.

"I'm reading some letters my cousin gave me. Do you know anything about Gudmund Hatt? A Danish geographer."

"Out of your field, isn't it?" Kari asked.

"A bit. There was a trial in Denmark after the occupation."

"I have relatives in Denmark," Kari said. "My uncle and his family. He's a communist. He told me a story the last time I saw him, a couple of years ago, about a new bike he'd bought in April 1940. He wanted to celebrate the bike with a picnic. He was getting things together, sausage, bread, cheese, apples to make a picnic basket. His wife had the radio on, and she was laughing at him as he gathered all the food. He stopped when the announcer said the Germans had invaded Denmark.

"My uncle was one of the communist officials in Allborg and had drawers of compromising documents in his office, so he rushed to the office and destroyed as many as he could. And then he returned to his house to collect his wife.

"There were two police officers going through my uncle's desk at his house. They were pulling books out of the bookcases for evidence. They told my aunt, 'We're taking these books and we'll take him too. There's no cause for alarm. Just routine.' He said almost four years passed before he came home. They didn't have any evidence against him. He wasn't a saboteur. He hadn't printed any incriminating newsletters. They took him to work camp, Horserade, in Zealand. He said it was fairly tolerable, but it had been hard on my aunt."

Hans was trying to concentrate on what she was saying. He wanted to be more involved in other people's lives. An ordinary person who ate breakfast every morning and made his bed, fed the dog, went to work without thinking every minute about Astrid's death.

"I asked him if he was angry at the cops who hauled him away. No, he said, it was all part of the way the government did things then. Not to rile the Germans. To stay under the radar, so they could keep on living their lives. It wasn't so simple, though."

"It seems like Gudmund Hatt got himself in the middle of the same kind of problem. He didn't get his hands as dirty as the Danish police, but still, it doesn't look good. He might have been an unwitting collaborator," Hans said.

"How did your cousin get the letters?"

"He'd sent them to our great aunt. His wife Emilie wrote the letters to him. She'd lived with my family before she married him. She was a painter and ethnographer and needed a tutor. They met at the University of Copenhagen. A friend introduced them. He was much younger, but they fell in love after a conversation about the Arctic."

"It sounds romantic, but how curious. She was studying your family?"

Hans laughed and moved his empty cup away. "It was something she always wanted to do. Live with a Sami family."

"She was naïve?"

"I don't think so. She wanted to immerse herself in a different kind of life. She was passionate about the culture. About the Arctic."

"So, what secrets are you unearthing?" She leaned closer.

It was a good question, but he had no idea what to say and pushed his chair back a bit on the tiles. "Nothing of interest yet." He stood and pulled his coat from the back of his chair.

"I'm staying at my aunt and uncle's apartment near Frogner Plass. They've invited you for supper tonight," Kari said.

It seemed like he should say he wanted to see her again. He thought he wanted to keep talking to her, but maybe staying home that night with Matisse made more sense.

Kari tore a piece of paper from her tiny notebook and wrote the address quickly. "About eight tonight?"

Hans knew Frogner Plass well. It was near a large park where he'd gone to a café in the summer. He'd taken a couple of days off and spent mornings drinking coffee and smoking on the terrace. Thinking about nothing.

The clipped grass of the park and the pond below the wooden café. The ducks with their half-grown ducklings and the toddlers with their mothers or grandmothers. The little kids were often pushing their own strollers. He'd desperately wanted to clear his head. Burn the last few months away.

The sculpture in the park was brutal bronze and granite. Vigeland Installation. Bodies twisted around each other on the huge stone tower. Phallic. And the wide avenues leading to the pond and fountains. In some ways it was everything he didn't like about Oslo. And in other ways it was what he craved. A world very different from his parents' close-knit community. Those few mornings watching the ducks in the murky pond below had given him a sense that somehow he'd trudge through the months ahead. Like he'd made it through the first months after Astrid's death.

When he sat down at his desk at the office, Kari's questions buzzed in his ears. It seemed like the body in the ravine should be connected to the sabotage, but there was no evidence of that yet.

The office was half full. Lars was typing slowly at his desk and Malin cradled her phone against her ear. She hung up, and he waved to her as she grabbed her long puffy coat and headed downstairs.

Hans worked on a draft of his report about the sabotage, and finished his notes on the death near Lismavarri. There was something satisfying about having these tasks to accomplish. The notes and typed pages were proof he was useful. Doing a job. Starting to put the pieces of a puzzle together. The light was brilliant coming in the row of windows.

He left work a little early. Solveig, a young woman who'd been an intern at Astrid's newspaper, walked Matisse at lunch. Matisse loved her. She looked like a goofy hippie. She carried a long macramé bag and wore tie-dyed shirts with Indian print skirts, but she was gentle and paid excellent attention to Matisse. Matisse was always waiting by the door for her, she'd said. He could tell when she was coming up the stairs.

Still, Hans felt guilty about the hours Matisse spent inside the apartment. He wanted to take Matisse for a walk before he met Kari at her aunt's. And he needed to stop at the dry cleaner's on Jens Bjelkes gate to pick up two sweaters he'd left there a couple of months before.

The owner said, "I thought you'd disappeared."

"Not quite," he said.

He passed the new Rema 1000 grocery store. He couldn't face the bright buzzing lights and boxes stacked up to the ceiling. Instead, he went into the pet shop a few doors down. It took him a while to find the bag of small dog biscuits that were Matisse's favorite. Glass lanterns on the sidewalk in front of shops lit the way along the street. Burning in the early dusk. The sun had set at about four and the sky was still tinged with a faint pink.

He took the shortcut through the Botanical Gardens in case the diurnal owl he'd been watching was still hunting. A northern pygmy owl with electric yellow eyes and deep brown feathers. About the size of a large woodpecker. Her head was spotted with confetti-size spots of white. Her chest marked with white streaks. She had two whorls of dark feathers that looked like eyes on the back of her head. He usually saw her sitting on the leader of a large fir tree. His bird guide told him she was about seven inches and weighed around two ounces. She nested in old woodpecker cavities in downed trees and sang a duet of toots with her prospective mate. She lived four brief years.

In the garden the roar of cars was muffled, a line of evergreens blocking the noise on Toyengata. No one else was walking the wet path across the empty brown lawns. A swish of feathers clattered out of the willows. The catkins swayed in the dim light. She clutched a field vole in her powerful talons. They were out of proportion with the rest of her small body. She landed on her favorite tree in a crook just below the top. It would take her about twenty minutes to tear the vole apart and swallow each piece of flesh.

21.

KARI POURED HIM A glass of Perrier. He'd thought about canceling. Telling her he had too much to do on the case, so he wouldn't have to leave the house. He wasn't even sure he'd felt well enough to go out again that night.

At their apartment, Kari's aunt and uncle were making a late supper in the kitchen together. They argued over the sharpness of the knives and whether to use bread or crackers with the salmon.

"They always do that," Kari said, as she sat down on the stiff sofa in the living room. It was warm in the room and nowhere else to sit except next to Kari or on a wooden chair. He took his coat off and put it on the back of the chair.

She was wearing a thin blue dress with tiny flowers. Hans liked it that it was so cold and she was wearing a dress he could pull quickly over her head. It had been so long since he'd wanted to touch someone. Since he'd felt anything at all.

"Antique," she patted the sofa. "Auntie loves this kind of thing. She used to drag me around to estate sales when I was a girl."

"I can't imagine anyone dragging you around." Hans perched on the narrow sofa.

"My father tried to badger me into becoming a teacher, but I always wanted to be a journalist."

Kari's aunt and uncle appeared with plates and forks and set them down on the polished coffee table near the sofa. Two small people with hardly any hair. They were so eager to make her happy. Next, they brought out dishes with fish and sweet buns and pickles.

He was thinking about what Gunter had told him. Three people had seen the body in the ravine, and they'd kept that secret from the whole village. Or had they? Was everyone else lying when they'd told the cops from Tana Bru no one had seen anything? And was the boy dying in the ravine a casualty of the plot to blow up the bridge?

"Thanks so much," Hans said. "It's very kind of you."

"Enjoy," Kari's aunt said. "We'll let you talk," and she disappeared into the kitchen with her husband.

"Auntie is always trying to make my life more interesting. She thinks I don't meet enough men."

Hans smiled. "Ah, but my mother wouldn't approve of you."

"Do you care?"

"What do you think?" He wanted to be anywhere but in the small hot room on the stiff sofa, but Kari's aunt and uncle had gone to so much trouble.

"It's funny Olav Elstad wanted a child so much but never married," she said, and picked up her fork. She scooped up some of the sliced pickles and positioned them carefully on a cracker.

"He's not so old. I understand why Ingrid wanted to move away. It's beautiful, but your whole life is that village by the river."

"Elstad seems to have worked around that, hasn't he?"

"No, he's tied to his parents."

"And you?" Kari asked.

"Me?"

"How did you decide to move so far away?"

"I had an older cousin who moved to Oslo and became a policeman. I thought it seemed like such a strange thing. It was so foreign."

"You went to the police academy at Bodo?"

"Yes. A bit funny, I know, but there it is." Hans wanted to eat something to make her aunt happy, and stabbed a piece of herring with his fork.

"Come on, tell me the real story."

"I saw a movie when I was young—just a kid. We went to Oslo. Some kind of meeting for Dad. They had a movie theater with red velvet seats and nuts for sale at intermission. My brother was too young to go and, anyway, Mom had to stay with the sheep. I think they argued about that. A kind of running argument. If she got rid of the sheep, she could do more things. You don't understand, this is what I like to do, she'd say. Oslo was lit up with electricity. Like a present for me when we got there.

"I liked the sheep, liked helping my mother. Holding the new lambs in my arms. But I decided after I saw glittering Oslo, it was the place for me. I was only six. I know, more noble if I'd decided I wanted to be a doctor or an astronaut. But I didn't know anything at all about those professions. The doctors I knew spoke Norwegian, not Sami. My aunt was afraid to go to a doctor. She wanted her priest to recite passages from the Bible instead. We saw *The Pink Panther*. It was such a cool idea—that you could solve mysteries like that. A different kind of power."

"But Inspector Clouseau. You've got to be kidding—it's so weird."

"I was only a little kid. I didn't say it had to make sense."

Now she was touching his hand, lightly. "My parents thought I was crazy, wanting to be in television, but my mother knew I wouldn't be happy stuck in a classroom."

She cut a little bun with a very sharp knife and put a sliver of salmon on the bread.

"I never wanted a life where you sit at a table to eat supper and your shoes are lined up in the closet by colors. I wanted something out of the ordinary. Something where I could make a difference. I never thought much of capitalism. And now here we are wanting to buy everything to make our lives like pillows. Very soft, expensive pillows. Don't you feel guilty sometimes that you're part of a kind of repression? Didn't it bother you that you ended up arresting a friend of your mother's?"

Hans moved her hand away and took a sip of water. "What do you want me to say to that?"

Why was she so annoyed at him? She knew he was a cop when they met.

"Want to see the garden? Get a little air?"

"Why not," he said. The room was so hot. Outside it was quiet and cold.

The dark shapes of trees, bare, hard. The outlines of bushes with black leaves. Brittle rhododendrons in the cold. The empty beds of the garden. Earth furrowed. Frozen in the late fall.

He pulled Kari to him and kissed her. His mind emptied. He wasn't thinking about anything except her lips, the taste of her lips.

"Let's do it here," she said.

"Christ, in the garden?" He laughed. "I don't think so."

He could feel her skin through the light dress, the wool of her sweater. The sky full of stars, no moon. All darkness. "You're a little wild then," he said. His mouth pressed hard against hers.

She leaned away from him. "I told you I get tired of spending my life in cities. I love to camp in the mountains."

He was cold suddenly even though his hands were still warm from her skin. He smoothed her dress down against her stomach, her thighs. Ran his hands along her back.

She whispered, "Later" in his ear, and they stepped into the light from the house through the French doors and into the living room.

"There you are," her aunt said. "It's so cold. Not the time of year for the garden, is it? You've been out there forever."

Hans could smell waffles cooking. Images flashed into his mind of his aunt making one after another heart-shaped waffle in her black waffle iron and stacking them high on a plate on the counter. He wanted those waffles with a strange hunger. They were light and sweet. He could slather jam on them. Smash the berries into their surface. It wasn't something his mother did—a good cook, but practical. "I never got the batter right," she told him when he was older. "Always sticks."

He picked up his coat from the back of a wooden chair said, "I've got to get home, things to do on the case before morning."

Kari frowned.

"Thank your aunt and uncle for me," he said and walked down the hall to the vestibule and opened the door.

"I will," she said.

He stepped onto the sidewalk and hailed a cab. He waved to her standing on the steps. She looked small against the light from the open door. He pulled the door of the cab shut, and she disappeared into the darkness.

The cab driver was an old man with folds of skin resting against his collar. Hans gave the address and sat back against the worn seat. The lights of the shops along Storgata were bright. His head started to throb again. The cab was hot and his heart beat strangely. He rolled the window down.

They stopped at a light and suddenly three men surrounded them and pounded on car. "Get out," one said to driver and started to throw punches at him when he opened his door. Hans flung the door open and held his badge up in the dim light. "I know who you are," the man said and pushed Hans against the door. The light changed and the three men ran off.

Someone was following him? The creeps pounding on the cab recognized him? His brother's friends were crazy, but not that crazy. And what had he ever done to them, except move away. Become a cop. Was that a sin?

"Get in the cab now," Hans said to the driver, resting his hand on the cabbie's shoulder. "You can take me to the police station near Gronland Park."

"I didn't know what to do," the cabbie said, shaking his head.

"You okay?" Hans asked, getting into the cab behind the driver. "You think you can drive?"

"Sure, sure. Those are punks, they can't hurt me."

"You're tough. We should get you checked out, though, don't you think?"

"The bastard barely touched me. I used to box. I'm younger than I look. You know those guys?"

"Don't think so," Hans said. "Come in when we get to the station and fill out a report for the desk."

The cabbie parked and they walked through the heavy door and stopped at the desk sergeant's.

"Trouble?"

"Your friend the cop here tells me I need to file a report," the cabbie said. "He witnessed it."

It took a few minutes to fill out the form, and then they walked out of the building to the cab. Exhaustion had caught up to him.

The cabbie drove to Hans's address and stopped near the door to the building.

"Here's my card. I drive limos too."

"Let me know if you have any problems again with guys like that," Hans said.

"Sure."

As he opened the door to his building, he remembered reading in Turi's book that when you think evil spirits are coming, make three fires and walk through them, then those spirits can't track you.

HE'D WANTED TO TELL Kari what happened to him so long ago. What happened to turn him into a cop. But she was a reporter, and it was the kind of thing she couldn't resist probably. His story about *The Pink Panther* was true, but it wasn't the whole truth. He still had nightmares about the winter solstice when he was fourteen. His cousin got him drunk and then his cousin's two friends beat him up. They kicked him over and over again. He was rolled up on the snow by the side of the road and they took turns punching and kicking him with their boots. They didn't like him, a skinny kid spending most of his time in the library. They didn't like that he was a good skier. Good enough to come in first in most of the competitions at the sports club.

They hooked him to the back of a pickup and dragged him through town on the icy road. The truck was grinding, and exhaust spewed into his lungs as the oldest kid drove faster and faster. He knew he was going to die. His cousin was a bastard, but he never thought he'd let him die. They'd slung him up in some kind of harness. Sparks snapped around him as the chains hit the gravel. He was lucky he was wearing a thick sweater and parka. He was bruised and battered when the nurses gently took his clothes off in the hospital, later. He didn't remember the jerks unhitching him. Like he was a horse.

Someone had reported him lying in the dark on the frozen road. Blood on the gravel near him, and when the ambulance came, there was a cop who told him he'd go with him to the hospital. He spoke Sami. He said they'd find out who did this. But Hans didn't want to get his cousin in trouble. He didn't say anything.

His father had seemed embarrassed about the whole thing. His mother, suspicious. She knew her nephew was bad news. His cousin's friends went off into the mountains for a while, and his cousin went south to live with his father in Oslo. Everything cooled down.

But he admired the officer who rode with him to the hospital and liked the idea he could help people if he became a cop. He just never told his father about what he wanted to do.

22.

A VOICE WOKE HANS in the middle of the night. At first he thought it was Astrid and got up, knocked the glass of water off the nightstand. Sopped it up with a towel. He felt more alone than he'd felt in weeks when he realized it wasn't her voice but someone else's. Someone older. Someone speaking a different language. Emilie.

She says she's worried about him, the way he stands in the doorway, the way he chews his pencil or moves past the windows. It's only death, Astrid was just one more death, but of course she didn't have to survive Gudmund's death. It was up to him to see her in her grave. Sometimes she thinks she can run her fingers on the tops of tables. Lick butter, spin light like cloth. Sometimes she feels like the only person she ever spoke to when she was young was Carl. Carl so alive, now dead. Carl consumed by his music. Their sails on the Limfjord, gray mist, the swirl of landscape around them. Carl so crazed with the body. Sensual and reckless. Carl deeply in love with her, flawed as she was. And so young. The echo of those years when first her father died and then her mother and then her sister. The emptiness of the house. The fields stretching off in all directions, plowed, smelling like manure. She's wondering about Hans. He has such soft hair.

Why he looks so sad. Why his wife stands just outside the door watching as he reads a report.

And then she was gone.

Matisse was barking to go out even though it was three. The city seemed to be perfectly quiet.

"Now?" He said to the small dog wagging his tail at the door. "You really need to go walkies now?" And Matisse insisted, so he threw on his coat over his pajamas and pulled on his boots. "Just a short one."

Matisse hauled him down the stairs and out into the night. There'd been a light dusting of snow and the streets sparkled. He was chilled to the bone but not from the cold. He recognized the voice in a stream of words from some time in his childhood with his grandmother and his aunts. There was no way he could have known Emilie. But it was her voice. He was sure of it.

He opened the door to the apartment and, inside, pulled off his wet boots. Matisse lapped up some water from his bowl in the kitchen and then trotted over to his bed near the radiator. Hans was wide awake.

He'd been doing too much and not sleeping enough. He couldn't remember if the symptoms of a concussion included hearing voices. A kind of dream state.

He put the kettle on and sat at the table shuffling Emilie's letters. It was too soon to get close to anyone. But he could taste Kari's lips on his, the warmth from her skin. He wanted to call her but wouldn't.

Matisse sighed in his sleep. Hans took the packet of letters to the chair near the window. The kettle whistled. He took a tea bag out of the box on the counter and poured water into his cup. He wanted to be able to feel again. But didn't know how to get there. His hands shook as he pulled the tea bag out of the steaming cup and dropped it into the sink.

He sat down on the chair. Astrid used to tease him about claiming the big chair for himself. "Matisse would love that chair," she'd said once.

"No way," he said. "You think I want it reeking of wet dog? I don't even like Matisse."

"He knows," Astrid said. "And when I'm gone, he'll torment you for that."

The men pounding on the side of the cab come back to him. His brother's face. Remote. Accusing. His mother's hand on Mikael's arm. Protective. The memory of the hitchhiker shouting to him on the road near Kautokeino, "You're in trouble."

It wasn't like him. Not like him at all to forget Astrid. A sudden kind of hunger to forget Astrid. Lose himself in the arms of a stranger. So different from Astrid.

Sometimes it hit him in the middle of doing something. A rush of longing so powerful it was electric. And then he couldn't do anything, not put water in the pot, or feed the dog, or make the bed, or brush his hair, eat an egg or an apple or a piece of toast. And he couldn't remember what it was like to be loved like that. It seemed like a mirage. Had there been someone who'd cared about him so much? Or was it a fairy tale? And the longer she was gone the more he couldn't remember her voice, what it felt like being near her, how her perfume smelled. The spaces around him were emptied out.

Hans held the letter in his hands, tipped under the light.

I'm not so sure what love is anymore. Is it comfort and companionship or what I felt for Carl when I was so young? I just know that the meeting on the train with Turi, so long ago, sparked a kind of love that had nothing to do with anything carnal but still was all about the body. The body in cold, the body sleeping in the sweet-smelling tent. The body wracked with pain. The body anything but clean those months with the old wolf's family. Yesterday I was painting a scene I remembered. The reindeer running and running in a circle around the corral while the men notched the ears of the calves with their marks of ownership. This was a time when the women would milk the cows, carrying pails up to the corral and back full of warm milk to camp. Earlier, the reindeer swam across a lake to get to the pasture on the edge of the mountain. It was dangerous for the calves. Sometimes men who were watching in their boats had to drag the calves out of the water. When they all got to shore the calves and their mothers ran around looking for each other. They shook themselves, a halo of spray cascading around each animal. I'd never seen so many reindeer struggling in a crossing. It was exciting and dangerous. My heart was beating hard, and I felt like I was on the edge of another world with much more miraculous events.

23.

IN THE MORNING HANS walked to the office in a cold drizzle across the Botanical Gardens past the empty beds. Bare trees, silvery branches. He stopped for a coffee at Zorba's and got another to go. His shoulder aching.

He didn't make coffee for himself anymore. It was too much trouble. When he first bought the French press Astrid thought he was nuts. "What are you, Michael Caine?"

"Not quite so debonair as he was in *The Ipcress File*."

"Just showing how clever you are that you remember," she said.

"I remember you thought he was ridiculous. A detective with that kind of coffee."

"Just shows how pretentious he is."

"So you think I'm pretentious."

"No, just silly sometimes," she said and kissed him. "But he was very clever and didn't trust anyone."

It turned out she liked the coffee, so they got a bigger version of the press, and he could laugh at her in the morning as she sipped her coffee. She was delighted with such a small thing.

When he arrived at headquarters Malin was sorting manila folders with little tabs on them marked in red ink. She'd cut her hair. It was very short. She looked younger.

"I'm hearing voices," he said and she glanced up.

"Voices, like weird voices from the beyond or people out on the street talking?"

"Voices from the beyond," Hans said.

"It's normal," she said. "Absolutely normal. Especially after a concussion."

"Not Astrid," he said.

"Not Astrid? Not normal then. Not God?"

"Not God. Emilie, the woman who lived with my family long ago."

"That's a relief," Malin said. "It's just the letters from the Danish woman, Hans, stop reading the letters. They're not doing you any good. What do you get out of reading those letters anyway?"

"I'm curious, swept into her life. Background research for the case."

"Well, sweep her away if she's driving you nuts. Especially if she's keeping you up at night. And what's this about an incident with a cabbie and some goons?"

"No big deal," Hans said. "A bit weird, but no one was hurt. Could be they were high on something."

"No possible connection to the guy who hit you over the head?"

"It's a stretch, but maybe," he said.

Lars walked into the office and kicked a small duffle bag under his desk. He took off his wet coat and hung it on the wooden coat rack in the corner.

"Any news?" he asked.

"There's an interesting development," Malin said. "We may have a solid lead on our dead person in the ravine." She tilted her head and scratched her forehead.

"Yes?"

"The Russian embassy in Stockholm has notified us that the son of one of the officials there, the press attaché, is missing. Yuri Zhukov. Gone north, they think, and not heard of for two months."

"Why did they wait so long?" Hans asked.

"They didn't want to arouse suspicions, get the kid in trouble before this. His parents thought he'd gone home to Moscow. His father arranged it. They often don't hear from him for weeks. They know he stayed with a woman in a village not far from the border with Finnmark."

"It doesn't sound good, does it?" Lars pulled a chair close to Malin's desk and sat down.

"No. So the body in the ravine could be the embassy kid. It's very close to where he was in Sweden. Bad news if someone in Lismavarri killed him. I don't think anyone wants an international mess from all this. I'll call and set up an interview with the parents. You can check out their story, Hans. We'll put you up in a nice hotel in Stockholm."

"Good. Just what I always wanted. A nice hotel," Hans said. "Can you take Matisse? He's bored with me anyhow. Won't even sleep on my bed. He likes his own better."

"I'd be happy to. Any luck contacting Ingrid Morland?"

"No. But I found out she's singing at a club not far from here. I thought I might check it out later today."

"You could leave a message at the university. She teaches a Sami language class in the Linguistics Department. Once a week," Lars said.

"This case is taking you all over the place. But I don't like to think of a boy murdered. If that's what happened," Malin said.

Hans took the folder Malin held out to him.

"The office in Tana Bru is convinced it was an accident. And they're not happy we keep insisting the dead man must be connected to the sabotage," she said. "The officer I spoke to yesterday was annoyed about talking to Jorgen. He said he'd send someone when he had a chance but it wouldn't be for a few days."

"Which means they're stonewalling us," Lars said.

"Yup."

"Nice haircut," he said to Malin.

"Hmm. A dramatic change, huh? Soren likes it. He says I look more spontaneous."

"Definitely not a word I'd use to describe you," he said. "I'll let you know how the conversation goes with Ingrid."

It was almost dark by the time Hans left the office. He was walking as fast as he could toward the university on his way to hear Ingrid Morland sing. It had seemed like a good idea to talk to her after her gig, but now he wasn't so sure.

Down the hill, up Karl Johans's gate toward the King's palace. The early dusk all around him. Lights from the buildings glowed on the sidewalk. Candles in big lanterns burned at the shop doors. The traffic rushed past. He checked the address of the club he'd written on a scrap of paper and turned left into a narrow alley.

Hans spotted the steep steps down to a red door. The hollow worn on each step. The door opened into another world. Dark, glittering. Ingrid Morland swayed under large foil stars suspended from the ceiling. He bumped his head on the edge of one. The walls were black. Heavy paint pulsed in dim light. The room was filled with smoke. People surrounded the singer, sipping red wine out of paper cups stained with lipstick and wine. They were sitting on metal folding chairs.

A few men wore sunglasses. One had a black beret tipped on his head.

Shabby. Women in long skirts gripped their companions' fingers. Temporary. Funny. And then she started to sing. He was embarrassed. She was *yoiking*. Should she be singing surrounded by all these strangers?

No one knew what she was saying. They were pulled along by the twist of her voice. She was darkly beautiful, far more beautiful than anyone he'd known. The dim light followed her lips, her forehead, the side of her cheek, the ends of her fingers. He'd seen her before, just a little girl in the choir. She'd sang with his brother. Something he didn't expect—this kind of connection.

Ingrid Morland's arms flashed with sparkles from the silver stars. The black walls came closer and closer. He got up. The room disappeared. All he could see was a pinprick of light. He stumbled over someone's legs and went out the door. Up the stone stairs. The smell of exhaust. Brittle leaves rustled. The glitter of water flashed between buildings.

When he got home, he called and left a message at the university that he needed to ask a few questions about an incident in Lismavarri.

24.

HANS WOKE EARLY AND took the long way to work through the gardens, past the owl's favorite perch. But she wasn't there. It was snowing lightly and he pulled his collar up. He was thinking about the Russian boy who ran away from his family in Stockholm. How could he blame him? And the clues in his pocket. A broken chain, a few keys, a pocketknife, a candy wrapper.

He'd tried to run away once. He was nine. His brother twelve, and he'd been beating Hans up for years. Kicking him in the stomach and the back. Once Hans ended up in the hospital with blood in his urine, and his mother insisted, when anyone asked, that it was kids at school who'd hurt him.

Usually, Mikael would wait until their mother was in the barn with the sheep or taking them off to their field to graze. Their father at work. Hans would hide in his bedroom closet barricaded by a box and read. This time their mother was spinning wool. His brother was pissed off at something that happened to him at school.

They'd gotten off the bus down the street from their house, and immediately Mikael started to scream at him. "You're a no-good loser, a stinking turd." Hans knew, unless his mother was in the house, there'd be trouble. It was the same time of year, early winter. November. Hardly any light. He'd told his father about his brother, but his father said, "It's nothing. Just something all boys do. You've got to learn to fight back."

When they got to the house, Hans opened the door and they burst into the living room together. There was his mother sitting at her spinning wheel. There was his father's desk. There was the pile of wood for the stove, the basket full of kindling. They took their rucksacks off and hung their coats on the pegs in the hallway, took off their shoes. He didn't have time to hide. His brother pulled him into the kitchen and started to kick his legs, pin his arms against his back. He was much bigger and it was hard to get away. When he tried to wiggle out of his grasp, Mikael grabbed his thumb and pulled it back. Hans didn't want to cry, didn't want to scream, he wanted to be tough. But the pain was so bad he started sobbing.

His mother said, "Cut it out, you boys. Can't you see I'm in the middle of work? I have to get this bundle of wool spun by the end of the week. It's a big order."

She kept spinning. It was long ago and maybe he didn't remember it perfectly. Maybe she did get up and haul Mikael off him and put her arms around Hans and tell him that his brute of a brother would never beat him up again, but he didn't think that's what happened. He'd slipped away once Mickael got bored and started eating some kind of snack in the kitchen. Hans was used to pulling his thumb back into place. He emptied the books out of his rucksack and put a heavy sweater and socks and extra gloves in the bag. When Mikael was out of the kitchen, he filled a bottle with water and snuck some cookies from a jar. Pulled on his ski clothes and put his school clothes in the hamper. He stuffed his headlamp into his parka pocket. His plan was to ski through the forest to a little hut near the waterfall. He was a fast skier and could get there in less than an hour. Once he got to the hut, he'd figure things out.

He opened the door as quietly as he could, but his mother heard him and turned. "Where are you going?"

"Got to prep my skis for the race tomorrow."

"Go on then but don't take forever in the shed, you've probably got homework to do. Don't you?"

"Not much," he said.

He opened the shed door and took his touring skis out of the rack. He didn't bother to wax them. He was scared his brother would guess where he was and catch up to him in the shed and beat the snot out of him. He fumbled with the switch on the headlamp and closed the door carefully.

He couldn't get his left boot into the binding at first. But once he jammed it in, he snapped on his skis, grabbed his poles, pulled on his pack, and took off into the woods on a track his father had set for him early in the week. He usually skied back and forth on the track. The snow could be heavy in the woods. His thumb was sore, but he was happy to be skiing away from his brother. Northern lights shot across the sky, and the headlamp lit the track a few steps ahead. But it was cold, very cold. His fingers were numb.

Once he was off the track, the snow was deep and he had to kick each ski ahead as he was breaking trail. If he didn't reach the hut he'd probably freeze to death. It was dumb he hadn't packed a sleeping bag or anything to make a fire. He sucked in cold air, his heart thumping. Just when he was out of breath, he heard a snowmobile. His father following him.

"I had a talk with your brother," he said when he caught up to Hans. "He won't ever do that again."

He was just hanging up his coat at headquarters when the package of photos from Tromso arrived. Malin slit the large heavy envelope with a tiny knife and pulled a folder out. She opened it and spread the photos on her desk.

"Not very many," she said, "but it will do."

Lars brought a magnifying glass to her desk. "In case we need one," he said.

There were ten photos taken from different angles and sides of the objects. So little to go on. And all the boy had left when they found him.

"For some reason this case is getting to me," Malin said. "It's kind of heartbreaking. A kid so far north. A kid who might have run away from his family. Only to die in a brutal place away from everything. And the uselessness of the sabotage."

Lars looked at Hans and he shrugged.

The keys were just ordinary, a Swedish brand of door locks, Malin said. And the candy wrapper was Swiss chocolate you could buy anywhere in Scandinavia. It was surprising it had survived in his pocket. The pocketknife wasn't anything special. Ordinary, not expensive like a Swiss Army knife. But the necklace was more interesting. It was more delicate than Hans imagined. A very thin gold chain with tiny links. It looked like it had broken at the clasp.

"Get that magnifying glass, will you?"

Hans held it close to the picture of the necklace. The clasp had a tiny gold disc. Smaller than his fingernail. A letter engraved on the gold.

"It's an A," he said.

"Shit," Lars said.

"Too easy for it to have been a K," Malin said, "but still it's something."

25.

HE'D ARRANGED TO MEET Ingrid Morland in the afternoon at a café near the castle. One of the places on the water with striped awnings, tables on the cobblestones. He arrived a little late. It had taken him a few minutes to find a free car in the motor pool, and at first the keys were missing. When he finally started the Saab and turned onto Nylandsveien, the traffic was stalled. He maneuvered the car into a side street. His hands were sweating. Sticky on the steering wheel.

Malin had told him to keep the interview informal. "Take notes, but don't alarm her." She might have some information they couldn't get from anyone else. Especially now that they knew three people saw the body and didn't tell anyone else. Or at least according to Gunter Schmidt.

Ingrid Morland was wearing a long skirt and a heavy jacket. Bright purple. The color was brighter than anything around her. She was sitting outside on a green chair. It seemed uncanny he was here in Oslo and she was here in Oslo and their past was somewhere else.

The taste of exhaust in his mouth as he sat down beside her. Outdoor café, a joke even in the summer. A perverse longing to be cold.

Just an informal meeting, he told her, to find out what she knows. "You'll be alright outside?"

"Of course," she said. "You know what it's like where we grew up. I know your parents," she said. "I sang in the choir with your brother."

"Ah," Hans said, "Mikael's all grown up now."

"And so am I," she said.

"Did you know what was going to happen? What Eric Paulsen had planned?"

"Yes, I knew about the bomb. I went with Eric to check out the dam site. I wanted a break from my life, from the exposure, the disconnection."

Was she telling him this to shake him up?

A waiter opened the door and stood above them on the sidewalk. He turned the propane heater near them up a notch.

Hans gestured at Ingrid. She pulled her coat tighter. "Just coffee," she said.

"Yes, coffee for me," Hans said.

Ingrid was looking at the fjord. Dark gray. Whitecaps rolling toward them.

"Was Olav Elstad your lover?" It was something he already knew, if Kari was telling the truth, but he wanted to find out what she'd tell him.

"Does this have anything to do with the whole thing?"

"I'm just trying to put the pieces of the story together."

"Olav was my lover, once. He was just supporting Eric at the dam. And Kathryn wasn't involved either. She's just a child. Eric was teasing me about that, about Olav and the American girl. It bothered me and I didn't know why. He was tormenting me," she laughed. "'Ah, Ingrid,' Eric said, 'I think you've lost Olav to Kathryn.' He thought I was jealous."

"And were you?"

"How could I be jealous of a child?" she said. "And how could I lose Olav when I'm the one who left?"

Ingrid was distraught about Eric's disappearance. His accident. She never thought anything like that would happen. Hans wanted to know about the German boy working on the farm.

She looked him straight in the eyes, "I'm sure Gunter didn't kill anyone. He's so naïve. A clown. We drove from Lismavarri to the bridge."

It was raining on the awning now, very cold. That icy wind they grew up with. So mild usually in Oslo.

She looked out at the street, away from him. "Eric was one of the hunger strikers, you know, in Oslo last year. I was with his mother and she told me to cry so the police would feel sorry for us."

Hans said, "I was an officer there."

"But an officer," she said and laughed. "One of the men in blue?"

He wasn't surprised she would see it like that. Like he was an enemy.

"We were on different sides, I suppose. Our division was called in when the protest had gone on for weeks."

"You look so unlike an officer now."

"It was the dress uniform," he said. "A show of force. The police apologized, didn't they?"

"But they still hauled everyone off to jail. I told Eric his mother wouldn't be happy with him if he did something irresponsible again."

Ingrid took the silver pitcher filled with cream from his hand, her fingers almost touching his. "I tried to imagine the vidda flooded, the river spilling over its narrow banks and running up to the tops of the hills in all directions. The grazing land down to almost nothing. The town wiped out. My family is from Máze. But everyone is either dead or gone.

My grandmother was the last to stay and she's been dead for three years now."

"I'm sorry." He looked down at his notebook. The wind was stronger now off the fjord. The heater hardly making a dent in the cold.

"Oh, she was a happy woman, a reindeer owner. And very rich. She had so many suitors, she told me, and they all just wanted her reindeer, she thought. Finally she married my grandfather because he was wild and kept bringing her gift after gift until she had a pile of shawls, one more beautiful than the next, and a box full of silver brooches. He was the most handsome too, even though he was the poorest. Something her father didn't like. But her mother understood.

"She wanted me to have her reindeer, but I didn't want anything to do with all that. I wanted to be a nurse. Instead my brother is very rich now, but he's moved. He didn't have enough grazing land there."

Hans drank the last of his lukewarm coffee.

"My grandmother was full of life, but my parents were sour as pickles. Father seduced my mother with his faith, his charm. I grew up in a house with no dancing or singing or drinking. Sometimes as my mother kneaded bread or sewed, I thought I could hear her humming under her breath. It made me happy. That little rebellion."

Suddenly water poured off the canvas near them.

"Let's go inside," he said, and he picked up their cups. Ingrid pulled her large bag over her shoulder and followed him inside.

Their waiter pointed them to a table near the window and they sat down.

"When we were at the bridge, Eric showed us where he would position the bomb. The river would be frozen in

November. He wanted to plan how he'd get away. It seemed like more of a prank than anything else. It was such a beautiful day. The warm sun, the calls of the birds. So much in bloom."

The waiter came with a carafe of more coffee and poured it into their cups.

"He was so ardent about the whole thing. So convinced a small gesture would get some results. But I didn't think he'd go through with it."

He asked her about the body found weeks after she'd gone to the dam site. Could she tell him anything about the people in the village. Anything about Olav.

"No, I hadn't been to Lismavarri in weeks. I thought it was an accident anyway. It was an accident, wasn't it? That's what the local police believe. Ah, but you believe something else."

"I'd like you to take a look at a couple of photos." Hans pulled his green canvas messenger bag off the back of the chair and popped the snaps. He pulled out a folder and opened it on the table, and slipped two photos out of their envelope. "We found various things in the victim's pockets including this necklace. Have you ever seen this before?"

"No," she said quickly.

"Did you ever see Kathryn wearing a necklace?"

She looked away and then back at him. She waited a little too long and then said, "You've got to be kidding. How could this be important? The only one I saw her wear was this sweet necklace, red and white beads, decorated with tiny elephants. You think someone killed the man?"

"Yes, I think someone killed the boy in the forest. I'm not sure why. But I want to find out."

"How do you know he was a boy?"

"Forensics. Teeth, bones, that sort of thing."

She seemed startled by the idea that the dead man was a boy. Maybe it was just that violent death for someone so young is always a tragedy.

Hans left Ingrid at the café. She lived nearby, she said. She didn't need a ride. She refused to let him walk her home. She wanted to pick up some things at the market.

When he returned to headquarters, Lars was at his desk, slowly taking bites out of a huge apple. The office was almost empty.

"Where's the boss?"

"At a meeting with the rest of the head honchos. A budget meeting. I hope we won't be the ones to get cut. My budget's bleeding already with all this baby stuff." Lars threw the nibbled core into the paper basket near Malin's desk. "Learn anything new?"

"Not much," Hans said, "but she knew about the plan to blow up the bridge."

"And she didn't do anything about it?"

"It seems, like everyone else we've talked to, she thought it was a kind of street theater. A loud gesture. She didn't think anything would happen. I think she recognized the necklace, but I can't be sure. I think there's a good chance it's Kathryn's. Who else would be wearing something like that?"

"So we still have only bits and pieces, to tell us what's going on."

Hans shook his head and pulled a chair close to Lars's desk. He sat and crossed his legs. His shoes and the bottoms of his pants were wet with rain.

"No suspect. No way to tie the death and the sabotage together. But the police in Tana Bru were wrong about it being an accident in the forest above Lismavarri."

"They wanted it to be an accident. Some tourist lost on the vidda. Someone not part of the community. It wouldn't matter then. Just a stranger who thought he could take off into the forest on his own."

Lars rubbed his eyes.

"Worn out?"

"Yeah. The baby was up most of the night. Just a cold the doctor said, but she's been miserable."

"I think it's worth the trip to Stockholm," Hans said. "To check out this disappearance, don't you?"

"It makes sense. The boy didn't just fall into the ravine. For some reason, he was a threat to someone in the village. Is Elstad the glue to the different pieces of the story? He was probably lying about waiting in the wings to bring Paulsen to the clinic. He had to have been part of the plan. He's lying about his affair with the American girl. And somehow her necklace ended up in the victim's pocket. I'd be way happier about all this if someone had interviewed Paulsen before he left the country. Bad luck we were too late. I'm guessing you could have found out something if you'd talked to him."

"Maybe, but what? I don't think he killed anyone," Hans said. "But then you know I've been tricked before."

26.

Malin picked Matisse up on her way home from headquarters. She handed Hans the tickets for the train to Stockholm and a piece of paper with the number for the hotel confirmation. "It's quite nice," she said. "I've stayed there. It's not far from the Russian Embassy."

The apartment was empty without Matisse, but he'd seemed happy to leave with Malin, a much more cheerful companion. Maybe it wasn't personality but space. She had a yard where Matisse could run.

He was tempted to walk down the hill to the store on the corner and buy some cigarettes. What did it matter if he started smoking again? He found the pack of Dentine and unwrapped a piece of gum.

Something had lifted. He knew it could be a rush of good feeling that in a moment would disappear, but he pulled the Mingus album, *The Clown,* from the bookcase, removed it from the sleeve, and placed it on the turntable. He'd bought the Bang and Olufsen stereo components years before. They should have been expensive, but he'd snagged them at a secondhand store. And the speakers were better than they should've been for the price.

He sat at the table and ran his fingers on the pad of paper, covered with notes about the case. He wanted the pieces to assemble themselves into a coherent story. Was Malin sending him to Stockholm on a wild goose chase? Maybe the evidence would fall together like those impossible jigsaw puzzles Astrid used to do. One color. This case felt like improv bop. It seemed to be all over the place but there was a theme. The theme was there was no order. Instead, everyone was lying about what they did and what the others did until the case looked like snow trampled by reindeer in the forest.

Strange to be reading letters to Gudmund. Hans never wrote letters. Only postcards, with the words as small as he could make them. The weight of her letters in his hands. The paper stained here and there. The ink a bit faded.

February 3, 1949
Kauslunde

Dearest,

I loved those days I spent with Turi's sister and her children, snug and close at night. The soft lips of the baby, her tiny hands, her head on my chest as she slept. I was so touched that Risten asked me to be the baby's godmother. I watched Karen too, a child of about two who would put her gentle hands on the back of their dog while he growled softly. She wasn't afraid of him. And even though he was a solemn fellow he would run with joy when the reindeer were moving. Everything had a name and a place in the tent that year. Boaššo, hearth. Smakko-muorra, woodchopping tree. We gathered the tent poles in the woods, and stripped them of their sweet skin. The children licked drops of sap. The black stew pot hung on the chain over the boaššo.

There were flat stones for the hearth. And each of us had our place around the fire. My pillow was a sack of rags, the sheepskin heavy on my back as I slept. In the summer the nets we hung over our beds to keep the mosquitoes from tormenting us. There was a wooden tray with cups, a soft red bag with sugar. Unroasted coffee beans smelled like moldy leaves in the cold.

Sometimes it's too painful to think about the babies I lost. Gone now, swept away. Just a peek at the second, perfectly still and beautiful. Her rosebud lips and tiny hands, kicking and pushing for months and then gone. I wanted to hold her, but all I could do was study her on that cold marble slab. I wanted to put her mouth on my breast, with my hand cradling her head. I never told you this, but when Anna and Niklas came to visit that time not long after her birth, I nursed their baby. My breasts were so full and he was hungry and I was so sad, it was a kind of comfort.

HER LOSS. SOMETHING SHE and Gudmund lived with. Put away. The speed of time sweeping away everything after death, even if you could hold the remnants of the person you loved, a dress, a scrap of paper, a comb, a cup. Astrid wanted to have a baby. When they were first married, she'd had one miscarriage and then another. After the second, it was so heartbreaking, they decided they didn't want to go through adopting a child either. Astrid was angry she couldn't mourn. She couldn't talk about losing the baby. Everyone just expected her to get on with things.

He gave up thinking it was something they wanted when some time had passed, and Astrid hadn't brought it up again. The whole thing so difficult. The doctor telling them there was no heartbeat. Sobbing in the examining room. Ushered out because the next patient was waiting.

He got up and put the kettle on.

"Do we seem like the type who would dote on babies?" she asked one night after dinner with friends.

"Perhaps," Hans said.

"But babies grow up and look what happens. Jail, broken teeth, stolen cars."

He read Emilie's letters until late at night. He felt more and more compelled to read them now.

And then there was her voice. Sometimes insistent, sometimes far away as he scooped oats into a pan or ground beans for his coffee. Hans knew he wasn't crazy, but he also knew it wasn't normal that the voice of someone dead for so many years, dead at all, could be his companion. The most obvious culprit was the blow to his head. He was hallucinating. But Emilie wasn't telling him to do anything violent.

Kauslunde
February 15, 1949

Darling one,

I admit I was thrilled when the old wolf came to where I was camped on the edge of the lake and led me to the Sami. Turi took me in a boat to the other side of the lake and we made a small fire on the beach. We hung a coffeepot on sticks over the fire. It was delicious and strange to be up at two—the light like morning light, translucent and clear. Once we started walking it was raining, but not cold, a cheerful rain and Turi told me it was good luck. And then, after, living in the hut on a slope above his lávvu, all dark wood and neatness. We were like a married couple. I catered to his needs and helped him accomplish what he wanted to do.

All for now!
Your only E.

EMILIE WAS ENCHANTED BY a life he couldn't imagine living, mired in the culture Turi was intent on saving. He'd never been that interested in his cousins and their reindeer. It seemed a waste of time, spending days following the herd, learning to throw a lasso as well as your father when you were seven. Their lives had always been much harder than his when he was growing up. It was interesting Ingrid had left that life, too.

He'd liked the days in the forest with his father fishing, or picking cloudberries with his mother—even though his father wasn't interested in that kind of life. He'd wanted to be a librarian. And he was ambitious and good at it. He became the director of the library. He was involved in the cultural center. His mother could keep the sheep she had, as long as it wasn't too expensive. She took up spinning then and her wool business flourished.

Hans unfolded the next letter.

Dearest,

Who was I before I knew you? A girl wanting to break free from my parents' lives in their little storybook town in the north. And don't remind me of how much I love the place. I thought about this during the terrible trial and those months before. Our friends turning away from us in the shop. Anna refusing to speak to me. The long dark days that went on and on. The cascade of articles, and your voice on the radio urging cooperation with the Germans. I knew you were not a traitor, simply stubborn, just following orders. You said in the trial you weren't sure it was right to prostrate oneself before the Germans. Those awful hours when they took you away in the middle of Liberation Day to make a point by picking up someone well known. Such a cruel punishment. It was a relief to lose myself in the smell of paint, the color blue, the bare trees I painted on bare mountains. And then I was in bed for months too sick to move. I felt cut off from you those days of the trial, all through the occupation. All those arguments we had, me yelling, you storming off down the street. You were just trying to do what you thought was right and what I thought was unwise.

The persistent throbbing in his head had returned. He got up from the table and went over to the sink. He'd let the dishes pile up. Not something that would have happened when Astrid was alive. He shook two aspirin into his hand and popped them into his mouth. The water was very cold. Even in Oslo the Akerselva was almost frozen this time of year.

In the north it was a surprise when the rivers started to melt. A rush, all of a sudden. Glaciers spilling into rivers and then spilling into lakes, and on the coast the waterfalls cascading off the steep sides of the mountains. You could see the breakup first in the lakes. Puddles of water reflecting the sky here and there on the ice, and then the edge crumbling, pushed forward by the momentum of melting chunks, one big plow tearing more and more ice from the surface.

He wondered if it was the months of sorrow. The way her voice echoed in his head. She wanted to help him, she was sorry to see his arm in a sling, she remembered days on the ocean near Frederikshavn, she wanted to be a great painter. She would have loved to meet Astrid. They would have been friends. Don't be so hard on Gudmund. He did the best he could. We all did the best we could during the war.

And what do you think of this painting? This one is pure light on snow, the line of reindeer, the sky coming to meet the snow, this one is the gift for Inga, a young woman on the horizon, all gray but illuminated, yes, illuminated. And the word echoed in his head as he washed first one dish and then another and another. The green dishes piling up on the drying rack.

(SUMMER)
KATHRYN

27.

THEY WERE DRIVING TO the clinic. His hands were relaxed on the steering wheel as they drove along the gravel road to Tana Bru. They were strong hands, and they could be soft as he caressed her. A funny word. Not quite what he did, but it felt like that, a caress, a kind of intensity. Paying attention to her, but here they were driving along the gravel road, the window half open to the wind. The smell of the forest close by, the tiny flowers of the orchids bursting in the bog and she was in love. That was it. Something she hadn't felt before ever, even though she thought she had. It was more than the kind of anticipation she'd felt with Joe, the man she'd met in the mountains.

But now she felt different, not herself at all near Olav. She'd finally become someone who was lost in someone else, not so bound up in her own mind. It was thrilling, even though she didn't want to admit anything like this. It could vanish. They were going to a doctor who could prescribe birth control pills.

Olav was careful with just about everything, even lust, if that's what this was for him. The office was small and clean and the doctor didn't speak English. The two men spoke Norwegian to each other. The doctor was professional, distant, businesslike.

They had talked about it before and Kathryn agreed it made sense to be on the pill. But later she wondered why.

She knew Olav wanted a child. But maybe he didn't want a child with her. And how could she be someone who could take care of a baby, when she couldn't even take care of her dog. But he was careful. She didn't wonder why he didn't use a condom. Maybe it was too late already.

The doctor's left eye twitched as he handed her the plastic container, yellow, round, as big as the palm of her hand. She didn't know the pills would make her dizzy and she'd fall down in the kitchen and Eric would bandage her cheek. Or that she'd fall again in a fight with Olav's cousin weeks later.

28.

GUNTER TOLD HER HE was summoning the other world. Playing the bongos. He hit one sweet spot and then another on the drums cradled between his knees.

"You can't do it," Kathryn said laughing, as she sat down beside him on the steps to the house. "You can't seriously get a spirit from the underworld to come to you."

"Hey," Gunter said, "it doesn't matter. You just have to believe, and anyway Eric has given me permission. I'm an honorary *noiadi*. He deputized this drum as sacred."

"*Noiadi*?" Kathryn pulled her hair into a knot at her neck.

"Sami shaman."

"I think that's sort of sacrilegious."

"If I do things the right way, I can get my soul to leave my body. Cool or what?"

"Why would anyone want to leave their body?"

"Too heavy, too filled with mechanical problems," Gunter said. "It would be like flying. Ultimate freedom."

He hit the drums lightly and looked up at her. "Sometimes the whole freaking cosmos was drawn on the skin of the drum. There were maps with figures. Sacred sites where they sacrificed reindeer, the place where you could dip your hand into water all winter. The drums were so powerful, Eric told me, priests destroyed hundreds.

"You could ask for luck from the spirit world for hunting or fishing or herding reindeer. There's a story about a *noiadi* who flew through the spirit world to a village far away and brought back a silver spoon to prove to a man out fishing that his family was alive."

Gunter moved his hands around the tops of the drums. "I feel like my cells are electric today. Something awesome's going to happen. A resurrection."

"It's the light. I read about it somewhere. All this light and no sleep. The kids outside playing at midnight."

"Fantastic, yes? Can you imagine that at home?" Gunter tapped the drums lightly. "The light drives me nuts."

Kathryn was jealous of the easy friendship Gunter had with Eric. She supposed it was because they were both musicians. It had to be that kind of connection.

"What's your village in Germany like?" she asked.

"Nothing much. Brick houses, a line of pear trees. My sister likes to sit on the front step eating cherries. I like the vineyards. There're all around the house. My mother and father and sister are just back from holiday. They're naturists."

"Naturists?"

"You know: camping, swimming, hiking. All in the buff."

Kathryn laughed. "No, honestly?"

"Yes. I used to have fun, but maybe now it would be awesomely embarrassing."

"I can't imagine doing anything like that with my parents. It's creepy just to think about it."

"Sometimes I want something different. I just want to get on with my life, get the hard parts over with. Breeze along. I'm not sure I want any more drama after the last few months."

"Drama?"

"I got into a fight with one of the bullies in my dorm. The dorm mutti called the police. I punched the guy. I almost broke his nose. I can't remember the argument now."

Gunter's face was pale.

"Did they arrest you?"

"They cautioned me," he said, "since the asshole started the fight. The provost told my parents and said I should get counseling."

"He must have provoked you with something major."

"I've blocked it out. All my days were shitty then. I had a mega meltdown. Left school. It had nothing to do with anything. I was curled up in my room in a ball. I stopped doing everything except listening to music. I'd go to the listening rooms and close myself into a cubicle, put the earphones on and listen to Kraftwerk."

"Kraftwerk?"

"Like your Switched-On Bach."

It was so quiet. The haze of the low sun seeping into everything. Drenched in light.

"And you're okay now?"

"Work helps. This kind of work. Not to go back to school yet, to get over the past few months, to think about things. I wanted to lose myself in any kind of work. Flipping burgers in the Burger King in Karlsruhe, wrapping packages, driving the tractor, poling the long boat down the river, knowing what I'm doing."

Kathryn leaned forward and rested her arms on her knees. "When I got home from England my junior year, I just sat out on the sand. We'd gone to the beach for a couple of weeks, and I watched the waves breaking. Over and over. It was soothing. I'd get up at dawn and spend hours there. I had a hard time talking to anyone. I felt like something was broken and couldn't figure out why."

She looked across the road where Olav was talking to his brother. "Do you miss home at all?"

"Not home, but I do miss my girlfriend."

"So that's your secret. What's she like?"

"Funny, very cool, a musician and smart."

"And beautiful?"

"Sure, like Christie Brinkley. You know, don't you," he said suddenly, "you can talk to me if you need to. I'm a good listener."

"I'm fine," she said. "Just tired. Why don't you call up the spirits on your drums? Call them up to protect you," she said and laughed.

"I can try," he said and slapped her on the back. "But I don't have the magic yet to get such a powerful wish."

"So, YOU ARE PRACTICING to be an artist?" Olav said that night, leaning over her shoulder, running his finger on the edge of the drawing she was doing. The paper was spread on the little desk in her bedroom. She set down her pencil and looked at him.

"You are, perhaps, an artist already?"

She laughed and opened the box of drawing pencils she'd brought with her. She slipped the pencil inside next to several other slim pencils in different colors and snapped the lid shut.

"That's right," she said.

"This is very good," he said. "I'm not an artist, but I like the way you've got the birch just so here." He pointed to the dark texture of the bark near the widest part of the tree. "And the sacred rock here."

The drawing was important. More important than she wanted to admit. It was the first one she'd finished since she'd traveled north. All the other sketches missed something vital she wanted to catch. Something close to sex. The sex she had with Olav. The minutes when she was caught up in someone not herself. Like when she was walking and couldn't remember who she was. Just moving through landscape. Her arms turned into wind or rain or bark. But she didn't tell him this. She needed to believe her work was significant. More than an exercise.

29.

SOME DAYS ON HER walks in the forest above Lismavarri Kathryn brought back flowers. Olav had given her a flower press. A large book with stiff cardboard and ribbons on the side. He had one, he told her, when he was a child.

She placed moss and delicate flowers and leaves between the thick pages. Sometimes she thought all she'd have of this time was smooth stones, pressed flowers, and brittle reindeer moss. Sometimes she felt like she was being pressed thin, like the flowers she collected.

You better watch out, her father said to her once, or you'll be as crazy as Aunt Margaret. Kathryn used to stand out on the porch when she lived with her parents, the light from the street running across the clipped lawn, and scream. They had a big yard curving around the side of the house and a three-car garage. She could get lost in the house when she wanted. She hid in the living room, sitting on the red couch reading, when everyone else was in the family room watching television.

Kathryn was always getting into fights with her father. She thought a spider had the same rights as any other animal. But he sprayed everything with bug spray. The tiny ants in the bathroom. The wasp nest in the corner of the porch. Yellow jackets on the hanging baskets.

She wanted something different. To be in a place that was wild. Towering trees, sap on her hands, rushing rivers. Not something safe and predictable with every minute planned.

Often it seemed like she was doing all the things she did to prove something. Everything she did was building into some kind of reservoir of good will for the future. If she worked hard enough, she could get what she wanted. She wanted to be stoic, energetic, persistent. Instead, she fell back into the person she thought she actually was. Shy, insecure, lonely.

Her first year in college she started to run. And it was better than anything else. Running those miles on dirt roads beyond the college buildings, past tall fir trees and the clanking of farm machinery, and then sitting in dry, still barns where the swallows dipped and swooshed past her face.

She loved the way her legs felt once she left the paved roads and hit the dirt. Open, relaxed, not afraid of anything, even running for miles in deserted country. But still she was depressed, and she went to the college therapist who gave her a test. The results showed that she wanted to do too much as a woman, he told her. She was too ambitious.

SOMETIMES OLAV TOLD HER stories, and the stories were an answer to a question she asked him.

One afternoon when they were walking up the village road Olav pointed to a blue house. "It was in the autumn," he said, "very early in the morning and light snow had come in the night, and the man from that house went out to his boat, a boat like that one."

He pointed to a slim black boat resting against the side of a house.

"He left his footprint on the boat. So they thought he was drowned and they looked for two days. And nothing.

His boat was there but he was gone. So his wife took in a lover, and the man gave her his picture and she hung the picture on the wall."

Kathryn laughed. "She was quick to figure her husband was gone."

"Just wait." Olav held his hand up and smiled. "In a week the husband came back and found the woman with her lover. And he took a knife and went like this"—he jabbed into the air—"to the eyes of the man in the picture."

"And where had he been?"

"He had gone off on another boat out to the fjord. The woman was not a widow like she thought."

"The other man must have been happy the husband only jabbed at the picture."

"I don't know what he thought about that," Olav said.

"It seems like the woman was just waiting for a chance to get together with her lover."

"Sometimes these things just happen," Olav picked up a stone and threw it into the grass.

OLAV SAID HE HAD business in Vadso. "Come," he said, "I'll show you Russia." They drove to the Arctic Ocean.

She was wearing her thin pink dress with a woven sash. It had been weeks since she'd had on anything except her jeans. The cotton of the dress was weightless. It was spring along the Tana River to the coast, though it was summer. People had put fish out to dry on wooden racks. Clothes were flapping on the lines in empty yards like bright flags.

They parked the car at a small church with white crosses all around. "This is one of the oldest churches here," Olav said and walked across the gravel lot.

She stooped to pick up a very round black stone in the courtyard of the wooden church. It was cold and she was surrounded by all kinds of grays: ocean, sky, piles of stones.

In Vadso she sat on a bench in the square, knitting a red shawl. She was horrible at knitting. Her mother could knit anything. She was knitting the red wool her mother had given her. Her mother and her sister were at the beach right now, sitting on the hot sand. She could feel her toes in the sand, the cold water as it sloshed around her body, the smell of seaweed and salt.

She was far away from the cocktail parties around the pool and her father, who wore madras shorts this time of year. Soon her mother would be stretching her smooth white legs under a beach umbrella.

She watched her hands as they pulled the red wool up to the needles and twisted the strand. All around her seagulls were calling for food. Tulips and other spring flowers were crushed into a small space in pots. Olav took a long time in the low building behind her. He was getting a watch repaired for his father. She grew colder and colder.

The Cape in summer came back to her as she waited. Beach plums, bittersweet, red. The smell of low tide in the marsh behind the house they'd rented. The smell of hot sand, salty, grainy. Like a kind of mustard.

The big house on the hill with its musty curtains and polished floors, smelling of lemon wax. And the smell of suntan lotion all summer long. Familiar, not anything like the smells of the north.

The wide sandy river that disappeared at low tide but pulled them along the bottom when the tide was coming in. Silver fish wiggling around their feet. When she was little, she had this world every summer. But now so far away from home, she was ready to give it all up just for the pleasure of these new smells of fish and tar, the cold clean wind surrounding her as Olav took longer and longer in the watch shop.

Soon they'd drive to Kirkenes, and she'd be able to say she was almost in Russia.

When Olav finally came out, he said, "Yes, Kathryn, I have a surprise for you. Put your knitting in the car and we'll walk along the harbor."

"What's the surprise?" She laughed. "A hat, a ring, a scarf?"

"Nothing like that."

They went past three or four wooden buildings with white-framed windows. Seagulls swooped, screeching and laughing.

"Just here," he said. And he led the way through a door painted bright red with white trim. They took one step up and were in a store that seemed to stock all sorts of things.

"Like a general store?"

"In a way."

"Like your shop?"

"Not quite. They do not sell food. Ah, here," Olav said. He stopped in front of two shelves of art supplies. "If you want so desperately to be an artist you need more than the pencils and pad you brought with you."

She ran her hands on the boxes of paints and the tips of brushes and the packages of illustration boards.

"I'll go get the things I need here and then meet you at the register. This is my present," he said and smiled. His whole face furrowing. He was the only person she knew who could smile so completely one minute and look so solemn the next.

She opened a set of Holbein artists' gouache and touched the little tubes. Crimson lake, cerulean blue, sap green. They were tiny tubes, but the eighteen colors in the box would last a long time.

When they reached the border of Norway and Russia, Olav pointed out the towers and the wire. "They will shoot you, if you take a picture."

"I didn't bring my camera. And why would they want to shoot me?"

"You might be stealing something."

There were no villages, only a house here and there and a barn. The rows of fish on racks. The violent piles of rocks on the edge of the road made her wonder how fierce the ocean was in the winter.

"The smell of herring is like money," Olav said.

30.

SHE SIPPED COFFEE BOILED in the shiny pot and nibbled the cake Olav's mother made each day for Kathryn's first breakfast with his father. She was thrumming with the light of the north. All her molecules lit. Her face shining with it.

The tips of her fingers flashed as they crumbled the soft cake and popped it into her mouth.

Olav's father chewed with his mouth open. The crumbs mixing with saliva. His heavy hands resting on the table.

She was thinking about the dead calf they'd pulled into a ditch Gunter had dug along the side of the road. It was almost eight miles away near the place Olav called the Storfoss.

They put a rope around the calf and pulled her into the gully. She'd fed the calf hay the morning before and stroked the stiff hair on her head. The calf licked her palm with her scratchy tongue. She was sad to see her head twisted to the side in the ditch.

"How did the calf die?" she asked Olav.

"She was pastured in that field a few miles down the road with her mother. She must have gotten out. A car hit her, I think."

They buried the calf there. "Now the buzzards will not eat her eyes."

SHE WONDERED LATER WHY she smiled then at Olav's father across the table. He was such an old man, hunched into himself as he swallowed the cake. Suddenly he reached across the coffee cups, his arm jostling the saucers, and patted her nipples. He laughed. She could still feel the heat of his heavy hand on her breasts as she jumped up from the table and banged her cup against the saucer.

She ran down to the cellar and pulled on her rubber boots. Then she ran across the road to the barn where Olav's mother was hooking the cows to the milking machines. She could barely say good morning to his mother, her head wrapped in a bright scarf bent over a pail of milk.

The floor of the stalls seemed to tilt as she shoveled the piles of manure steaming in the light from the spattered window. It was hard to catch her breath. Maybe it was nothing. There was so much she didn't understand. Her longing for Olav, the laughter in the loft at night. The delight and pain of the sauna, her nose burning with heat. The words swirling around her.

Olav told her, "I feel for you a little more, not less. You see, I don't know what this word love means. I am only an old bachelor. Don't worry about words, Kathryn. They are nothing. Stop all this thinking you do about everything."

"WAS THAT SOMETHING MR. Elstad should have done?" she asked Ellen, later as they washed dishes. Both Maren and the baby were napping. The water was burning hot, and she sloshed the suds quickly on the plate.

"No, it is not something he should do," she said.

"I thought maybe it was cultural."

"No, he would never do anything like that to me."

"Ah, but father is always joking," Olav said when she asked him. "And often in a sexual manner. It's nothing. I will tell you something about father. It is the only way he knows how to talk to other people, this kidding, and most times in a sexual way."

The more she thought about it, the weirder it seemed. She couldn't imagine her father doing anything like that. She was so far from home. The land stretched out all around her, the repetition of hills and little trees and river. In the winter, Olav told her, it was dark for three months. Sometimes she tried to imagine that darkness. Thrilling but terrifying. Like being trapped in a cave.

She pulled a sweater and a book out of the tiny cupboard in the narrow room where she slept and stuffed them into a small backpack. She wasn't sure yet what she'd do. She didn't tell anyone where she was going. It was late but the sun still smoldered, a spark on the horizon. On the way up the road to the forest, she saw Olav's father nailing a reindeer hide to the side of the shed.

"I'm very angry at you," she shouted. He wouldn't understand what she was saying.

He laughed and said, "*Hva?*"

Maybe he thought the father got to share the son's lover. She wanted to hit him over the head with one of the clubs they used to kill salmon when they hauled the nets in.

She wasn't sure what time it was. Sometimes she lost track of the days. She walked through the birch woods, the trees even with her shoulders. She was headed for the cloudberry man's cottage. When she'd looked in the windows on one of her hikes with Olav in the forest, she saw a little black stove and reindeer skins piled in a corner. "In late summer," he said, "families come and pick berries in the bogs around Grandmother's Lake."

When she got to the hut, she couldn't find the key. Olav had told her it was hidden under the step.

She curled in a hollow in the moss near the cottage and rested her head on her pack. Twigs and leaves and spores of moss glowed with light. She pressed herself into the ground. She could hear the whole world moving under her.

A bird she didn't recognize called out again and again like a liquid bell.

She was alone on the edge of the vidda. There was something standing near her. She could hear its breath. Something pulling grass from the mound near the cottage. She was afraid to look. Mouth touching grass. The small rip of the meadow hay. Maybe it was something she shouldn't see, but she looked up. A large white reindeer, bent to the new grass near her head. His coat was shining. Not cream and brown, but white. She was almost close enough to touch his legs. His antlers furred, curved above his dipping head. It was a gift she wouldn't get again. A secret to keep for herself.

Would anyone miss her if she stayed out another night on the vidda? No one had come from the village to find her. Olav knew she was upset. And he knew where to find her. He'd been her guide in the forest.

She pulled on her pack and started walking toward the waterfall above the ravine. It was the wildest place she'd ever been. That roar of water breaking over the cliff. The sun at midnight. The screech of the fledged hawks near the rim.

She followed the narrow tracks rutted deep in the spongy taiga. In a couple of hours of slogging across the damp green hummocks she was nearing the waterfall echoing through the clusters of willow brush and stunted birch. The leaves of the birch as small as her fingernails.

The willow brush caught on her arms. Twigs snapped in her hair. It started to rain and soon the rain poured down her collar. The drops shimmered on her sweater. She heard Olav say over and over again, "I feel for you a little more, not less. I don't know what this word love means."

She was crying now and wiped the tears away from her face, still wet with rain. She didn't want to cry. A huge stone Olav had shown her near the waterfall glowed. The old Sami, he said, thought it was sacred. It was split in the middle and taller than she was. The sides streaked with whorls of green lichen shining in the cold rain. She was almost close enough to touch the stone when a man in a green parka appeared suddenly.

He stumbled toward her. He had a gun, and the gun flashed in the rain. Glinting for a moment. It was small. A pistol.

The man was saying something over and over in a language she couldn't understand. Nothing she'd ever heard before. He was close, waving the gun around her face. He was young. Near her age, not a man at all. His face was rough with a sparse beard. Now she could see blood smeared on the right side of his face, matted in his dark hair. He was close enough to grab her neck. She reached out quickly and pushed him. He fell. He fell too easily. He was so light. As if he were made of air.

She touched her neck, her throat. She could feel the dirt from his hands on her skin. Grainy. Wet.

Shouldn't he have tried something? Shot the gun. But he crumpled and she heard a crack as she turned and ran. Had he hit his head? Had she hurt him somehow? She kept running over the uneven ground until she knew she was at least a couple of miles away from the waterfall and crouched in the moss. She could see the petals of the orchid she'd found once before. The white flower cut like lace. Her heart was pounding. She waited until the beating in her ears faded away, drank some water, and got to her feet. She walked steadily for hours until Lismavarri appeared below her on the river.

When she opened the door to the house, Olav said, “Ah, Mother thought you had been eaten by a bear.”

31.

KATHRYN PUT MAREN INTO her crib for a nap at two before going into the barn with Olav. In the loft, the scratchy hay on her back, the smell of the field below them. His lips on her breasts. "Don't worry," he said, "she's fine. She's sleeping."

When Kathryn went back inside the house to check on Maren, she expected to see the soft side of her cheek, the dark curls on her head, her fist clutched around the blanket. But the crib was empty.

The heat blasting.

The house silent. Ellen and Jorgen away at the clinic with the tiny baby for a checkup.

She couldn't breathe. She sat down on the floor and tried to take slow breaths. Outside, the sheep were calling to their lambs in the field. She'd never been this cold. Now Olav was gone too, taken off in his car.

She should have told Olav about the boy in the forest. They would have looked for him. And now this was her punishment. Maren stolen.

She got up slowly and started to search, first the closet. Each room, under beds, calling "Maren, Maren."

So many places the child could be. The barn, under a car, in the river, taken by a neighbor, in the forest. Her heart thudded in her ears. Maren, Maren. Her hand sticky on the banister to the basement. She ran out into the yard and then the road. She'd start with the nearest house.

Her bare feet burning on the gravel. Her vision blurring, the panic so thick. Her heart beating but everything else frozen. Her arms hanging. And then she saw them, Olav's mother and Maren standing in the yard of the blue house in the thicket of birches. The beautiful singer standing near Maren. She rested her hand on the child's head. Maren fluttered her little hands and shouted something to Kathryn.

Too far away, she couldn't make out the words.

32.

"COME, WE'LL GO GATHER the hay now," Olav said as she sat on the steps to the house, and they walked down the village road to the farthest field perched on the edge of the river. Everyone in the village was helping with haymaking.

When they reached the field, Olav's father handed her woolen gloves. He'd left a bag of oranges by her bed. A peace offering, maybe. They were valuable. He'd traded a salmon in Finland for the fruit.

Gunter and Eric had mowed the hay early in the morning. Two wires strung on poles ran all along the clipped field. A boy from the village was hammering the third wire to a row of sticks. She pulled the gloves on and bent to shake the cut hay and pile it on the wires to dry. First darker green, then golden as it hung for a week or more. The fields closest to the river, wet, matted. Smelling like lemon.

She did this again and again until her back ached and her hands were stiff.

They stopped for lunch and sat in a circle, or leaned against poles supporting the hay.

Olav's mother cooked strips of fish on sticks over a fire she'd lit at noon. She was sitting on the clipped field on a plaid cloth surrounded by a basket of bread, a pile of whittled sticks, glass bottles full of water. Gunter started to laugh, his mouth full of sweet salmon.

"You look crazed," Kathryn said.

"I am, and I will eat you with my sharp teeth, my pretty."

"Never." She picked up the loaf of bread and cut a slice off with the sharp knife Olav's mother handed her. "I have the knife." She shook it at Gunter.

Olav's mother chuckled and nodded her head, wrapped up in a bright scarf.

Eric had finished tossing his pile of hay onto the last row of wire and walked toward them. The sheep chewing peacefully in the next field.

When Eric reached the fire, he carefully lifted one of the sticks into his hands, sat down near her, and bit into the fish.

"Paradise," he said, and closed his eyes. "All we need now is beer."

Gunter took a long drink from the bottle of water. "The beer here isn't at all bad."

"Not bad, but expensive." Eric turned a stick in the fire. Olav's mother pushed a piece of salmon onto a stick and handed it to Eric.

"It's still so tied up with religion. You're supposed to get your ecstasy from confession, from the redemption of confession. From shouting your sins to the world."

"I grew up in a family who believed in confession," Kathryn said.

The taste of the fish, the smoke from the fire. The heat on her face as she chewed. She thought about the man in the forest. The blood on his face. The way he fell so easily. She was running away from Olav's father when she ended up in the forest. Couldn't the boy have been running away from something?

"Not a kind of redemption I want," Eric said. "I used to watch my mother and the other women asking forgiveness in the church. We'd travel a long way after we moved from Kautokeino. We had to. The nearest church was days away. There wasn't a road at the end, only a long bridge across the river where there was an old church. It was a place where we came for hundreds of years and then the settlers came there too.

"Everyone prayed together. We stayed in a *kota* with some of mother's relatives. It was a big party until the service. And then I couldn't stand all the wailing and fainting. The settlers had their own cabins. My favorite part was the river. I'd spend hours playing there. It was cold, came right down from the mountains. When my older sister was married, we took the long trip there again. I always thought it was odd we didn't just go back to Kautokeino, but Mother's family were from Sweden and that's where we went twice a year to confess our sins."

"Where was the village?" Gunter asked. "It must have been an awesome trip." He held a stick with grilled salmon near his mouth and tempted Kathryn with it. She didn't want to play anymore. Her eyes were filled with the smoke from the fire. If she didn't confess, how could she get absolution?

"It was deep in the mountains south of here. We took days to get there and it was eerie. All those graves. My mother told me about her sister's child born when they were going up to spring pasture. Burning up with a fever in his cradle on her back. All the bright ribbons moving in the wind, but he was so hot and she couldn't do anything about it. So hot and even the cool water that she bathed him in didn't calm him. He stopped crying as they got farther and farther into the mountains. One day he just died. They wrapped him and put him in a tiny birch bark coffin, carried it to the church. They had the child blessed and buried. She wanted to show me his grave and I said no."

THAT NIGHT IN THE sauna she shook branches filled with cold water from a pail on her skin. She was perfectly alone lying on the bench near the little stove. No one had possession of her. The wood was against her back, heat from the little stove rising above her. Fields dropping off to the smooth river stones and then the river and then Finland.

She wanted to go away and come back to Olav after she'd learned how to live by herself in the woods. In a tiny cabin at the edge of the forest where it stopped on the hill above the village. She wanted him to tell her he loved her. She wanted the way her body tricked her mind to stop. To stop tasting his lips, his hand, his stomach. Why wasn't she as smart and brave as those women she'd met in the mountains in the West? Tall, strong, with blond or red ponytails, as clever as the men. Scaling granite cliffs, walking to the top of Denali. Not afraid to die.

33.

A SMALL ROUND WOMAN was cutting the grass near the blue house. She leaned over and, with a series of sweeping motions, cut the grass low. Her rhythm perfect as she swung the sickle. Her arm in an arc across her body. It was peaceful to sit on the steps of the house and watch the woman work. The tall birches near the house and the shining river beyond, across the large field. There was Olav walking from the shop to his uncle's house. There was Gunter coming in her direction. Everything seemed to be in slow motion. The beating of her heart, the pulse in her wrist. The progress of the slim black birds across the sky.

Kathryn wanted the moment to last forever. Gunter laughed. Olav slammed the door to the house. The birds began to call.

Later, she crossed the river in one of the long black boats with Ellen. The house they visited was old and small. They had to bend to get through the door. There was hardly any light. "They are cousins of Mrs. Elstad. A family who has many reindeer." An older woman was washing a toddler in a tub on the table. There were cardboard boxes and piles of skins in a corner.

Ellen gave the grandmother a package and they sat on chairs pulled up to the table as the woman washed the little girl, who stared at them. Kathryn didn't understand what they were saying, but they started to laugh and she smiled too.

The little girl giggled, and her grandmother wrapped her in a towel. The sun was brilliant outside, but in the small house the dim light pooled on the shiny tub on the table.

Ellen paid the woman some money, and she went to the corner of the room and opened a wooden box. She handed Kathryn a pair of boots made of reindeer skin. The most beautiful things she had ever seen.

"Olav wanted you to have a pair and I thought the little trip would be fun."

Kathryn slipped off her sandals and pulled the boots on. They were soft gray and trimmed in blue, red, and yellow wool cut in patterns. Yarn twisted in delicate ropes tied the boots snug around her ankles. "The old Sami would stuff the boots with straw to make them soft and warm," Ellen said.

"Thank you," Kathryn said. The boots fit perfectly.

She wanted to be part of this life but didn't quite belong to anyone yet. She could see herself slipping the boots on and bending to strap her skis over the curved tip.

"A terrible life," Olav had told her. "It's dirty, dangerous. In the winter the tents smelled. The fur parkas they wore over their tunics reeked after those cold months. They smelled of smoke and food and their bodies. The parkas were very heavy. And most of the work is on snowmobiles now, Kathryn. Not like you imagine."

Slowly the night was coming back. The willow and the birch would soon turn yellow in the forest. Night would start its fast return to the north and the silky light of midnight would disappear. It was almost dark enough to see the moon.

Everyone was asleep in the small house, curled in their beds. She could almost hear the house breathe with the weight of their sleep. Olav was beside her in the narrow bed. In her room. His mouth against her ear. His arms around her shoulders.

"There must have been something wrong with your boyfriend," Olav whispered.

Kathryn didn't answer right away. She was thinking of the dark light of a low building in the mountains. The trees rimmed in snow. The track through the valley where a slope could slide at any minute.

"No, there was nothing wrong with him. He wasn't my boyfriend. Things just didn't work out."

Olav's mouth had been on her shoulder as she slept. Now his lips were on her lips. The blanket was wound around them like a sleeping bag. Outside the door someone was knocking. His mother waking her to go to the barn. His hand was on her stomach, now again his lips were on her lips. She was unable to remember where her body began.

"I was only in love once before," Olav said, "and that was ten years ago."

"With the singer?

"Yes, with Ingrid. But she was not singing then."

"Oh, so you are in love, then?"

"Perhaps," he said.

34.

THE NEXT MORNING AS she was sweeping the steps of the house, she watched two men in matching clothes open the door of the shop across the street. They wore khaki pants and safari vests, the kind with all the pockets. Baseball caps and heavy brown boots.

Olav held the door as the men entered the shop. They disappeared and reappeared a few minutes later. One was straightening his cap. The other shook his head. They walked down the road in the direction of the sauna, and got into a Land Rover parked on the grass near the little shed.

Someone was shouting in the shop. Soon Jorgen appeared flinging the door shut as he walked toward the dairy.

"*Du*," Olav's mother yelled from inside her house, "*hit*," and Kathryn leaned the broom against the step and went inside. It was strange Olav's mother never called her by her name. Was Kathryn so hard to pronounce?

"They were probably salesmen," Gunter said later after lunch as they walked down the village road kicking up stones.

"You have meat between your teeth," Kathryn said.

"I can't imagine they'd be anything else. You are suspicious for an American."

"What's that mean?" she asked and walked faster.

"You ask an awesome amount of questions for someone from a very incurious country."

"Just salesmen. Two salesmen so far north. And what are they selling?"

"Fishing gear," Gunter said. "The shop carries all sorts of things."

Jorgen ferried his mother and Kathryn across the river in one of the narrow black boats in the afternoon, and she bought bananas and yogurt and oranges in Finland. He was silent as he poled the boat fast across the shallow river.

When they returned to the farm, Jorgen and his mother argued. Or Kathryn thought they were arguing. Their voices were loud. His mother hit the kitchen table with her hand, covered in flour. Kathryn was halfway through the door of the kitchen and she stopped and turned around. His mother pointed her finger at Kathryn and muttered something about "the English."

Ellen was setting the big table in the living room with plates for dinner.

"Where did the men go when you saw them leave the shop?" Jorgen asked as Kathryn carried cups into the living room.

"I saw the men get into their jeep," she said.

"Both men?"

"Yes."

She was uncomfortable alone with Jorgen, so different from his older brother. Never laughing, always businesslike. His dark hair slicked back from his forehead. She was trying to see what Olav saw in him. A different version underneath this one. So different from Ellen, who was delicate and warm.

He was looking carefully at her face. Searching her eyes. What does he know, she wondered. What does he want to know?

Even though she wasn't quite sure what people were saying, she knew everyone in the village understood she and Olav were lovers. It was plain on their faces. She couldn't tell if this was good or bad. Jorgen seemed to think it wasn't good. He was protective, defensive and never had anything kind to say to her. But Ellen was the opposite and Kathryn was grateful about that. She could talk to Ellen, even if she couldn't tell Ellen anything about what she felt for Olav. They never had that kind of conversation.

What she felt for Olav, though, seemed to cancel any questions she had about her life in Lismavarri. Sometimes she was absolutely convinced she'd never been this happy before.

Jorgen walked out of the living room down the steps to the basement.

She set the cups in a row on the table and swatted at a mosquito near her ear. "What's Jorgen so angry about now?" she asked Olav when he joined her, balancing more cups in his hands.

"I'll tell you something. Jorgen doesn't like complications. He likes things to be black and white. Nothing for you to worry about, Kathryn." Olav said.

His mother motioned to her from the kitchen and asked her to get the milk for the table. She left Olav and walked across the street to the dairy. She could feel the night in the small room. The first night in almost three months. It was sudden and quiet, sneaking up on them.

She dipped the metal dipper into the milk can and filled the white pitcher. The light was on and the first cricket chirped in the new darkness outside. How could she forget what the cool night tasted like?

She crossed the road to the house and opened the door. Ellen had set out cloudberries and cream and salted salmon and little buns with butter on the table in the living room.

Olav and Eric were sitting at the small table in the kitchen. Kathryn set the milk pitcher on the table and sat across from Eric, his plate filled with salmon. Small pieces of cake were piled on a dish near Olav.

"Men have come to the village asking questions about the forest," Eric said.

"The two men in safari vests?" Kathryn asked. She carefully spooned the ripe berries into her mouth. "Why?"

"A construction project. Something to do with geology. A special kind of rock. They're interested in the small mountain near the hot spring."

"But they can't build anything there. Can they?"

"They can try. Jorgen thinks it's a good idea. It would be practical to lease the mountain to them. Uncle doesn't think so. There's good pasture all around that spring," Eric said, his mouth full.

"What's it like for the reindeer herders when it gets cold?" she asked, reaching for a piece of cake.

"It's very hard following the reindeer," Olav said.

She was curious. How many people keep track of how many reindeer? Where do they sleep? How many reindeer does his uncle own?

"You can't ask someone that. It's like asking a man how much money he has," Eric said and laughed.

"Oh, I thought it might be like owning cattle." She took a sip of the coffee, dark and bitter, and bit into the light cake.

"Nothing like that. Yes, it's very hard following the herd. Sometimes lost in the snow. The worst time is the autumn when rain and snow mix together. This makes things bad."

The last time she'd walked in the forest she saw the sheep, moving higher up. The birches turning yellow near the cloudberry man's hut.

35.

THE NEXT DAY THEY took one of the black boats to go to the Cowfest. In the boat, Gunter stood behind her and pushed the long pole into the river, guiding the narrow boat to Finland. Kathryn laughed as he maneuvered the slim boat through the shimmering water. Eric's band was playing, and he'd asked Gunter to join them on a couple of songs.

The chill came down from the top of the world. The sound of the band warming up on the bank of the river drifted across the silent water.

The boat crunched against the gravel. They got out on the cold sand and Kathryn carried her shoes in her hand. The sharp sand cut into her feet. Gunter pulled the narrow boat up on the bank.

"Gunter," Eric yelled, "come over here, guy!"

His hands felt a little cold, Gunter told Kathryn, and he was starting to feel nervous about playing with the band. He ran up the small slope to where Eric was standing. Magnificent, Kathryn thought. Eric dressed in his Sami tunic with red and blue embroidery and bright blue pants and a sash like a pirate.

"You sure it's okay, dude?" Gunter asked.

"Oh yeah, it's perfect. You'll be perfect."

Olav and Eric had built a dance floor in the field, and people had come from all the villages along the river. Olav pulled Kathryn toward him and danced with her on the smooth wooden floor, dipping her this way and that.

"This band can't play a waltz," Olav shouted. Kathryn laughed, holding onto him as he twirled her around. Her heart was beating hard against his shirt. She wanted to feel weightless forever. Maybe they could all leave their heavy bodies, ascend into heaven for a few minutes. Ellen and Jorgen were dancing, too. Ellen was smiling.

"We're having a party," one of Olav's cousins said, shouting into Olav's ear near Kathryn's face, the smell of beer, sweet, spoiled on his breath. "Come after the dance. Jorgen and Ellen are coming. A celebration for Magnus. His birthday. He's going to Bergen soon. Studying to be a doctor."

Olav said, "Sure, sure, sounds fine."

"Not so fine," he said, when the music stopped and they stood on the wooden floor. The bodies stilled around them. Cold coming from the river. The hazy light of the summer sky. The musicians packing up their instruments. Guitars hidden in their cases now. "It's never fine with my cousins, but I would like to talk to Magnus, so we'll go."

They caught up with Ellen and Jorgen walking on the road and headed south. They stopped at a low wooden house, the door thrown open, filled with men drinking beer. Two black and white dogs were curled up in the corner.

Someone handed her a bottle and she squeezed onto the lumpy couch with Olav. Jorgen stood in the doorway talking to a tall man with long hair pulled into a knot at his neck. The dogs had woken up and ran around eating scraps people threw at them until a woman came and shooed them outside. "Not so nice for the party," she said and smiled at Kathryn.

Suddenly Jorgen started punching the tall man in the chest with his fist. "What's he saying?" Kathryn asked Olav.

"He's trying to convince Magnus that the men who want to lease the land near the mountain have a good idea. It would be a smart thing for the village and bring in money for the schools and sports club. Magnus and his brothers think it's a bad idea. The loss of more grazing land for the reindeer. Magnus is getting angry, but he'll walk away. You'll see. He has other things to worry about."

"I can see that." Kathryn laughed. "I'd be angry too, if Jorgen was hitting me."

"Jorgen's harmless. Just a little worked up about something,"

Magnus backed away, but another man took Jorgen by the shoulders and pulled him outside.

Olav had turned to talk to a woman standing over him, holding a tray of cakes. Her hands were covered with scars. She whispered something and looked at Kathryn.

"What did she say?" Kathryn asked.

"She told me I will lose the American girl."

"How's she know this?"

"She's very stupid. She thinks she can practice trolldom and make things difficult for me."

Kathryn was dizzy, drinking the beer too quickly. It was hot in the little house.

"I'm just going outside to get some air," she said to Olav and he nodded.

She went out into the yard where the man, a cousin of Olav's, was punching Jorgen over and over again.

She couldn't watch Jorgen standing there, covered in blood and dirt. They wrestled each other to the ground. Kathryn ran at the men just as they struggled up from the ground. Jorgen swung around and hit her on the forehead.

She touched her skin. Sticky, wet. Olav appeared suddenly and pulled the two men apart.

"You're hurt," he said. He looked old suddenly, helping her up. Everyone else was laughing, but the man was shouting at Jorgen.

"What's he saying?" she asked.

"Nothing for you to worry about. He's a hothead. Magnus's younger brother."

She'd seen Jorgen fight once before, but with Eric. They'd come back across the river late from a party, the sky gauzy with faint stars. Like a gift from some wizard. In her bed, she'd woken to voices. Someone shouting. Bottles breaking.

She rubbed her fingers in the corners of her eyes and pulled herself out of bed. Olav was working late in his office in the basement. When she looked out her window she saw Eric and Jorgen fighting near the sauna.

Eric's wife appeared, brushing her light hair back from her eyes. She shouted something at both of them, looking from one to the other as she yelled.

The baby started to cry deep in the house.

Olav ran out and pulled Jorgen away. He was laughing. So odd, that he was laughing. But there were lots of strange things she didn't understand.

Eric took his wife's hand and they walked away up the road. Kathryn watched until they were out of sight behind Olav's uncle's house. Who was taking care of their little girl? Olav picked up the broken bottles scattered on the grass near the sauna.

36.

Kathryn had seen Gunter in the forest a couple of times when she was running. Once he was kneeling, bent over a mound of moss, photographing the tiny red trumpets popping up from the green moss. Another time he was standing at the edge of the forest, his camera held steady pointed toward the fields they'd just hayed in early August. All the long grass was thrown over the wires strung along the field. Heavy bundles drying. Olav was hoping it would dry quickly before the weather got bad.

The forest smelled of wet leaves now that it was late in August. Her bare feet on the hard dirt of the village road. Kathryn turned the corner and there were the fields in their rush to the river and the bank above the wild cold Tana. The single birch trees at the margin. Dark birds flying in a messy group to the water. Soon the sports club appeared.

When she first got to Lismavarri she'd gone to the sports club dressed up in a Sami tunic and a pink shawl.

"Are you a linguist?" someone asked her.

"No," she'd said, embarrassed that Olav's mother had dressed her up like a doll for the party.

His mother had laughed as she gave her the blue tunic trimmed in red and yellow and the bonnet with the long red ties and the silky shawl finished with hundreds of twisted pink cords of silk. At the sports club, everyone was crowded into the room, sitting on small chairs. Pictures of skiing champions covered the walls. How strange she'd felt wearing someone else's clothes.

Now as she ran, she couldn't quite make out what it was propped against the wall of the sports club next to the door. Something big. Not a person or a box. Not a tool.

Something bleeding but not alive. White and bristly. Beautiful but dead. A torso. A body without a head. The heavy antlers bleached gray. The gentle mouth gone. She knelt in the grass by the reindeer.

Everything had come to this. The white reindeer she'd seen in the forest by the cloudberry man's hut. The good fortune she'd had to be so close to the reindeer erased by what happened later. The secret of the man in the green coat, crumpled on the moss as she turned and ran. She wiped her face with the back of her hand and got up from the wet grass.

She ran back to the Elstads' house where Olav was working in his office and told him about the dead reindeer. By the time they walked back to the sports club, the body was gone. No trace of the animal. "It was there," Kathryn said. "Is this some kind of joke?"

"Not a joke," Olav said. "The animal is valuable. No reindeer owner would do this. I must make a call. A man I know. One of the reindeer police. They take care of such matters. But this doesn't happen. Not this, but theft, disputes. Sometimes people fight when the men are marking the calves, things like that."

He leaned over the blood and hairs on the ground. "It could be from anything. One of the men slaughtering animals for the winter, a neighbor skinning a hide."

"But they wouldn't do that in front of the sports club. Would they?"

"No, not here, but there's not enough proof that the body was left in this place."

"I didn't imagine it."

"I know, Kathryn. But even if we did find the body, there would be no way to tell whose reindeer it is. So the reindeer might have died and then someone brought it here. To say what, I wonder."

"Something to do with your cousins and Jorgen?" Kathryn touched the matted grass.

"No, that was nothing," he said, but she could see he didn't believe it. He turned away from her. Rubbed his hand along the back of his neck.

The slaughtered reindeer was a warning but she wasn't sure what it meant.

(NOVEMBER)
HANS

37.

He took the early train to Stockholm to interview Yuri Zhukov's parents. What kind of life had their son lived in Stockholm, restricted by the embassy protocol?

The pine forest all along the tracks, plowed fields coming into focus as the light grew. Every day there was less daylight.

He pulled Emilie's letters from his bag and propped them on his lap and flipped on the light above. His cousin Sara had called a friend in Stockholm, a curator at the Nordiska museet, who would meet Hans to show him Emilie's paintings.

His reflection in the train window flashed as the train sped across the dark fields, through deep woods, past little villages with their dim lights, the animals waking in their barns and sheds. A man bent over the pages of letters.

The death in Lismavarri was haunting him. Before Astrid's death, he was more practical about matters like these. They were outside of him, puzzles to be solved. Now he wasn't so sure. The train swayed and the letters scattered across the aisle. He jumped up and picked them up quickly. An old man sitting in the seat opposite him winked.

"Letters from a lover, heh?"

Hans laughed. "Not quite. But I suppose they could be."

In one of her letters Emilie talked about losing Turi. The old wolf. A lawyer had sent her a letter. Turi wanted some money from the British edition of their book, and Emilie said she tore her hair out about it. It wasn't long before Turi died. They were so old suddenly and he was so different from the man who'd missed her terribly those years before. The man who thought he couldn't live without her. The man who wrote her letter after letter. As close as two souls could be after those weeks working together in the miner's cabin on their book.

He knew he wasn't as focused on the case as he could be, tracking down both Turi and the Danish woman who might have been in love with him. But here he was, about to spend an hour or so taking a look at her paintings and some of Turi's things that Per, Turi's nephew who'd disappeared in America, had given the museum.

His mother liked Per the best of all her aunts and uncles. Hans had looked at Per's drawings on graph paper of the mountain near her village. Reindeer herders traveled over the mountain to reach summer pastures. They were sketches of the peak from different directions and distances. Per drew the glaciers and snowdrifts. The crags and meadows. The dark stone of the mountain, the brown slopes leading up to the summit, rough red shadow of bushes along the flank.

His mother wasn't sure why, or when, he'd made the drawings.

"He was always trying to make some money from the tourists," she said. "Maybe he was leading a climb up the mountain. It was very popular then with people from the south."

THE CARRIAGE SWAYED ON the tracks as he opened one of Emilie's letters.

Kauslunde

Darling one,

I've been painting frantically. The images are pouring forth. It's intoxicating. I don't remember when I last felt like this. I sleep on the cot in the workroom and wake at dawn and paint for hours. This morning I made coffee and sat out on the patio, the lilies opened wide with their pearly throats, and an image came to me of a boy bent over his long black boat pulling it out of the water at midnight. The bright blue and red of his coat, belted at the waist, the long narrow boat in a curl as he pulled it over rocks at the edge of the shining lake. His body bent to mimic the curve of the tip of the boat, the long poles crossed in a "V" on the thwart in the polished interior. I saw the sun pouring like a river of silver over the flat surface of the lake. All light, nothing more, the water turned into something beyond reflection. There were still patches of snow in the mountains. June, as I remembered it there.

Love, E.

AT THAT MOMENT, HE wanted more than anything to see her paintings. Going to the museum was a way to postpone the bad story, the one with the Russian boy who might be dead.

The farms grew larger as the train rumbled toward Stockholm. The narrow trees in the woodlots like sentinels around the barns. He got up and shuffled the letters into their folder and slipped it into his briefcase. A new addiction, this longing to hear someone's voice again and again.

He walked to the dining car and ordered breakfast even though he wasn't very hungry. He picked at the pre-packaged breakfast meats and cheese. His head throbbed. Not something he wanted to admit. He shook two aspirins into his palm and swallowed them quickly with the last of his coffee.

The train rocked as he walked back to his seat. It was just pulling into the station. Hans lifted his duffle off the luggage rack. Wrestled into his coat and grabbed the briefcase. He had about two hours before the Nordiska museet closed.

He got on the tram to Djurgarden. He always felt like a poor kid in Stockholm. All the fancy cafés and shops with expensive cloth arranged in cascades in windows. Business-men with dark suits. It was raining. He got off at the wrong stop and had to walk up the long avenue.

Everything was gray. He was tempted to pay the admission to Skansen and see the bears on the way to the museum. Astrid had always liked them. They'd gone to Stockholm on a holiday once. "I want to stay in an expensive hotel," she said, "and eat expensive food, and drink expensive wine, and spend most of my time watching the bears in Skansen. Those bears with cinnamon-colored fur."

"Okay," Hans said, "whatever you want." It was a warm spring and the bears were sleepy. They watched one small bear climb high up in a tiny tree. She loved the seals too. Astrid was happy that day, even though they both knew soon she'd be too sick to travel.

He was wet and cold by the time he reached the museum. The curator, Evan, took Hans to the basement, where he signed a document to see Emilie's paintings. He was pleasant and wore one of those tailored vests with a bright shirt.

"Sara told me you're both looking into Emilie's life," he said as he pulled on a pair of white cotton gloves. He seemed surprised Hans was interested in the paintings.

"Yes, I know it's a little weird, isn't it, for a cop to be so off track."

"There are photographs and artifacts, too. Would you like to see those?"

"That'd be great," Hans said.

"Then you'll need these," he said, and handed Hans a pair of white gloves.

Evan led him down the stone stairs into a room filled with paintings, each framed in the same plain wood. They hung on movable frames, one after the other.

"A brilliant artist. She said, and forgive me if I misquote some of this, that she understood finally color as sound, the mystical power of color. The veil fell from her eyes, and she understood how she should paint, how deep in her soul, she'd always wanted to paint. It's one of those moments artists have when everything comes together, if they're lucky."

The curator pushed his glasses up on his nose. "I'll go find the other objects in the archives and then come and get you."

"Thank you." Hans walked from one painting to the next. Rubbed his shoulder. Maybe his brother was right. How could he have left the place reflected in the paintings to live in an apartment with narrow windows looking out at the street? His slick kitchen and bedroom with built-in shelves. Books arranged neatly. Everything so sterile since Astrid's death. A fiction, perhaps, that he liked living in Oslo. An exile he'd chosen.

Emilie's paintings brought him back to his mother's childhood in the mountains on the border of Sweden and Norway. His mother hadn't been to those places since she was a young woman, but she carried the landscape with her. Turi's country. Hans remembered his grandmother telling him about the long trek from Sweden into Norway following the reindeer. When they started to see the coastal forest, where there was grass and leaves, it was beautiful and pleasant. Or the word they always used—*havski*. And when they started to hear the cuckoo and all the other birds singing, that was pleasant and they began to *yoik*.

Sustenance for body and soul. It's pleasant in the *goahti* with the fire going, coffee boiling, good pasture, reindeer grazing. The baby, wrapped in the *gietkka* on the long migration, is happy. The older children spend the ride on the reindeer, cold, sometimes too cold to hang on, she told him.

Emilie was painting years later what she remembered of the time with his family. In one painting a boy was pulling a narrow boat onto the sandy gravel of the riverbank. In another it could be one of his great uncles tugging a reindeer off jagged rocks in the mountains with his lasso, the vidda at dawn. Or Turi's brother and his children gathered around a fire, the coffeepot above the flames. The stark trees of the forest bare in winter, reindeer pawing through frozen crust for moss.

When Hans was a little boy they traveled to Sweden. His mother wanted to see her sisters. He went out with his cousins to the place where thick grass grew under fir trees near their *goahti*. It was the place where they cut grass for their boots. He liked the way it smelled like lemon. Silky and shiny in his hands.

They knew how to cut efficiently. Gather the grass in their hands and swiftly shear a hank with their sharp knives. Even his cousin who was five had his own knife. They gathered the grass and twisted it into handfuls, pulling the burrs and stalks clear, beating the roots against the trees.

He'd felt important, in charge of the bundles. He carried them to the little yard in front of the house where the dogs were sleeping. They used a special comb to pull the grass so it was smooth. Then they braided each hank into a *pil'ka*. They'd get about fifty, enough to last the family for the winter. Soft hay in a nest to pad their boots. Warm, easy to dry when it got wet. They carefully heated the soles of their feet by the fire and beat them with birch branches to make them tough. The hay was like a cushion, much more comfortable than Hans's boots.

Hans compared the dates of the paintings. Several were painted in the 30s and others during the Occupation. In his favorite landscape it was high summer. The sun swinging around the horizon at midnight, more like a moon than sun.

Some of the paintings were darker. The trees bare and twisted. There was no one there. Just the reindeer, bent under their heavy antlers, pawing at the ground. The date on these paintings was during the war or just after. Something had happened. Not just the war. Something happened to Emilie.

Evan appeared and said, "I've found artifacts for you to take a look at. Interesting that you're related to Turi."

"My mother thinks I'm a little obsessed about this connection."

The curator laughed. "My mother thinks my profession is crazy."

Hans smiled and followed him into another large room. The objects were in open shallow drawers, covered with heavy muslin cloth. Evan drew the cloth to the side and pulled the first drawer out.

Turi had been not only a hunter and writer but an artist, Hans realized, as the curator picked up a knife Turi'd made for Emilie.

"It's very beautiful," Hans said.

"I agree. He would have bought the blade and then attached the hilt. And carved the sheath out of reindeer antler. See how it twists here at the end?"

What kind of man would give a woman a beautiful knife? A man who valued the knife above all. Who lived with his knife. A man who was perhaps in love with the woman.

The knife the curator held in his gloved hands was small and carefully made. The blade straight and dark, the handle incised with decoration on the antler, burned patterns of tiny dots and stripes with a flare at the top. The sheath was skillful. Dark reindeer skin, the most valuable color, the skin of a calf, wound around the top, a supple drawstring with a silver button on the end.

The curve of the body carved with a design like the rickrack on his mother's Sunday dress and the letters J.O.T E.D., the date 1909. She would have worn it on her belt. Their names linked together by a simple design.

Why did Emilie give it away? The curator said the museum acquired the knife in 1940. She'd kept it all those years and then let it go.

Evan put the knife away carefully and moved to another aisle with more drawers. "And here, some things of Turi's." He pulled the drawer out slowly like a magician.

Turi's hat with a worn leather brim and red woolen pompom appeared. "It's incredible to see his clothes," Hans said. "Makes him more real." His boots were small. Hide polished from years of wear. And his pants, the most amazing. The knees still bent with the imprint of his legs, fur on the cuff.

"I have some photographs for you too. Let's move to the table over there," Evan said. There was a blue cardboard file box on the table. He opened the box and took out several large envelopes.

"I'll let you take your time with these," he said, and disappeared again.

Hans put on the pair of white gloves. He slipped his hand into the envelope and placed the photos on the table.

There were several photographs Emilie had taken when she and Gudmund visited Turi in the 1920s. The caption was, "Turi with the largest wolf he ever killed. Going to America." Turi held the wolf for the photograph with his hands on the ruff of the animal's neck and fur of its back. The forelegs bent in the snow by his boot.

The wolf was magnificent, coat thick and shining even in death. Hans didn't see Turi as a contract killer, but that's what the caption seemed to imply. A trophy for some rich American.

He shuffled the other photographs and stopped at one of Emilie. Her cap was like a crown on her head. She wore a tunic belted at the waist with a woven belt. She was smiling, coaxing a wolf cub closer to her with a piece of meat. The dog she painted so affectionately in her paintings was standing near her as she crouched by the three pups.

He'd looked at evidence, held it in his hands, turned it over and wondered about the person who'd owned it, but this was different. The room was windowless and cool. He could be entombed with the relics of his ancestor. The photographs of a woman who knew much more about Turi's life than he did.

It seemed like Emilie had pushed through difficult times in her marriage. Losses calculated and then boxed up, put away. But the paintings told a different story.

HE'D MADE A MESS of things with Kari. She'd written to him. A short note. He'd thought about her. The way she laughed. How unpredictable she was. Not what he expected.

She wanted to see him again, wondered if he was okay. He'd almost called her. He wanted to tell her that he wasn't okay. He wasn't anyone she wanted to get involved with. But he hadn't. He left it at that. He wasn't thinking straight, dropping off a cliff into a ravine that looked like the gash in the forest above Lismavarri. The thunder of the waterfall crashing over and over again.

It was dark by the time he left the museum. His head hurt and he rubbed his neck as he walked over the bridge along the water to the tram stop.

38.

THE INVESTIGATION INTO THE missing boy seemed straightforward when Hans read the report at Police Headquarters in Stockholm the next morning. He'd walked to the office from his hotel near the Observatory across the bridge to Kungsholmen. The rain had stopped and it felt good to be striding across the streets as if he knew what he was doing.

He couldn't feel his body sometimes. Everything numb. But the man he'd become after Astrid died was walking across the bridge like nothing was wrong.

He sat in a stiff chair across from Detective Mattson, a man younger than he was. Other officers were at their desks. Looking busy. Dialing their phones, sorting folders. A plate of pastries sat on Mattson's desk. Hans was feeling hungry, but the detective didn't offer him a croissant.

Hans could tell he wasn't happy they'd already wasted time on this. His colleague, a very young woman with a shaved head, sat in another chair nearby. She stood out in the office full of men.

Mattson nodded toward the woman and said, "Hilde Berglund. She's been working on the case." Mattson brushed his dark hair away from his forehead. "We think Yuri Zhukov might have a gun."

"How did the boy get a gun?" Hans asked.

"We don't know," Mattson said. "His guide near Saxnas told us he had one. We lost his track south of Kiruna. You can look at the material. There's nothing to indicate he made it to Finnmark. You can follow up if you want, as I told Chief Inspector Lund. Let us know if you need anything." He seemed annoyed, distracted.

"So, you're satisfied the boy is still alive."

"We think he's alive and Annika Johnson, a woman who gave him a place to stay, knows where he is, but isn't talking. We interviewed her by phone. We've told the parents that. It could be Yuri Zhukov's defecting. It could be he doesn't want to tell them where he is. He's a man after all, not a boy."

Likely they didn't want to waste resources on this, and Mattson wasn't happy his chief had brought Hans in. It complicated things.

"Here's the file. Hilde will give you an office for the morning. She'd be happy to answer any questions. She conducted the interview."

"Thanks." Hans smiled. "His parents think something's happened. I'd like to at least double check."

"It makes sense. Though I can't see how you'll connect it to the case you're working on. Sounds like reindeer herders contaminated the site in Lismavarri before anyone got there. There's the problem of local police not knowing how to handle the body," Mattson said.

Hans wanted to argue with Mattson. He wanted to rant about the thoroughness of police training in Norway. It was the same old crap about the north.

The young woman led him down a brightly lit corridor to a small room with a table. An interview room. Hans opened the closed window.

"We don't have the resources right now to work on this," Hilde said. "A missing person is not a priority. Finding him could be more of an embarrassment. He just walked out of town and went north. Everyone feels uneasy about the case. His parents thought he'd taken a plane home to Moscow. Yuri must have paid off the driver, a guy who quit soon after Yuri disappeared."

"I understand."

"Let me know if something's not clear in the notes."

She disappeared and then returned with a croissant on a paper plate. "I thought you might be hungry," she said.

Hans smiled. "Starving."

He bent over the pages of the report. Yuri Zhukov's parents had found a scrap of paper in his room with Annika Johnson's address written on a napkin from a club. They told Mattson that the embassy security police warned Yuri he shouldn't be going out to bars. His parents hadn't heard from him for weeks and finally contacted the Swedish police. Mattson had tracked down Annika Johnson and called her.

Hilde Berglund followed up with a conversation with Mrs. Johnson that lasted an hour. Yuri had gone to a club in Sodermalm and met someone who had stayed at the hostel in Saxnas where Mrs. Johnson worked until recently. Yuri wanted to see the north.

In the report, Mrs. Johnson said Yuri told her he'd slipped over the fence of the Russian Embassy onto the limb of a large tree at midnight. Yuri wasn't happy with his parents. He didn't like the idea he had to be escorted out of the house. He wasn't a child. He didn't want to go back to Russia. She liked him. He was smart. When Yuri's parents thought their son was on his way to Moscow, he was heading north instead.

Annika Johnson said Yuri told her he took the train to Ostersund. No one checked. His parents hadn't reported him missing yet.

In the notes Hilde asked, "And you have no idea what he wanted to do?"

"No, no idea. I knew he'd already be in a lot of trouble for traveling north. I didn't want to make it worse."

"You told inspector Mattson he had a gun."

"My nephew told me. He led Yuri into the forest. A small pistol. A Tokarev, a Soviet Tokarev."

"You have no idea where he got it?"

"He said he got it in the mission. He said if he didn't get away, he'd go crazy. He was a nice boy. He wouldn't shoot anyone. I think he just wanted it for protection. He had a romantic idea about the wilderness. He was really a city kid."

It was such a strange breadcrumb for a parent, a paper napkin. Their child slipped over the fence and followed his own trail into another world.

No one had retraced Yuri's steps. There wasn't a sense of urgency about the investigation. The Swedish government thought it was the parents' problem. Hans figured the supervisor was sure there were KGB people involved in the search.

"I'd like to look into this," he said to the detective as he handed the file back to him in his office.

"Yes? You think we didn't do such a great job?" Mattson asked.

"It's not that. You did the job you thought was necessary. It wasn't connected to a body at that point."

"And you think the body found in your ravine is this Russian?"

"I'm not sure. It seems far-fetched. But the whole case is strange. It doesn't make sense that he would go any farther than Kiruna. It's wild around there and easy to get lost. You'd have to be prepared to camp for several days."

"Unless he thought he could disappear in the north and hitch a ride on a boat to America," Mattson said and turned away from Hans.

"I'll talk to the parents first and then try to follow his footsteps north. Annika Johnson might have something more to say, too. It may be that she was reluctant to tell you everything she knew. She might feel she needed to protect him, if he was determined to defect."

"I THINK IT'S A good idea. Go ahead, follow up on this," Malin said when he called her from the hotel. "We don't want any trouble from the Russians."

It was important to understand Yuri Zhukov's journey. Where he went. What he did. Often people left details out. Sometimes a phone conversation wasn't the best way to handle an interview. Someone's missing child seemed important enough for this kind of journey.

He made an appointment with Yuri's parents to meet at their apartment on Grevgatan near the embassy later in the afternoon.

His head started to throb again, and he took three aspirin. He cut a thick slab of cheese he'd bought and a hunk of bread and opened Turi's book to one of the chapters on hunting wolves. Turi wrestled with wolves and stabbed them with a knife. The wolf in the picture, though, seemed unharmed, if dead. You can also, Hans read, trap a wolf with a hidden shears-trap or poison a wolf with baited reindeer.

He closed his eyes and leaned back against the narrow padded chair. He knew he'd carry Emilie's paintings with him for days. Like a song stuck in your brain. A mix of joy and sorrow. The brushstrokes layered with light. She'd painted them so long after her years in the north. And the cold swift river in the ravine. The picture of Yuri Zhukov the Swedish detectives had given him. A tall boy with very dark hair. His thin face almost breaking into a smile for the photographer.

THE RUSSIAN EMBASSY WASN'T far from police headquarters. Hans walked past the courthouse with its turrets. Fallen leaves. The sun dissolving.

Yuri's parents lived in a narrow stone building. Iosif Zhukov opened the door to the apartment. His wife Larissa stood beside him. The setting sun flashed into the room.

The walls of the drawing room were painted dark red. The draperies pulled back with gold twine. Hans wondered if they'd decorated the apartment themselves or if someone else had. It was so ornate.

"I'm so glad you are now involved, Inspector Sorensen," Larissa Zhukov said. "We have been tearing our hair out. He was such a sweet child when he was young. So practical. He never argued. He always listened to me. A child with a beautiful voice."

Hans sat down on a chair carved like a small throne. He told the boy's parents he wasn't sure the police could help, but he wanted to know all the details.

"Not because you care," Yuri's father said. "But you want to solve the case you have. A body in Finnmark." Yuri's mother winced and touched the yellow curtain, adjusted the folds. She was a reporter, Mattson had told him, but he suspected she actually worked for the KGB.

"True," Hans said, "but there's only a small chance this case has anything to do with your son. You know strange things sometimes add up. Is there anything you can think of that might give us a better idea of where your son might be?"

"North, he is north," his father said. "He has been obsessed with the north since he was a little boy. He went to the Nordiska museum, full of all that Swedish history. He found carved wooden idols, he told me, *seite.* He was very interested in Sami culture. Someone told him there might still be hidden holy places. He knew he couldn't travel without permission, so he was spending hours at the museum."

"We told the Swedish police this," his mother said. There was nothing sinister about her, she was a slight woman with long red hair.

"He wasn't supposed to travel beyond Stockholm," his father said. "But you know children. Once he became a teenager he became a rebel."

"Not easy to live with?"

A woman came into the room with a tray filled with steaming cups and cake on gold rimmed plates.

"We love Yuri, of course. Though I had a hard time when all he did was listen to that American band. You remember, Larissa?"

"Yes, The Eagles. I thought it was such a strange name. Their lyrics weren't exactly something we approved of."

"He met people in a club. Americans his age. I found poetry in his room here that could make your life hard if it was discovered in Moscow. We think he went north to find a woman who knew about the wooden idols. We found her address in his room on a napkin from the club."

"Did you know the police interviewed her?"

"No," his mother said.

"We knew from our contacts that he's been in Ostersund," his father said and touched his wife's arm. "He was supposed to go back to Moscow this fall and start university there."

Hans balanced the cup and saucer on his knee. It was delicious coffee. Strange that he could think about coffee as a boy's parents told him about his disappearance. He never understood the way his mother's sheep were so frantic when their lambs were out of sight for a minute. They'd run from one track to another calling, calling until their lamb would answer. "You know I can trick some of the sheep who've lost lambs with the skin of their dead lamb tied to the back of another motherless lamb. But not all of them. That's why you ended up with a pet lamb now and then," his mother said.

"I shouldn't have talked him into coming here." Yuri's mother gestured to the windows, the doors. "A terrible place in some ways. Colder than Moscow. So dark."

"Let's take a look at his room," Hans said and placed the coffee on a small table.

They walked single file down the narrow hallway to a small room looking out at a park where a woman walked a tiny dog on a very long leash.

The room was cluttered with clothes and books and albums scattered on the floor. Hans recognized the names on two of the covers. *Undertakers Cirkus*, *Aunt Mary*. So Yuri liked folk rock bands. There was a pamphlet of poems by Joseph Brodsky. He picked it up and turned it over.

"He is just an ordinary boy. Nothing special. But very funny. Very quick."

"We thought Yuri would be back soon," his father said, his hand on his wife's arm. "He was supposed to go home for a couple of weeks and visit his grandmother. We didn't want to have him think we'd been looking through his things."

"But you have."

"Oh, yes," his mother said. "That's how we found the poetry, the music."

"Did you have a fight before he left?"

"Nothing more dramatic than how we usually disagreed." She smiled ruefully.

"He said he was bored by Communism. He wanted something more. He liked to taunt me with his ideas about democracy. We tried to use our own people in the north, but couldn't find out anything," his father said, pulling the heavy curtain over to block the sun shining into his wife's face.

"You told the Swedish headquarters about this?"

"Yes. Of course they weren't happy, but what could we do? They don't want a diplomatic disaster. Something that would be all over the papers," Iosif Zhukov said.

"We miss him terribly," his mother added. Her face as still as a stone.

It wasn't a fairy tale at all, but it was feeling more and more like one of the stories his grandmother used to tell him. A lost child. A body pecked apart by buzzards, a mother and father grieving.

Hans walked fast back to the Hotel Birger Jarl. Someone was following him. A fat man with a dark hat, pulled low over his eyes like a cartoon detective. When Hans moved, the man moved. When Hans turned, the guy looked somewhere else. He was probably KGB.

He was cold. Very lonely suddenly.

39.

Getting to Annika Johnson's house was a two-day trip. Hans took the train north to Ostersund, retracing Yuri's steps. On the way the train stopped on a stone bridge across a river in a midsized city. The narrow spire of a church, houses painted in bright colors, streets packed with bicycles and delivery trucks.

And then the cities disappeared. There were only frozen fields with sheep and horses. Cows in bunches near barns with peeling green doors. Small red and gray summer houses on lakes. Miles of bogs and then forests logged over, all the slim birch and narrow pines cut down, piled in heaps.

He stayed a night in Ostersund. He couldn't sleep, so he walked along the lake. No moon but the sky full of stars. The lake and sky merging. Lately he'd felt like an imposter. Not quite in his body, but not quite vanished into another world. It was easy to pretend he was just as efficient as he'd always been, even if he was covered in sweat and had to hold his hands steady against his thighs.

The next day he took a bus to Vilhelmina, the church town hours away. The bus was packed, with people standing in the aisle. Old men with small rucksacks and women with bright scarves knotted at their necks. Girls studying their faces in small mirrors. A man about his age sat next to him, picking his yellow teeth for most of the ride.

The bus went farther and farther into the forest on a narrow bumpy road. Whole swaths of trees chopped down, ruts in the mud from logging trucks. Sometimes there were farms with newly painted barns and fields right up to the doors of the large houses.

At a stop in the middle of a stretch of deep woods, a very old man got on. He stood stooped in the aisle near Hans's seat. He had a rucksack and a walking stick. A grimy hat pulled down over his eyes.

"You can have my seat," Hans said in Norwegian and started to stand.

But the man spoke to him in Sami, "No, no, just on for a few stops and then I'm off. I knew your great uncle."

"Oh yeah?" Hans asked, switching to Sami.

"You look like him. But you're taller. Johan Turi. You're from that family, aren't you?"

"Yes." He laughed. "Hans Sorensen. You must have been a little boy to know him."

"Knut Pedersen," the old man said. "Very little. My father got hired now and then by Mensch and Turi to take their clients out wolf hunting. Sometimes they were very fat. Father had beautiful draft reindeer and pulks that flew across the snow. One man was so big I thought he was a bear." He leaned against Hans's shoulder.

"Turi hired me to help with hauling water and firewood when he was living with a lady called Emilie. I fell in love with her, too, even though I was a little boy. She was so gentle with the animals. Father told me she was pregnant and couldn't chop wood or haul water from the lake. I don't know what happened to the child."

"Did she have a child when you knew her?" Hans asked.

"No, I think she lost that child. I remember she was sad, and later she was not so sad. Then she went away and I grew up, didn't I? I know all sorts of things, but we don't talk about them, do we?"

Hans pulled his coat over his shoulders. The wind was seeping around the edges of the window and the darkness filtered into the bus like water.

"What do you remember about Turi?"

"Very smart, very kind. I liked to help father on those long journeys across the vidda. But mother sent me to school. She didn't want all that for me. And here I am. Lost for many years in the mines and not half as rich as your family."

"We're not so rich."

The man got off the bus and said goodbye, tipped his cap and disappeared.

After a few hours there wasn't anything except a small cabin or a shed miles away from the next. Reindeer running beside the road, their light flanks flashing in the twilight.

Hans barely remembered those days he went with his grandmother as they moved camp and travelled from their winter pasture to summer pasture with the reindeer. It was one of the last times his family was part of that. He was only five or so. And he'd forgotten that summer until he started to read Emilie's letters.

So much had changed. It was a strange thing to remember. His delight. His grandmother beside him as he balanced on the pack reindeer. The smell of spring. Grass greening under the snow. His grandmother laughing.

The colors first. The deep red on the horizon as the line of reindeer pulled sledges across the frozen snow. The creak of the reindeer's tendons, someone singing the verse of a psalm, and then quiet. He was there to have fun, but for his cousins it was all business. Not long after, his family switched to snowmobiles and the long trips stopped.

He'd watched his uncle tame a reindeer on that trip. One of the draught animals. Like a cowboy breaking in a horse. His uncle threw his lasso down over the reindeer and fought to keep a steady grip as the animal stretched the rope. He kept pulling the rope shorter. The reindeer struggled and they fell in the snow. Sweat ran down his uncle's face and the hair of the reindeer flew around, torn off in tufts.

His grandmother told him, when he was older, the reindeer decided when to move. An area grazed off, or ice and snow cutting the animals off from their food. Then the camp moved to a new area where conditions were supposed to be better.

If a reindeer's pushed to the point of exhaustion, she told him, it dies in a few days. You've got to unhitch a fallen reindeer and leave it. It may be a beloved tame draught reindeer that can't go on any longer. It gets up and staggers along after the others. The owner clenches his teeth, the two will never see each other again.

His cousins didn't see the reindeer very often. The older cousins were swaggering, calling out who owned each reindeer. Hans remembered them trying to catch the most domesticated with their lassos. But their parents shouted at them to stop.

He remembers his uncle loosening the tent canvas just before they left. The canvas sliding stiffly, rigid and sooty, down from the support of the kata. Swiftly folded along its traditional folds. The tent poles gathered in two bundles and placed, one on each side of the draught reindeer, dragging along on the ground. The last poles from the floor placed on the fire. When they've burnt down, there's only a small round spot left.

It was late by the time the bus got to Vilhelmina. There was one hotel near the bus station, and they served a bad breakfast with packets of cheese in plastic and stale bread and dishwater coffee. In the morning, a boy with a black and white dog was waiting patiently on a bench in front of the station. He had an extraordinary face. Kind, open, scarred with chickenpox. Hans asked him if he took the bus north from the town often. "Every two weeks or so," he said. "I'm in school here. But I'm training her. Brought her back this time with me for a few days."

"She's a reindeer dog?"

"She's young. A bit unsteady. My first dog. I'm not sure she'll be good."

"Do you remember this boy?" Hans pulled Yuri's picture out of his jacket pocket.

"Yes, I remember him. It was late summer. I hadn't started school again, but I came into town for groceries for my mother. He wanted to know about *seite*. He was Russian but spoke a little Sami. He said he taught himself. I thought he was clever."

"And you never saw him again?"

"No."

The report he'd read in Stockholm said that Yuri Zhukov had gone north to a town near the Norwegian border. The road was blocked with snow now; then he would have been able to hitch into Norway.

Hans thought he had a chance of tracking him down. He wanted to be able to tell Yuri's mother Yuri had gone in another direction. It was impossible he could end up in a cold ravine in Lismavarri.

He caught a ride from Vilhelmina with the school bus to get to the tiny village where Mrs. Johnson lived. He'd called her the night before and told her he wanted to talk about Yuri. He was afraid there was a chance police in Finnmark had found his body.

The driver doubled as the mailman. He was a skinny guy with no hair and didn't say much of anything. He'd dropped the kids off and now was on his mail run. Hans zipped his coat up to his neck and pulled his light gloves out of his pocket. It took almost an hour to reach the village.

Annika Johnson was waiting at the door of her house as the van pulled up. The driver handed Hans her mail, and he walked across the sloping field to her farmhouse on the edge of a narrow lake. There were mountains all around him. Everything was polished. November. The light crust of snow vibrating with the reflection of the sky.

They'd passed a couple of summer houses on the way to the village, but there were only a few places along the road once they got to the end.

Hans handed Mrs. Johnson her mail and she nodded. "I called yesterday," he said. "Hans Sorensen, Oslo police."

"I know who you are," she said, and took his hand. "You've come so far. Don't worry about Yuri. He's smart, even if he's impractical. It can't be Yuri's body you've found."

"My grandfather built that cabin." Mrs. Johnson pointed to a shed in the next field. "He was famous. They wrote a book about him." She was small, her gray hair twisted in a knot on the top of her head.

"A book?"

"Yes, first settler in this valley. Cold today. Come in. You're stuck here for a while until the van comes back with the kids."

She carried the mail into the main room of the house. Hans ducked through the door. Spotless, filled with succulents on the windowsills. She deposited her mail on the table in the center of the room. She pushed the sleeves of her heavy blue sweater up to her elbows and set the kettle on the stove.

"The rest of my family left, but I stayed," she said. As the coffee boiled she took cake out of a metal box and arranged it on a plate. "Sit, enjoy!"

"They went to America?" Hans asked as he sat at the table.

"Yes, they were so poor. It was hard to live here. But I've done all right. Married a reindeer herder and then divorced him. Worked in the hotel down in town."

Hans was hungry and picked up a square of the lemon cake, crumbling in his fingers.

"Yuri came in late July and stayed for a week or so."

"What did you think of him?" Hans asked.

"I liked him. He was trying to learn Swedish. We laughed a lot about that. I told him he should let his parents know where he was." Mrs. Johnson filled two cups near the stove with coffee and brought them over to the table. Put one in front of Hans.

"They thought he was back in Moscow."

"He was a cruel boy not calling his parents. But he'll grow out of that. Mine did. Now all he wants to do is talk to me."

She waved a milk pitcher near Hans's cup and he said, "No, thanks." She sat down next to Hans and poured milk into her coffee.

She patted his knee. "He'd never go to Finnmark. He was all worked up about some holy place north of here. Someone in the village told him there was a sacred tree there. I don't know who it was."

"Did you know about this place?"

"Of course, everyone does, but we don't go telling anybody about it. It's been there forever. Been there for so long most people don't even go there anymore. My first husband used to stop there on the way north with his reindeer. It was a special place, this valley, for the Sami. My ex-husband's family burned down my grandfather's cabin and all the wood he'd cut for winter. My grandfather had been making the place ready for my grandmother and their children and came back to find everything was cinders. There was a great blaze they could see down the valley.

"My grandfather was so poor, wanted more land. It was free for the settlers. But the Sami used the valley for grazing their reindeer. The reindeer would come through in April on the way to the calving grounds near town below us. The flat mountain you see over there," she pointed out the window toward the north. "That's the place where the reindeer herders would come through the high peaks from their winter grazing lands. Now they use trucks, but then it was a long walk. My ex-husband's family didn't want Swedish settlers in this place. But my grandfather came back and built the cabin again."

She turned to Hans. "Are you married?"

"I was," Hans said. "But my wife died. Cancer. It happened too fast."

"How old was your wife when she left you?"

"Not old at all. Thirty-six."

"And you're not so old. You've got your whole life ahead of you. Look at me. I've been living forever. Let's go see the cabin, since you've got some time before Axel comes back with the children." They stepped into the soft light. Wind rustled in the birches by the lake, but everything was so quiet.

Their boots squeaked as they walked across the matted grass. Just a light dusting of snow. "We should have more at this point, but it's been a strange autumn," she said.

A lean-to sheltered the cabin door.

"Your grandfather must have been determined to move here. When he lost everything."

"Ah, he didn't have much in the south and he had all these children. He was dirt poor. Land was free. You could just take it. He liked adventure, liked being out in the wild. He said it made him think better."

She opened the door and they stooped a bit under the lintel. The cabin was compact. Her grandfather fit thirteen children in two beds. There was a stone fireplace and a table. A small chair. The hearth. Rafters for drying food, making candles. A big bowl. That was about it. An entire family compressed in this tiny house. From the little window you could see the lake, frozen now.

Her grandfather had been making a statement: this is my place now, not yours. Hans could see why the reindeer herders were incensed. It had been so wild and then there was a family by the edge of the lake.

Looking at the cabin, it seemed like everyone was just trying to grab what they could from the Sami. The settlers. The government.

As they walked back to her house across the frozen snow, Hans said, "So you think Yuri set out to walk to Norway."

"He may have, yes."

"How long would it take to get to the place where you think he disappeared?"

"Oh, not more than a couple of hours, not much snow—probably two, and then two to get back."

"Could I get a guide to take me?"

"My nephew, Robin, might do it, but he lives in the town, works at the hotel. You could talk to him. Why would you want to go there?"

"Intuition, or something."

Mrs. Johnson opened the door to her house and Hans bent once more under the doorframe.

"I'll show you a map of the area," she said. "You still have time before the driver gets here." She opened a drawer in a cupboard by the stove and pulled out a folded topo map. She shook it open and placed it on the table. They stood over it.

"Here's where we are," she said, and pointed to the lake. A light blue shape cinched in the middle. And here is where Yuri walked with Robin. She ran her finger up the dotted red line through the forest to the taiga along the foot of the mountain.

"Chasing after Yuri would be a waste of your time. Here's your ride." She pointed out the window at the school bus parked on the side of the road. Two kids got out and waved as they ran up the street to the small house at the end.

40.

HANS DIDN'T KNOW WHAT he'd find in the forest near the mountain, but Robin agreed to lead him into the place where he thought Yuri disappeared. They drove up the long road with the smell of Scots pine, hot and bitter, so different from the softer citrus fragrance of spruce. Into the high valley, deeper and deeper away from his own life. Robin parked the car at Mrs. Johnson's house, and they pulled their packs on.

"It's not a long walk," Robin said. "Less than two hours probably. You look like you're in pretty good shape." He was shorter than Hans and thin, wiry like a rock climber.

"Okay shape." It was the brightest time of day, the low sun shining on the crusty snow.

"I don't think anyone's been there for a while. Too bad there's not more snow. It's an easy ski in."

"So Yuri just disappeared?"

"Yes. I liked him. Worried about him, set him up with some supplies, told him it's easy to get lost here. But he took off one morning on this same path and we never heard from him again."

"Was anyone angry he was going into the mountains past a sacred place?"

"Oh, not many people have much truck with all that stuff anymore. A few of the older ones and the reindeer herders maybe, but even then it's all superstition, isn't it? Not very cool."

He couldn't tell whether Robin was telling the truth. It seemed like no one was telling him anything close to the truth in the days he'd been looking into the case.

There was so much loss. Of people you loved, of faith, of land. Turi was angry about this, but he wrote a book. It was so practical. A way to get the word out.

He followed Robin through crusty snow into the forest on the slope of the mountain the reindeer owners thought was sacred. He could be walking with his father in the forest near their house, going to the lakes on the vidda to catch fish. Sweet spotted char.

"I'll take you to the place where he went first, and we can look around, but I don't think you'll find anything. I was up there not long after he disappeared and there was nothing to show where he went. There were lots of tracks then, reindeer herders, hikers, people from the village going fishing. There's a lake nearby. I could have found someone who's a great tracker, knows about all that, but we didn't know Yuri was missing."

"You thought he was smart enough to make it out to the road?" Hans asked.

"I gave him a good map and detailed directions. So I think, yes, he could have made it to the road and then hitched north. My aunt told me about a tree, a tree with a human face in the forest where people long ago used to leave sticks smeared with blood. Grisly sort of things like that. Her mother-in-law from the first marriage told her that. But this place where Yuri was headed was a bit different. You'll see."

Hans was having a hard time catching his breath and couldn't figure out why. Too many days in the office? They climbed higher and higher through the bare forest, the fir trees very still. The smell of pine evaporating as they climbed.

"Here it is," Robin said and stopped at an overhang. Two huge rocks resting one on top of the other like a table with a tilted surface, rocks covered with gray and green lichen in whorls. Tufts of moss tucked in the cracks. Just enough room to squeeze through into a small cave. They dropped their packs. First, Robin and then Hans went into the cave.

There were bones, but not human. It was still. Light seeping in from the north. He wanted suddenly to just sit there in the quiet. Sink down into the cold dry dirt surrounded by reindeer bones. Their swift lives just whispers in the cave. And all the intricate memories of his life so far, just this. The stillness. His breath going in and out, in and out until his spirit was part of the cave. He was tired of putting one foot in front of the other. He didn't want any attachments. He didn't want to be responsible for anyone. He'd been trudging through darkness. Past lakes. Cabins. Knotted trunks. The old man on the bus prodding him with his fist, like some ghost from Emilie's paintings.

Robin said, "You can see there's not much here. There was a *seite* at one time. You know, a kind of wooden idol. Small, carved. The size of a large doll. It disappeared in the '50s, my aunt told me."

Robin's words suddenly sounded far away and Hans could barely make out each syllable.

The damp smell of stone, and the sound of branches in the wind.

They dipped their heads and stepped out of the cave onto the little mound outside the overhang. Their feet crunching in the thin layer of snow.

"My aunt told me this is where they used to sacrifice reindeer for good luck. Dressed them up in silk ribbons, all different colors—blue, yellow, brown, red— slaughtered the animal, ate the meat, then counted all the bones to leave for the *seite.* Even if they were missing only the tiniest bone, they'd have to do it all over again.

"There's a story in the village that once there was a *noiadi* who told the *seite* that if the *noiadi* had a son with a certain woman he'd give his son to the *seite.* This woman had a boy and the *noiadi* fought with her to take him away. She wouldn't give him the baby, but he stole the child from her when she was asleep and left the baby here for the *seite.* The *noiadi* had too much brandy one night and people heard him *yoiking* to the *seite. Alas, my poor woman's weeper, where is he now? Alas, my poor woman's weeper, where is he now?* Then the woman understood her son was lost forever."

"Do you think this was true?" Hans asked and laughed.

"No, just a ghost story. We used to love listening to my aunt's stories when we were little. I don't tell my kids this stuff."

41.

When Hans called Malin from Ostersund on his way home, she told him there were more complications in the case. She'd just had a call from the desk sergeant in Alta that Jorgen Elstad had been killed. It seemed like an accident. He'd gone out at about ten on a snowmobile up to the vidda. The medical examiner figured his blood alcohol content was high enough to make him drunk. Crushed under the machine. The police thought it flipped. He was going too fast. In the morning, though, they saw tracks that seemed to tell another story. In the daylight, when the officers conducted a more thorough search, they found more tracks, at least two other machines.

"Could he have killed himself?" Hans asked Malin.

"Why would he do that? A happy family. His brother told me they'd gotten permission to build their house near the forest."

"You think this could be proof that he had something to do with the boy's death?"

"Guilt? Perhaps," she said. "It turns out the office in Tana Bru was too busy to interview him and no one checked out the tool shed on the farm for the suspected murder weapon. They thought it was a waste of time. Go look into it. Get some answers. Transportation on this case is going way over budget. But you're more than halfway there in Ostersund. You'd better fly north again, Hans. I'll set it up for you with the travel officer. He's starting to call you a rock star."

"Cool. Can I have my own private jet?"

"Forget it. It's the mail run again for you."

An officer from Tana Bru picked him up in Lakselv and they drove to Lismavarri in the dark. It was the same cop he'd met on the vidda in the ravine, tall, bearded. Ivvar. Annoyed with him this time around.

"Here's your warrant," he said. "It was signed off yesterday, but we've had a shakeup in the office and no one free to take care of this."

"It's too bad you didn't at least get someone over here to interview Jorgen Elstad."

"You can say that again."

Everything felt like it was holding its breath. The shop in the old house. The barn with the cows in their stalls. The low green wooden house with the wide door across the road. The bare birches by the blue house down the road, the fields sloping to the river, crusty snow glittering in the lights from the buildings. He'd been waiting for the second death and now here it was. The unease he'd felt when he bent to touch the frozen ground in the ravine had been following him. He hadn't understood that until he stepped from the officer's car onto the gravel of the village road.

He was getting nowhere talking to the people who knew Jorgen. A difficult man, one of his employees told him. But fair. Moody, a woman at the shop said.

Olav's mother refused to talk, and his father was in bed. He wouldn't move. Olav had gone to Tana Bru to make arrangements for Jorgen's funeral.

He walked across the wind-swept snow around the barn to the tool shed next to the sauna. The warrant was in his pocket. It seemed almost completely quiet on the farm.

If the mallet was the weapon, there was probably no way it was still hanging on the wall of the shed. But guilt does strange things to people. He opened the door and pressed the button on his flashlight. Pulled the string hanging from the ceiling and the light came on. It was a meticulously-ordered place. Small tools on the work bench lined up and the larger tools hanging on the wall above it.

Was it too clean? He turned boxes over and searched through the shelves. Maybe it was something about being a shopkeeper. There were two rakes and several shovels. Everything was spotless. He couldn't find anything that looked like a mallet. Was this where they'd made the bomb? He turned the light off and latched the door.

Ellen Elstad placed the cups, saucers, tiny napkins, and the pot of coffee on the narrow table in the living room. She adjusted the striped cloth and finally looked at Hans. She was still living with the Elstads. Her new house half built up near the forest.

"What do you want me to say? I didn't know he was going out that night. He doesn't drink. It's very strange. He doesn't do things like this. He's very responsible. He loves his children. He wants to do well and make a lot of money. He wouldn't do this to me."

"I'm sorry I have to ask you these questions." He put his hand on her arm. "Why don't you sit down? Sit down and we'll try to figure this out."

"I told the inspector from Tana Bru all this already. We've had so much happen. So much lost."

Her face was pale. Her dark eyes, dark hair against her white face. He felt brutal questioning her. He wanted to tell her Jorgen was fine. It was a story they'd made up. A story to get to the truth.

Just like after Astrid's death. He'd wake up. Reach out to touch her hand and she wasn't there. Sometimes he'd dream she was alive, living in another city. He'd left her alone. A city with winding streets, children sitting on bundles of clothes, begging on cobbled streets. It was his fault she was dead. He wasn't clever enough to figure out how to save her.

"Why did you call the police?" he asked Ellen.

"He hadn't come to bed. I woke Olav, and he said he was probably working in the office late. He never works this late, I said. You know he never works this late. The baby was crying. I held her. I walked up and down, up and down looking out the windows, sure he was going to pull up on the snowmobile. I knew he was going to open the door. Olav didn't want to do anything. I thought he knew something and didn't want to tell me. Jorgen has a lot on his mind, he said, don't worry. It could be he's just gone for a ride. He never goes out so late. You know that, I said, he never leaves us. He wouldn't leave us," she said, and looked at the cups and saucers. "I forgot to pour you some coffee."

He watched her move the cup to the saucer, move the cup and saucer to the tablecloth, carefully ironed, and pour the coffee slowly.

"Thanks," he said. A car pulled into the yard outside. The sound of shoes on gravel. A door slamming. "Was he having problems with anyone?"

"Problems?"

"An argument, someone who might have a grudge. Anyone who'd want to hurt him."

"There was a fight," she said. "A pretty bad fight with some cousins. But it was not anything. Not enough to make them want to hurt Jorgen like this."

"A fight about what?" Perhaps this was something, finally.

"Leasing rights on a mountain near here for some Americans. Jorgen saw it as a chance to get money for the village. His cousins thought it was just one more way to lose grazing land."

Hans knew about these kinds of fights. They could be violent, but usually never ended in murder.

"I know this is hard for you."

"How can you know anything? How can you know anything at all about me?"

"Did Jorgen put up some stakes around your building lot at some point in the summer?"

"Yes, what's that have to do with anything?"

"Do you know what he used to hammer the stakes in?"

"I suppose a mallet. I'm not sure."

"There's no mallet in the tool shed. Do you know what happened to it?"

"Do I look like I have time to keep track of something like that?" she said and started to clear away the coffee cups.

Hans climbed down the stairs to Olav's office and knocked on the door.

"Ah," Olav said when he opened the door. "I was getting some work done. Let's take a walk. You're used to the cold, aren't you? You know not everyone was happy about the protests."

Olav moved slowly as if he were suddenly a different man. All the light gone from his face.

"I'm sorry about Jorgen," Hans said.

"I know, it's very sad. Ellen won't recover. Or at least not soon. Two young children."

They walked along the village road toward the sports club. "This is where Eric's band used to practice."

"Ingrid mentioned that."

"Oh, so you've spoken to her?" They turned off the road and followed a track that led across the fields to the river.

"Yes, I'm completely unprofessional talking to you like this. But my supervisor's given me permission to ignore protocol."

"Something you don't do very often?"

"I'm usually a rule-driven kind of guy."

The fields glowed under the full moon. Hard, brittle, shining. Their boots crunched on the track.

"A little boring," Olav said. "I don't see you like that. I think you hide a lot under your skin. Keep things tightly wound. Your anger flares when you're pushed, I know."

Hans laughed, thinking of the broken plate sitting on the counter in the kitchen. "Maybe. And you?"

"I suppose I like to think I tell the truth, but sometimes I don't."

"Just like you're not telling the truth about your brother, are you?" Hans asked. He needed to gather as much information as he could, even if it meant making Olav uncomfortable.

"This is usually the first field we hay in the summer," Olav said and turned to face Hans. "It's ripe quickly once the weather warms. I put the sheep just there, that next field over. I like to see them looking happy, eating to their hearts' content."

"Ellen told me about a fight, a big fight with some of your cousins."

They were standing in the middle of the field on the path and all around them the frozen fields were silent.

"That was nothing," Olav said, and brushed some dirt off his jacket. "No one would kill Jorgen. Not enough at stake. They were drunk that night. It was a party in the summer. Jorgen got one or two of them mad. He poked his finger too many times into their brother's face."

"Did anything happen after that night? Anything that might tell you they were angry. Had some kind of beef about this."

Olav started to cough and then turned to face the river.

"My cousins didn't tell us if they did. You keep some family things a secret, too, don't you? There's nothing here that connects the fight with his death. It was all over the next day. My mother had a long talk with her sister."

They were walking again, and Hans could hear cars on the village road. Two cars driving fast, one after the other.

"Was it odd for Jorgen to be so worked up?"

"Not so odd, but yes, he's usually practical. Only bad-tempered about small things."

"Wasn't it unusual for your brother to be out so late at night?"

"Yes, completely out of character. But he'd been brooding about something, so I wasn't surprised."

"And drinking?"

"Yes, father's the only one who drinks."

"So there's something that doesn't add up. I took a look in your toolshed."

"And did you find anything?"

"I didn't find a mallet."

"That's strange," Olav said. "We use that mallet a lot in the summer, but not so much now."

The frozen track curved across the uneven surface of the fields. The snow was pounded down, slippery. Every time he talked to Olav, he felt like he was being tricked. Olav fed him facts, but it was difficult to know if the facts had anything to do with the questions Hans asked.

"You know," Olav said, "it's so easy to get lost here. I'll tell you about that. We were up in the forest above the sports club with the tractor, and a cousin of mine, and his woman, Marta, and her friend were also nearby picking cloudberries. Marta and the woman lost track of him. They found us and we said, there. Look over there. We see a tractor and a tent.

"They said, 'Oh no, it's not our tractor, not our tent.' People who are lost often won't believe even something they can see. So they stayed with us. My cousin told us later that he looked and looked for the women, then went back to Lismavarri. There were about five men out looking, but they, Marta and her friend, were with us the whole time picking cloudberries."

They went down the steep slope to the river where three narrow black boats were pulled up on the gravel. The dim light polished the river, the bent birches, the low hills of Finland across the river. Hans took a deep breath.

"You don't have any idea who could have hurt Jorgen? Maybe someone you know who'd be angry about the protest."

"Why not go after me, then?" Olav asked.

"People in the village told me Jorgen wasn't a popular guy. He could have made someone angry."

"Ah." Olav picked up a stone to throw. "As I said, my cousins would never drive Jorgen off his machine. They can be mean and thoughtless, but they wouldn't kill someone. Especially someone in the family." Olav laughed and then coughed again. "Not angry enough to kill. So tell me about Ingrid. You've heard her sing?"

"Yes, she's very beautiful and talented."

"You only have to hear her sing once."

"And then you're bewitched?"

"Yes, bewitched. I'll tell you something. Be careful with Ingrid. She left me once. She'll never be happy with a cop."

Hans kicked an ice chunk along the frozen river. "There's nothing going on between us." Moonlight swirled above the white floes backed up against each other on the surface.

"Tell me something else, since we're talking off the record here. Was Ingrid at the dam with you?" Hans asked.

"Perhaps," Olav said. "We told her it was dangerous. It might ruin her career if something went wrong. For Eric, it was more bravado."

"So she may have been with you?"

"Perhaps," he said again. "I can't be sure about these things. It was very dark and cold."

Hans put his hand on Olav's shoulder. And then they climbed up the slope again, away from the cold river.

42.

His cousin Sara carefully folded a dark linen jacket and placed it on his bed. And then a bright yellow sweater, still heavy with Astrid's perfume. Sara was staying with him in Oslo for a couple of days. She had an interview at the university for a fellowship.

They were almost finished sorting Astrid's clothes. Throwing the shoes out. She'd worn the soles thin on all her shoes. Her cowboy boots. They were putting clothes that seemed almost new in a large cardboard box to bring to the church across from Toyen school.

He was haunted by his trip to Lismavarri. The silence as he stood on the riverbank with Olav, ice floes piled haphazardly on the glassy river. The deep night of the north stretching out around him except for the dim lights in the barn, in the house, in the shop as they climbed up the slippery bank to the track through the fields. Sara was a welcome distraction.

"Are you sure you want to go through all of Astrid's things now?"

"Yeah," Hans said. Though he wasn't sure how smart it was, since Matisse was sniffing everything. Malin had dropped him off the night before. Hans threw a squeaky red ball to him, and he chased it into the kitchen and then brought it back.

"You know, it might make him feel better," Sara said roughing up his fur.

"Or make him feel like shit," Hans said.

"He seems happy right now. Are you reading Emilie's letters?" Sara asked.

"I'm more than halfway through them," he said.

She held a shirt against the light. "Grandmother said she remembers Emilie spending months with her family when Grandmother was eight. Her Uncle Johan arranged it."

"Turi?"

"Yes. It's the time she writes about in her letters. She seems to have fallen in love with that life."

"But then she went home, didn't she?" Hans said.

"I think she used that time, though, to call up something she needed when things got too painful."

"All those paintings as evidence, I suppose," Hans said.

"She painted so many those years after the war."

"It's strange Grandmother didn't talk about Emilie before."

"A little strange, but then I never asked her about that time. She remembered how Emilie smelled at first. She said like tin, metallic and sharp."

"It must have been her clothes," Hans said.

"And then the longer she stayed with them, the better she smelled, sweet like hay. At night Grandmother slept curled near Emilie. She said Emilie loved the dog called Benno. Grandmother's favorite too."

Hans rummaged in the closet and handed Sara a skirt, a ski jacket, a twisted scarf. Astrid. It was such a trap thinking you could live with the ghost of someone you loved. He couldn't do it. What you had left was so little compared to their skin, their breath, their hands, their lips.

"Any more?" Sara asked.

"Just a few. One more drawer to go."

"This is lovely," she said as she smoothed a navy blue wool skirt and folded it once.

"Take it," Hans said. "She'd be happy you're wearing it."

"It will make you happy," Sara said, "that you've done this, finally. Even though they were all packed away, you still knew they were there, didn't you?" She shook out a silk scarf. "Beautiful, so shimmery."

"It's yours," Hans said.

"I saw your brother." She folded the scarf and put it with the wool shirt folded on the bed.

"Where'd you see him?"

"Dinner at my mother's."

"Christ, I thought she couldn't stand him." Hans laughed.

"She's mellowed. She took a jewelry making class and now she's mining whoever she can for information. You know my mother."

"Single-minded."

"Possessed."

Hans laughed. "How's Mikael?"

"He seemed fine. Not so wound up about things. His girlfriend's brought him around to laying off the secret meetings in smoky huts. Stuff like that. I think he's sobered up quite a bit too. And no, he didn't even mention you."

Hans folded the flaps on the top of the box and shrugged.

"My mother kept him on track. His girlfriend's nice."

"I only met her once, when I almost beat him into the hospital."

"You're kidding. That doesn't sound like you," she said frowning.

"No, a long story."

"When I was very young I remember him kicking you over and over again in the kitchen. I was about five. Even then it seemed like he shouldn't be roughing you up like that. But my mother and your mother were more interested in the new spinning wheel in the living room. How beautiful it was. How it would make it so much easier for your mother than using a spindle. Your parents do seem protective when it comes to Mikael, but I know they love you dearly."

Hans laughed. "Let's get this stuff over to the church and then," he paused, "some Chinese takeaway."

He picked up the box and put it near the door.

"What did you think about Emilie's paintings?" Sara asked later. She put the teakettle on the stove and pulled two cups out of the cabinet above the sink. Hans dropped teabags into the cups, and then filled Matisse's bowl with kibbles.

"They were great. Powerful."

"It must have been difficult to keep on painting. Her friend Christine was determined to be successful. It was so hard to be a painter as a woman. The critics in Denmark complained the shows were filled with women's paintings. Not half as serious as the men's.

"I've been thinking about one of her letters," she said as she walked over to the table and shuffled through the pile of letters. "She's remembering the War. You can see how upset she was in those late paintings at the museum."

Hans handed her a cup of tea and she said, "Ah, here it is," and read: *Inga sent me letters about the north. How everything changed for some families. I knew Jouna and Anne were cut off from Norway. They kept their reindeer on the Swedish side of the mountains. She missed, she wrote me, the pastures of the sea kingdom. The fearsome mountains above Ghost Lake. Their life was easier, but not quite as happy. Down in the valley near the sea lay the Sami's small green homes. You could mistake them for rounded tussocks of grass if a fine coil of smoke hadn't risen from some of them. At the end of the valley lay the mountain with its snow-packed kettle depression, and the river ran shining bright between the green hillocks deep in the valley bottom. In the sunshine and quiet all of it resembled a prehistoric landscape from a dream. Now all that's gone. The turf huts probably crumbled into the field.*

I know it turned out we were wrong during the War. The Germans were worse than the Russians, but we couldn't know that. Or, I suppose we should have once we knew about the camps. My heart aches thinking about all those murdered. In the middle of the war, I felt like there would never be peace. The War would go on and on and the commotion and anguish continue until after my death. I didn't think I'd live this long, but I have, love. But it did seem logical that for a while at the beginning we thought it would be bad if the Germans lost.

"It's hard," she said, "to understand why they wouldn't be furious when they knew what was going on. So many people did help the Danish Jews to escape to Sweden."

"Almost eight thousand people overnight. In fishing trawlers and motorboats and sailboats. Like the little boats helping the English out at Dunkirk in June 1940. Shit, we know what it was like in Finnmark from our parents. All the cities burned and many of the villages. Incredible destruction. Everyone knows someone who suffered. Do you think Gudmund was a collaborator?"

"No," she said, "not according to Emilie. Just stubborn. He wanted to do what was right for Denmark. He listened to the wrong people and wrote speeches for the foreign office and editorials that seemed to side with Germany. But he was only being pragmatic. He wanted to keep the country whole, stay under the radar like so many people. He thought he was doing what the government wanted.

"My friend Kristin remembers being a little girl sitting on her father's shoulders, watching the king ride through the streets of Copenhagen on his horse Jubilee during the Occupation. Everyone would run along beside him as he trotted around the city. Her parents thought it was a sign of resistance."

When Sara was asleep, Hans spread Emilie's letters on the table in the living room. He should give them back to her to take home. But he couldn't. Not yet. He wasn't quite finished with them, and he had a few he wanted to look at again. A few more letters about the War. Emilie's thoughts about Gudmund. In any case, Sara wasn't going home but to Tromso. She wouldn't be home until Christmas, so there was plenty of time to get the letters back to her mother.

He opened his sleeping bag on the couch, closed the door to his bedroom, and picked up the letters on the table. Once he was under the sleeping bag propped against the arm of the sofa, Matisse curled up at his feet.

Dear One,

It doesn't seem fair, I agree, that you were called a traitor during the war, even when you stopped doing the radio talks. Even though your World Survey was by the government's request. It doesn't make any sense. But by then everyone wanted to live the story of the Occupation. How everyone was against the Germans. No one wanted to cooperate, when really everyone just wanted to get on with their lives, without bloodshed, to get on with their work. It was a kind of compromise, and then no one would admit it. I think you were a scapegoat. Though it does gnaw at me sometimes that you could have said no. There wasn't any possibility they were going to execute you. If you'd known all the facts, darling, would you have said no? But after your talks stopped—we had peace at least for a while and got a lot of work done. It was hard for you—so hard for you when you were trying to explain the conditions in the world in a reasoned way. The problem was reason was splintered then. With all the deaths of the war there wasn't any reason left.

Sometimes I have dreams of the damn saboteurs' bombs. Murder and destruction everywhere. The house shaking. How the war ate us clean through. Though we were better off in Denmark than other places in the world.

E

Everyone wanted to live the story of the Occupation. He supposed that's what interested him so much. These different versions of the truth. Eric Paulsen had stepped out of his story into another place. A different country. Olav was, like Hans's father, convinced there was a way to explain everyone's choices by a kind of reckoning that had nothing to do with the facts. Especially the people you loved.

Did Jorgen kill the Russian kid and then kill himself because he was so troubled? Or was it an accident? But anyone could commit a violent act. Especially if they were threatened. It was amazing there weren't more murders. And was the body still sitting in the morgue Yuri's body or some other Russian's? He had a gun, that much was true.

He thought about the path he followed to find any trace of Yuri. Up the road smelling of pine into the forest walking behind Robin. Animal tracks, grouse, field vole on the surface of scattered snow patches, the glowing light of November. But Yuri hadn't left any tracks. It was an invisible trek across the border into Finnmark. If that's what Yuri had done. He knew the story ended in death for someone.

Even though Emilie wrote to Gudmund *you could have said no,* she was loyal to him, made excuses for him, continued loving him. How much did it take to convince herself her marriage called for this kind of betrayal?

Was he kidding himself by believing protecting his brother and his brother's friends, even if they might be destructive and dangerous, was part of the whole package of family loyalty?

SARA WAS SNORING IN the bedroom. She'd done that as a little kid. Purring. He shifted around on the couch and then unfolded the next letter and held it tightly.

Kauslunde, March 15, 1949

Dearest,

It's been weeks since I heard the patter of your slippers on the path by the birch, or your laughter, or felt your hands on my face. I never told you this, but Signy said our marriage wouldn't last. We were sitting in the café near your office on Krystalgade. Gudmunds's too young. It's just a marriage of convenience. You get respectability. He gets a wife. A beautiful wife. A brilliant wife. But soon you'll be old, won't you? Don't give up on your art. Marriage is such a cliché, so bourgeois. Why do it now, Emilie? Soon you'll have a show and the critics will love it. I don't think so, I said. They haven't loved anything yet. The last review said my work was old fashioned. She said, bBut he's a child, hardly a man. And that improbable beard. Signy would have to eat her words, wouldn't she, if she'd lived this long.

She'd been telling me about her first encounter. How she was 14 and the man much older. How they made love in the forest. Flowers crushed under her back, how she stood up and the wind caressed her breasts. I laughed and asked her, but were you happy then, Signy, were you happy you were so alive? He was embarrassed, said someone would see me, Signy said.

I always felt spoiled, a pampered daughter. She glued boxes in a factory when she was 14, right after her confirmation. So I let her say what she wanted.

Love,
E

One of Emilie's paintings in the Nordiska museet was painted just before the year she wrote the letters to Gudmund. He'd examined it trying to figure out that painting. All the rest were filled with life. This one had three white reindeer on a low hill. Their antlers against a sky as neutral as the landscape. No color anywhere. Was this what it had felt like for her? Hardly any movement. Stripped trees against the white sky. Gray stones. Gray waterfall.

Sara told him Gudmund was arrested in Vordingborg, Denmark, on liberation day and paraded with other suspected traitors through thousands of people spitting and screaming. He was released without charges after a week. A communist underground paper called him one of Hitler's creatures in Denmark. Gudmund was bitter and angry. One colleague said he ought to be shot.

43.

IN THE MORNING, HANS met Malin and Lars at Zorba's. "So this is your joint?" Malin said.

"Just since Astrid's death. She wouldn't be caught dead in here." He laughed. "She didn't like Greek food. She thought the coffee was bitter."

"Just one of those rolls and coffee." Malin pointed at the bar when Fausto appeared, wiping his hands on his apron.

"Sorry," he said. "Sometimes I'm the dishwasher, too."

Lars said, "Just coffee."

"Inspector?" the waiter asked, smiling.

"Just coffee for me."

"Let's start with the Russian boy. So, what happened?" Malin asked, when Fausto turned toward the bar.

"Annika Johnson didn't know. He left one morning with supplies he'd bought in the tiny store near the hotel in town. Took off toward the mountain, she told me, where her ex-husband's reindeer came through in the spring. He was headed for a holy place, she thought. He wanted to see if he could find a wooden idol, a *seite*."

The waiter returned with a tray balanced on one hand.

"It's just superstition, she told me, but her husband thought it was a good idea to leave an offering each time they came through there with reindeer. I held Johan Turi's pouch for offerings in the Nordiska museet. Small as the palm of my hand, very soft skin with striped fabric sewn around the top. Tassels to pull the mouth closed. There were coins in the bag."

"Pretty primitive, isn't it? Could something have happened to Yuri Zhukov messing around in this place?" Malin asked.

"I don't think so, do you? No one would feel threatened about that, unless it was worth money. I've been reading about *seite*. People scooped them up early in the century and they ended up in museums. I saw several in Stockholm. One about three feet tall. Wood. A little weird. But I don't think someone would harm Yuri if they found him poking around."

"He could have gotten hurt," Lars said, pouring milk into his coffee. "Your wife was right. It's bitter."

Hans looked away. He hadn't gotten used to thinking of Astrid in the past tense. Lars hadn't hesitated a second.

"Could have, yes," Hans said, "but I spoke to the only other people in the village and they'd been hunting or through there with reindeer and hadn't seen anything. If he'd gone that way, they would have known, they told me."

"So we're back to the beginning again." Malin tore the brioche in two and took a bite.

"No evidence to link the body in the morgue with Yuri, except for the Russian dental work. Not much to go on," Hans said.

"And no luck in Lismavarri. No more information about Jorgen Elstad?" Malin asked.

"I'll write it all up, but no. I'm feeling extremely frustrated. There was a fight in the summer, but Olav thinks it was nothing. It doesn't seem to have anything to do with the death. Just a family spat about leasing rights. And there's no evidence to prove Jorgen could have killed the Russian boy."

"It's convenient he's dead," Malin said.

"Too convenient for my taste. Maybe there's some kind of love triangle," Lars said, draining his cup. "Any thoughts about that? It seems strange that, as you said on the phone, suddenly Jorgen starts drinking and goes off to the forest on a snowmobile. What's his marriage like?"

"I couldn't tell. It seemed okay."

"Any connection between his wife and Eric Paulsen?"

"Not that I turned up. It seems like someone might have said something. But they didn't."

"They wouldn't say anything to you. You're a cop from the south. One who arrested their cousin or mother," Lars said and stretched.

"No mallet?"

"Nothing, but a seriously clean tool shed."

Malin looked at Lars and said, "Check out the story about the fight and the leasing rights. Who wanted to use the land and why. You might turn up something. Write the report up, Hans, and then we'll go over the pieces again after you talk to Kathryn Cole tomorrow."

Hans worked several hours on the case in the office. He called Robin and asked him a few questions about the details of the last day he saw Yuri. He wanted to make sure he wasn't leaving anything out. Two men who were passionate about Sami culture, Eric Paulsen and Yuri Zhukov, might be connected after all. Their paths could have crossed, or not, before Paulsen ended up in the clinic in Alta.

Hans caught a bus and walked along Karl Johans gate to St. Olavs Plass on the way to the University of Oslo's law library. His stomach growled. He hadn't eaten anything since breakfast. At the law library he flashed his badge. He asked one of the librarians at the main desk for the transcript of Gudmund's trial. "In Denmark?" she said, moving some books on the counter to the side. "You want the files of the prosecutor of the Extraordinary Disciplinary Court for Public Servants in microfilm in government documents. They're in the basement."

Hans wasn't sure he needed to do this but was hooked on this story. He'd finished his report about the investigation and thought the diversion might trigger something about the case. He was afraid Gudmund was guilty. It was as if Gudmund was a suspect, his photo pinned on the murder board.

It smelled like waxed linoleum and cardboard in the basement. The acrid whiff of microfilm. So much of the past was hidden in boxes, or on film, in recordings and stories people told to each other year after year after year. He was craving a smoke and pulled a piece of gum out of his pocket. A grad student, nametag hanging from her thin neck, found the shoe box size container with smaller boxes of film for him.

He stood for a minute in front of the microfiche machine. There was no one else in the room. He felt like he was on the verge of something that could snap the pieces of the case together. But there'd been so many false summits on this trek. He was wasting time chasing after Gudmund's secrets. Just then the air changed in the room as someone opened the door.

The microfiche was a pain in the neck. Slippery, hard to read. His father had told him stories about the resistance in Norway. There was one person, the head of the resistance, who hid out across the border in Sweden for years. When he was arrested and locked in a cell alone, he told his story on toilet paper with a pin he found in his cell at Mallagta 19. On the seventh day of his prison stay he wrote, "Feb 2 1944. Have been 2 interrogations. Was flogged. Betrayed Vic. Am weak. Deserve contempt. Am terribly scared of pain. But not scared to die." He numbered and rolled the sheets carefully and dropped them down the ventilation shaft.

Could Gudmund have been working for the resistance in Denmark as a kind of undercover agent? It didn't seem likely. The way Hans thought about Emilie could change. He'd been slogging through shifting perceptions of the truth. He wanted to think the boy in the ravine was not Yuri. That no one in Lismavarri was capable of killing the boy. That somehow Yuri would reappear at his father's door. His mother would feed him borscht and apple vareniki. He didn't want the boy whose picture he'd seen in his parents' opulent apartment to be the body in the ravine.

It took him about two hours to read through the trial transcript. In July 1945, according to the documents, Gudmund was the one who asked the court to investigate his activities during the Occupation. He was indicted in winter 1949. He'd waited that long for his name to be cleared. And it wasn't. He could keep his pension, but he had no duties at the University of Copenhagen.

Hans thought about his father's work in the library as he read through the papers, twisting the machine up and down. Why did it matter what the truth was? He wasn't sure. And why did it matter that Paulsen had tried to set off a bomb under a remote bridge? Fierce loyalty was something his father admired. Hans had chosen to work for the government in Oslo. Not what his father would have chosen for him. He wondered how many decisions he'd made that compromised his father's sense of what was right.

In one of Emilie's letters, Sara told him, Emilie said Gudmund only saw black and white. He thought he was being a patriot. Emilie warned him that others might see it differently.

But Gudmund didn't listen. He was convinced the policy of the Foreign Minister was the only right one under the circumstances. He acted in line with government policy.

Hans wasn't sure whether Gudmund was guilty or not. It seemed like he did what he thought he had to do. Hans didn't think Emilie would have stayed with him if he'd set out to be a traitor.

Many of the articles written after the trial said the verdict was unfair. Gudmund was just doing what the press and the government did during the Occupation. But Hans kept thinking Gudmund could have said no to the Foreign Minister. Refused to cooperate. Kept doing his own work. He could have thought about Emilie more—what it could do to Emilie.

He walked up the marble stairs from the basement and out into the evening. The sidewalks were crowded and it was raining. Women in expensive trench coats, wool scarves wound around their necks, and men in camelhair overcoats, their black shoes spattered with mud, walked quickly past him.

Were they thinking of dinner, buying bread, sick kids, a torn elbow on their jacket, the incessant rain, a ski trip up in the hills, bills and sick parents, too sick to move? It was difficult for everyone, wasn't it, to take a breath and enjoy anything in the middle of this daily rush.

He pulled his collar up and ran across the street to the bus. The emptiness he felt suddenly had nothing to do with forgetting to eat lunch back at the office.

HANS TURNED OVER AND punched his pillow, the sound of Emilie's voice. Rain hitting the window. The sound of her voice again.

She wasn't a saint, she guessed he knew that now. Angry at the resistance for blowing up factories and trains, giving her heart away again to Carl when she knew she loved Gudmund for years and years, covetous, angry, lost at times. Suspicious. Wanting fame when she'd traded that for loyalty to Gudmund. Jealous of her friend Christine. Christine of the beautiful paintings and successful shows, Christine of the famous brother, Christine of the teacher who loved her best of all, Christine who had a life only filled with her art. She's at the window and all around her are frozen clods of earth. Just that. The water a line of pewter on the horizon. The apples are furred nubs on the trees in the orchard. This doesn't make her happy. Her heart is ice cold. The steady beat familiar, normal. Not like those months in bed when she couldn't walk more than a few steps each day. Sometimes she can't remember what love feels like. Jealous of Gudmund's youth at first, his travels later when she could only see white sheets, white walls, the color white all around her, days in the hospital, her heart betraying her.

44.

He was hoping Kathryn Cole could fill in the missing details in the case. Her parents had told Malin she was living in a cottage in Wales. A friend from university had offered her a small stone house on her farm. Kathryn had decided to apply to art school in Bangor, a bus ride away.

There was no phone where she was staying, so Malin had contacted the chief constable in the nearest town. They'd settled on a time to talk, and he'd let Kathryn know she needed to appear at the station near her friend's farm.

He had no idea what this young woman would sound like. If she'd be defensive. Or afraid. It was always a toss-up. You could never tell how someone would react to the kind of questions he wanted to ask. Questions about Olav. Intimate, invasive. This wasn't a part of the job that he liked much. It felt worse, somehow, than strip-searching someone. Maybe he should've asked Lars to do this interview. Or Malin. She was skillful at ferreting out information from a reluctant witness. It was a bummer sometimes that she'd been promoted.

His notepad with its list of questions waited near the phone in the small interview room at headquarters in Oslo. He dialed the number and the phone rang and rang. Finally an officer picked it up. They spoke for a minute and then the constable said, "I'll hand the phone to the young lady now."

"Hello?" Tentative. A young voice.

"Hello, Kathryn? Hans Sorensen, Oslo police," he said. He scratched his head, shuffled the notes one more time, cleared his throat. His English was fine, but he always felt a little awkward speaking it. "I would like to ask you some questions about your time in Lismavarri. I know this might be strange that I am calling like this."

"Yes, a little strange," she said. "Has something happened?" She sounded distracted.

He'd decided to be as direct as possible. She might know something that no one else had told them. It was crucial to maneuver her into telling him something that might give them a break in the case.

"I wanted to tell you about a body reindeer herders found in the ravine above Lismavarri. We have been talking to everyone who was there this summer. Is there any chance you saw something strange in the gorge on one of the walks you took?"

"A body?" she asked. And then she was quiet.

He wondered if she would admit she was on the walk with Paulsen and Schmidt when they'd discovered the body. He had no idea how honest she'd be. Sometimes it was difficult to tell what anyone would admit to.

"Yes," he said.

"I saw the body," she said.

"You saw it?"

"Yes. It was awful. I was hiking with Eric and Gunter. We all saw the body."

"Tell me why no one reported the body. I might have gotten it wrong," Hans said. He was writing notes as he talked. It seemed like this was something. A kind of guilt that might lead to new information. Hans was curious about her. What would she think of Olav's version of the days they'd spent together?

"Eric told us he'd planned a protest at the dam site. He didn't want to report the death. There'd be too much activity just before they were about to set off their bomb. They were passionate about the whole thing. But it was a mistake, wasn't it?"

"It did not end well. It never does when there is a bomb involved."

"What do you mean?"

He hadn't thought about whether she'd heard from Olav. Why hadn't anyone written to her? No one had filled her in. Maybe Olav was telling the truth. There was nothing going on between them.

"Eric Paulsen lost his hand," Hans said.

"That's terrible. How? What happened?"

"From what we can tell the bomb exploded early. Olav took him to the clinic in Alta."

"So Olav is okay?"

"Olav is fine. They were lucky. Eric could have died." There was silence for a few beats on the line.

"But he's okay?"

"Yes," Hans said, "he's okay. Were you close to Olav?"

"Yes."

He was being too easy on her but he didn't want to make her more guarded than she already was. Her answer along with Ingrid's comments was enough to solve that mystery.

"On your way back to the village that day, you didn't have a feeling that anyone in your group could have killed the person in the ravine?"

"No," she said too quickly. She was hiding something. "Strange things had been happening. Someone left the body of a reindeer on the grass near the sports club. It was tragic."

"Oh," Hans said and rubbed his eyes. This was something new. Something no one had told him about yet.

"Yes, a couple of days after a party. I thought it might be because of the fight at the party. But Olav said no."

"A fight?"

"A fight with Olav's cousins. Jorgen was hurt. I fell and had to have sutures above my eye."

"No one told me you were involved."

"They wouldn't. Everyone seemed embarrassed. But Olav said the dead reindeer had nothing to do with the fight."

"But you thought it might be connected."

"Yes."

"Is there anything else that seemed strange, just a little odd?"

Her silence was so long he was convinced she had something to confess.

"Did the fall kill him?" she asked.

"Who?"

"The boy in the ravine."

"I can't tell you about that," he said.

It was such a strange question. How could she know the dead person was a boy? "I have to tell you something, though, Kathryn. Something about Jorgen. He was killed. Riding a snowmobile. Less than a week ago."

"Oh, how terrible," she said. "Poor Ellen. It's not possible he's dead."

"So Olav hasn't written to you?"

"It's difficult. I live in a cottage down a track from my friend's house. I haven't sent the address to anyone yet."

"I just have one more question. Did you lose a gold chain at some point this summer? Maybe in the forest?"

She didn't answer right away. Hans underlined the word necklace on his pad.

"I don't think so," she said. "Unless it was when I fell running above the village in the woods. Yes. I could've lost it then. I realized it was missing when I packed. I hadn't been wearing it for weeks. Maren liked to pull it. I was afraid it would break."

On his walk home from work it started to snow. Light flakes drifting down on his head as he passed the gate of the Botanical Gardens and the empty flowerbeds, the bare trees filling now with snow. It was like living in the tropics for him when he first moved south. Summers so much longer. One spring Astrid made him tear out all the tulips they planted in the community garden plot on a steep hill above the river. She said the color looked like blood.

There was a tiny red cottage that came with the plot of land, and sometimes he'd bring coffee in a thermos. He'd spend time pulling weeds and transplanting lettuce he bought from a woman who sold plants near the rows of neatly trimmed gardens. Her thumbs cracked, black with dirt.

His hands were so smooth now. City hands, the hands of a man who doesn't do much work. Not weathered like his father's. Who still spent time checking his snares in the forest. Fishing in the lakes near his house.

The streetlights glowed on the wet snowflakes, melting once they hit the pavement.

Kathryn's voice echoed in his head, "It's not possible he's dead." She was so young. She knew more about the dead boy than she was willing to confess. She seemed very far away when he asked her about the necklace. He might have gotten more out of her if they'd been talking in person.

(FALL)

KATHRYN

45.

SHE WAS DRAWING IN her notebook while Olav slept, sketching the stove, the slim birch logs piled on the floor, Olav's head resting on his arms as the fire burned.

"You have a small problem," he'd said before he fell into a deep sleep in the little hut.

Reindeer skins were piled high in the corner. Their musty smell, the brittle feel of the fur. On the stove was a kettle.

She plucked the lace in the windows with her fingers, her other hand on the closed notebook. She listened to him sleeping curled on the floor, his head on a sweater. Olav's soft breathing as he slept was almost the only sound.

The fire was low, she thought, and opened the door of the stove, stuffed a log into the coals. She was perfectly happy, several minutes after walking from one side of the hut to the other, the morning light warming her arms and legs as she stooped to pick up her clothes, thrown in a pile on the cold floor.

When Olav woke, she said, "A problem?"

He shifted the heavy hide and stood up, shaking his head like a bear. "Yes, about living in Lismavarri."

He pulled a sweater on and then bent to add two logs to the fire. "It's a tricky stove, isn't it?"

"Not so tricky. Not so tricky as you are," she laughed.

"But that's not it, is it? Not what makes you wonder if you can live here. And it's not the long dark winter either."

She was afraid to ask him for something. For something that sounded like the word love. She didn't trust him. She wasn't sure he loved her enough or loved her at all. Sometimes she felt powerless even though she pretended anything was possible. She didn't know if it was possible to love someone the way she loved Olav and still be passionate about your art.

"You know the story of the old boy?" Olav asked, as they started to pack for the walk home.

"I remember. The man who lived in the forest."

"Well, there is an old girl too in Lismavarri. In the little white house. And one night two brothers slept with her and from that night she got a child. One of the brothers, Olapeer, was the richest reindeer owner in the world. He owned above six thousand reindeer and his sons each almost two thousand. But the other, Tore, was very poor. He owned only four hundred reindeer."

"So she slept with the richest reindeer owner in the world and his brother who was so poor?" Kathryn asked, laughing.

"She did."

Kathryn remembered the woman hanging her sheets on the line to dry. They were walking to the field by the river. The wind was strong and each time the woman reached up to hang another sheet, the wind blew it back into her face. Her hair was very long and white. As they walked past her, she turned and waved. Kathryn wanted her own little house by the edge of the forest, high enough to see the river and the town below. She walked quickly and turned back to see the woman pick up her basket and go inside her house.

"So was her son poor or rich?"

"She kept the son for herself and both brothers helped her with the child."

"Was she happy?"

"How can I know about that?" Olav shrugged. "But I grew up with her son and he thought he'd been lucky to have two fathers."

THAT NIGHT SHE DREAMED the vidda was flooded and silent. It was winter and dark. Everything frozen. The little village submerged. The tracks of reindeer erased. Willow grouse hidden in their icy bushes. She was flying overhead in a small plane filled with white sacks. "There," the pilot said, "there you see where the village used to be, and there in that dark stretch we found a man who disappeared."

And then she saw Olav's father hitting a salmon with a club. The boat was bloody. She saw the narrow boat move silently through the frozen night. She was out on the river with Olav and his father to check the nets. Olav at the prow of the long narrow black boat. He was huddled in a winter coat and hat and gloves facing her, seated beside his father. The river was as smooth and flat as a lake. Her pale face reflected in the water.

There were fires on the Finnish shore and the white peaks of tents. Olav pulled in close to some buoys, and his father dipped his hand into the water to pull up the net. He tugged it once, twice, to see if there were any fish. They did this several times and then Olav rowed them back to shore. They passed two other boats, checking their nets. But the boats were empty, the nets pulled by invisible hands.

46.

SHE CAMPED WITH ERIC and Gunter on the very edge of the waterfall where it fell over the rocks into the ravine. Olav was busy in the shop, something to do with accounting. Gunter was leaving soon to meet his father in Paris, and Eric had taken them on a hike up to the vidda.

Everything was thundering. The cold water crashing over the cliff. The dark night like thunder after weeks of sunlight. She could taste the cold water on her lips. The mossy smell of it.

"Ah, my friend Gunter, don't be so sad about leaving. You can always come back," Eric said. He unrolled his sleeping bag with a snap.

Gunter shook his head and wandered off to collect small branches for the fire.

"Tell me about *yoiks*," Kathryn said.

"When the priests first came here from the south, they saw *yoiking* as primitive and dangerous. They thought it was a threat to their power."

Gunter circled back to the fire, his arms full of slim branches. He was bent over the brushwood, cradling it in his arms.

"Your parents didn't talk about any of these things?" Gunter asked.

"It wasn't polite. No one wanted to talk about the past. The settlers from the south never believed we were quite human. They didn't like our religion or our tents or our clothes. They took our land and plowed it and planted hay. For years, the people in the south thought we were dirty, ragged, not very smart."

"But no one thinks that now, do they? It's bizarre," Gunter said.

Eric laughed. "Don't worry, Gunter, they can think what they want. It's what they're doing that I'm angry about. The dam site is near where my great grandfather was beheaded. I want to stir things up. Start a conversation. This will all disappear, if we let them build the dam and flood the forest."

"Why are you doing this?" Kathryn asked. "There's no way this will stop the construction, will it?"

"Ah, it is important to do something. One last thing." Eric said, feeding the fire with small sticks. "The *yoiks* are like Johnny Cash's songs, but with reindeer instead of cattle. The same kind of land. The *yoik* was like a lullaby to keep off wolves. Men would sing their songs around the fires at night. From the beginning of time. The fire, moon, wolves, and the reindeer. It sounded like this. Oulu, oulu, oulu. To soothe the reindeer."

Eric's voice hollowed a place in the darkness. The fire was blazing. The sticks disintegrated as they watched.

"If you knew a man and wanted to make a song about him or a place or a woman you missed, you would think about them and make a melody—slow or fast or peaceful—and then the words would come. *Yoiks* weren't only about the reindeer. I am right now beginning to make a *yoik* about you, Gunter, a fast song to show how you ran up the hill with the wood. Ingrid does what she wants with the idea of a *yoik*. Twists it all around." Eric started to sing wildly.

"And who ever heard of a *yoik* accompanied by bongos?" Kathryn asked.

"Touché." Eric laughed, and poured Kathryn more coffee in her metal cup.

"I like the way you jazz up the tempo," Gunter said.

"It's a *yoik*, but I'm taking Ingrid's cue and experimenting a bit. She says your voice is a mirror of your soul, you know."

"My music teacher talked a lot about what he called sonic acts of remembrance," Gunter said, as he held his hands near the fire, "The *yoik* as an act of remembrance. A willing yourself into existence. A way to make who you are blend with the universe all around you. I listened to some of the records this guy in Finland made in the '60s. He'd *yoik* and there were musicians playing drums and guitars. The sound of reindeer and dogs barking."

"Ah," Eric said, feeding the fire with more sticks. "Valkeapaa. He's a mentor for me. He left his life. The life of his parents. He couldn't stand the reindeer slaughter in the autumn. He felt closer to birds, to wind, than he did to his family."

They were awake until late at night.

IN THE MORNING THE whole earth was glowing. She woke slowly, warm in her sleeping bag on the edge of the river. Eric crawled out of his bag and stretched.

Kathryn pulled herself out of her bag. She looked down at the foaming river where it slowed and turned. A few feet away Gunter was taking pictures.

"Take a look at this," he said. She walked over and he handed his camera to her. When she looked through the telephoto lens, she saw something dark and green on the rocks near the edge of the water. It wasn't an animal. It was hard to make out exactly what it was.

Eric walked over to where Kathryn and Gunter were standing.

"There's something down there," she said quietly to Eric. She couldn't figure out what it was at first. Green cloth, the yellow finger, the head broken, bent, turned, a cheek withered. Not a skull but a face still there.

A body broken. Pieces attached to a coat. But some of the bones gnawed almost clean.

She knew she recognized the coat but wasn't able to admit it at first. Even to herself. His green down parka was matted, covered with mud.

She'd buried the moment in the forest with the boy. She still hadn't told Olav what had happened, but this was proof she hadn't killed him. The boy had walked to the edge of the waterfall.

Gunter said, "What the fuck?"

Kathryn was so still she forgot to breathe.

"What do we do now?" Gunter asked, throwing his pack on the stones at the edge of the cliff.

She looked through the telephoto lens again and could see the head turned away from her, the side of a cheek shriveled and yellow. She wondered if maggots would have stripped the carcass clean after wolves chewed pieces of flesh off. It was so cold. He'd been trying to kill her. But she didn't want him dead.

"We do nothing," Eric said. "There's nothing we can do to help him. It's a stranger who fell, perhaps, from the waterfall."

"Someone must be looking for him. People don't just disappear," Kathryn said.

She knew a reindeer herder or someone fishing in the lakes would find the body just like they'd spotted it. In the gorge, bent, alone. There was no chance all this would just disappear like magic. The boy in the forest, the flash of the pistol. The wind in her ears, her heart thumping. It was indelible now.

Someone would report the body to the police. Lying there, the green coat. Off the map, surrounded by wilderness.

"There was a deserter who fled into Kirkenes, they think. Olav was there not long ago and heard the sirens, the Russian sirens from the base across the border," Eric said.

She took a deep breath. "But aren't we a long way from there?"

"Not so far. We should go now." He pulled his pack on.

The wind had come up and it was colder, so cold she could barely feel her fingers as she adjusted the straps on her pack.

"He's dead, Kathryn, we can't help him."

"We have to report it, Eric."

"If we report it, police will be all over the place."

They were quiet all the long walk back to the village except when they stopped for water and Eric handed her a shank of dried reindeer meat. She chewed slowly. "But you'll tell someone about the body after you blow up the bridge?" she asked.

"Yes, of course. The body won't go anywhere in a month. Soon it will be covered with snow."

They were almost to the main road when Gunter stopped and threw up on the rutted trail. Eric was ahead of them at the bottom of the hill and she yelled to him. Gunter sat down on the mossy edge of the trail. He was holding his head. "It's okay. It's nothing. You go ahead. I'll catch up."

"But you're not okay."

"I'm just a little dizzy. You got any water?"

Kathryn handed him her water bottle, and he poured some of the water into his hand and splashed it on his face.

47.

The stiff leaves of the birches were gold. Tiny red leaves of Finnmark rose brushed against her legs. Dwarf willows burning yellow. The lichen-covered rock. Pools between the tussocks, cushions of electric green moss. A couple of weeks before she left Lismavarri. They walked up to the place where the reindeer owners marked the calves, not far away from the waterfall and the body.

If she wanted to, she could tell Olav. She could tell Olav about the man who waved his gun in front of her face. The boy she thought was going to shoot her. And how she pushed him and now she wanted to know his death was not her fault. Olav might convince her of that. It wasn't like he'd do anything about it. Would he? She was panicked about what might happen. Eric said there'd be police and an investigation. And Olav would have to tell the cops what he knew.

Someone must be searching for this boy. Someone must be wondering where he is. And if she'd harmed him in any way, if she'd caused his death, that made it much, much worse. She'd convinced herself she had to run away, but he may have been asking for help.

Kathryn could hear shouting before she could see anything.

And there was the roar of the waterfall, not far away at all. She could take Olav there and show him what they'd found. Maybe there was nothing at all. Not the body broken on the rocks. Not the narrow face half gone. The skin like wax. Not the pieces of dark hair, or the leg missing a foot. Not the hand cupped around a rock. Not the worms curled on the ear. And the glint of something that looked like a gun.

She stumbled and Olav touched her elbow.

"Are you alright, Kathryn? Your face looks a little odd."

Olav's uncle was shouting at his dog.

She said, "I'm fine. Nothing's wrong. Nothing's wrong at all."

"We don't have to watch this, if you don't want to. They will kill some calves. I told you that. They separate them from their mothers and kill them for their skin. But it's later. We'll just watch the first part."

Kathryn rubbed her eyes and said, "I'm okay."

"You're not okay. All this is too much, isn't it?"

He took her hand and they went up to the corral where the calves were running and running, crying for their mothers. The dogs circled the herd just outside of the corral. It started to rain and the cold seeped into Kathryn's shoulders through the thin layer of her jacket down her arms to her hands.

"Their skin is valuable, brings a lot of money. You see that dark brown calf there? Her skin is like gold. The mothers will call for their calves for three days, not more, and then they give up."

"It's sad."

"Yes," Olav said. "Sad, but so much of this life is filled with this practical sadness. It's part of business, Kathryn. Everyone has to live somehow. Some are slaughtered for their meat. The old Sami people would flay the calves and remove the innards, wrap up the other parts in fresh birch twigs and load them on the draft reindeer. They tied up dried jerky in scarves."

Olav dropped her hand and went over to his uncle. They leaned toward each other in the rain. Kathryn pressed against the fence. Two boys snapped their lassos out to catch a calf. It was raining hard now and the rain poured down on the calves panicked in the corral.

Olav walked away from his uncle who was giving orders to the dogs, calling one back when she was chasing a reindeer too close to the corral.

"He will beat this one when she's very bad and violent with the reindeer," he said when he neared her. "But that's seldom. You see, they're proud dogs and won't respect Uncle if he humiliates them. They refuse to work." He took her hand again, smoothed her wet hair back from her face.

One of Olav's cousins, a thin man with a wool cap pulled low over his forehead, held a calf between his legs and cut his mark into the calf's ear with a quick motion of his sharp knife. She watched him do this many times and put the slices of ears from the calves in his mouth. Later, he put them in a pocket, and after all the calves were marked, threaded the slices on sinew, and counted the number of calves.

48.

HAD SHE UNDERESTIMATED GUNTER? How could you truly know who people are? He was barely here and then he left. He promised to send her a bottle of wine from his aunt's vineyard.

She'd woken in the middle of the night not long after he arrived. The sky still bright, filled with light. She looked out her small window toward the sports club. Gunter was running from the shop toward the long jump. He jumped and flew through the air for seconds until he landed in the sand pit and shook himself off. He did this again and again. So many times she lost count and went back to bed. He must be covered in sweat and sand, even though the night was cool.

He'd told her about what happened to his grandmother in the war. "I'd read the Russian army moved in huge columns, soldiers in black helmets driving tanks. Cossacks on big horses, guns slung across their chests, bags of fruit and hunks of cheese, bottles of wine, tied to their saddles.

"My mother told me she watched them come across the fields from far off. She was standing with her mother and father near their cherry trees. The cherries were ripe and her mother told her that tomorrow they'd pick the cherries. My grandmother would climb up, and my mother could manage the basket below as her mother collected the cherries in her apron and then, when her apron was full, dropped them into her basket. They were going to make pie. My mother loved cherry pie even as a little girl. They hadn't been eating much. There was so little food. The bunch of soldiers was growing closer. They were laughing and hitting each other like little boys. They're drunk, my grandfather said. We'll go inside."

He told Kathryn that he wanted his mother to stop and said she didn't have to tell him about it if it was too hard—she was having to keep her hands from shaking.

"But she said, 'No, Gunter, you need to know about this.' When the soldiers came up to the house the family was sitting down to dinner. Her parents must have thought if they acted like there was no danger, they'd be fine: the soldiers would pass by on the village road and leave them alone. But they were wrong. A young Russian pulled the door open and smashed the wall with his fist. He gestured with his gun that my grandfather should come outside and my grandmother, too. My grandfather refused and said my wife stays here with my daughter. Many soldiers crowded into their small house. They threw the cold dinner onto the floor and pulled my grandparents into the yard. They left my mother alone."

His mother told him she stood at the window and watched as they dragged his grandmother past the orchard and into the shed where his grandfather kept his pruning shears and the long pruning pole and ladders. His mother saw them push his grandfather into the shed too and heard the screams from his grandmother and then a shot and then another.

"Then, there they were, singing and laughing as they got back on the road and made their way into town. My mother was too afraid to move from the window and started to count the cherries in the tree. She wanted so much to see my grandfather lifting the ladder up for my grandmother and my grandmother filling her apron with cherries," Gunter said.

After a while, his grandmother came out of the shed and his mother ran out of the house. His grandmother held her a long time, crouched in the yard. There was blood on her mother's hands and in her hair. Her arms were bruised. There were streaks of mud on her legs.

Gunter said, "I put my arms around my mother and we stood in the woods for a long time. She said, it was a long time ago, and my mother was very strong like other women who watched their husbands die. They were too guilty about the War to tell anyone about it."

This story about his grandmother wasn't something Kathryn expected. Painful, intimate.

49.

ONE OF HER LAST weekends in the north, Olav led the way across the forest to Eldor's earth hut. It was autumn. They had three days to be alone. It took them all day to walk up the path he'd traced on the map the night before. His finger touching the little lakes and streams and the tufts of grass that showed where the bogs were.

The hut was on the edge of Grandmother's Lake. It perched there, covered in moss with two tiny windows that looked out at the birch forest. They unloaded their gear on the floor, and Kathryn examined the tiny benches built into the sides of the hut and the table with two chairs. "Like a fairytale," she said.

Olav laughed. "I will split some wood and get the stove started."

She shook their sleeping bags out and arranged them on the benches and took a long sip of water from one of the bottles she'd carried. Little birds were chirping in the trees by the lake.

A short walk up the hills and they'd be on the vidda, where there were no trees to break the wind. Through the tiny window she watched Olav splitting the birch logs into smaller pieces for the stove, the ax cutting through the soft wood and the smooth skin, cleanly.

Soon they had a fire and Olav set a battered pot with a little water and reindeer meat on the top of the stove. She sprinkled salt on the meat, and chopped carrots and potatoes and added them to the pot. The stew smelled delicious as she sat and read on a little worn stool, and Olav slept under the sleeping bag on the bench.

There was so much to lose all of a sudden. The summer light, the taste of cloudberries freshly picked, the sound of his voice. Their socks were drying on the oven door, open a bit. She sat as close as she could get to the stove. Reindeer hair littered the table and she swept it off with one hand.

They'd left the door open, and the wind came from around the lake and lifted the few scattered leaves still on the birches like a skirt.

That night Kathryn dreamed that the beautiful woman who was once Olav's lover killed an owl and took it apart. Ingrid threw the body into the birch woods and then placed the feathers, gray, black, and silver, in a pattern on the table to show Kathryn.

"What does it mean?" she asked Olav in the morning, her head close to his.

"Sometimes these things don't mean anything," he said. "But the owl can bring good luck."

They walked up to the vidda past a waterfall. An eagle soared above them, a bird with dark brown wings with white markings. Her nest was a pile of sticks suspended on a ledge covered with orange and green lichen. Willow grouse foraged in the brush.

"You can find willow grouse bones in the eagle's nests," Olav said.

It was such a watery world on the vidda. Water rushing over stones, through the spongy moss, shining in the lake and in small pools. Sometimes soft gray, sometimes brilliant blue. Torrents cascading over smooth rocks, the shimmery lakes full of trout. Water boiling in the coffee kettle on the liquid coals of fire, water splashed on her face from the pools surrounded by moss.

On the way home, they crossed the big bog to reach the bottom of the hill. Her boots squished through the watery grass. Soon, her socks were wet. Olav told her about the old fence half stuck in the soft earth.

"My mother's grandfather cut the grass here with a cutter shaped like a little sleigh. The farmers cut the bog grass in the forest because the field grass was still so poor without fertilizer. My father cut hay here too. He would start mid-June and cut all summer for three or four cows. The last man to cut up in the forest was Eldor's father in 1950 or so. No one cuts here anymore."

"But you told me the woman who lives in the little white house at the end of town used to get her hay in the forest."

"Ah, yes, but not as much as the other farmers."

As they walked down the hill toward the river, she couldn't feel her hands. They were so cold they could be someone else's. The river spread out, glittering in the rain. The sky darkened and cleared. One star twinkled. The first in a long summer of daylight.

"You see the star?" Olav asked.

"Yes, I'm wishing on it right now."

IT'S HARD TO REMEMBER, but Kathryn knows Olav didn't tell her he loved her when she left. He woke her early. She could hear the baby crying. Maren would still be sleeping.

Everything was telling her not to go to Wales. The cows in their warm stalls, the sheep in the pasture, the dark birds flying across Olav's uncle's fields. She couldn't think, couldn't see as she woke up. Her head was pounding and her chest hurt. She was afraid to ask Olav what she should do. Afraid he might tell her to stay.

She started to pack. She decided not to bring the dress Olav's mother had given her. A pretty flowered dress that someone else had left at the farm. Or the old jeans she'd worn every day for months. She wondered if Maren would remember the English words she'd taught her. Ball, water, splash.

The wind was blowing hard, and they got into the small blue car without saying goodbye to anyone. His parents were in the barn tending the cows. The fields were shorn. All the haying done. Puddles of water stood in the lowest fields near the river.

50.

When Kathryn walked off the ferry in Newcastle, the pavement was tilting. The light so different from the glowing light of Finnmark. She'd traveled away from Lismavarri by plane, and then ferry. Farther and farther away from where she wanted to be.

She pulled the pink scarf Olav gave her out of a pocket on her pack and held it to her lips. Beautiful shimmery silk with thousands of twisted threads along the edges. A marriage shawl, Ellen told her.

"But he didn't ask me to marry him," Kathryn said.

Ellen had smiled and smoothed the sheet she was ironing.

Yellow leaves covered the sidewalks. The change in the trees shocked her, used to months of tiny Arctic birch. Everyone was speaking English. It was loud, very loud. Those months listening to conversations in Sami wrapped around her like a cocoon.

The north called her again and again like a drug. The smell of the wind. The miniature leaves. The shallow, glinting river. The small waves lapping on the gravel bank.

Her loneliness was so strong she couldn't breathe. Smoke stung her eyes as she walked to the train station. A bomb had detonated in a mailbox not far from the station, long before it opened. The work of the IRA, everyone said.

By the time she reached the station to catch the train to Wales, her heart was beating against her ribs. She paced back and forth, back and forth in the large waiting room. She was afraid she was having a heart attack. Every part of her was numb. Her hands, her toes, her arms, her legs, the muscles in her throat. Soon she wouldn't be able to swallow. She sat on one of the long benches near the gate. The wooden bench was cold against her legs. She leaned her head against the wood, the station humming around her. She felt as if she had no skin. Soon, she couldn't move at all, and she strained to see the clock on a pillar. She couldn't miss her train. Gwen would be waiting at the station.

"Can you help me?" she asked a woman who sat down across from her.

"What's wrong, love?" she asked. "Sick to your stomach?"

"I can't move."

The woman yelled to a guard, "The girl here is very sick, I'm afraid. Can you call an ambulance to help the lass?"

"Stay still, miss," the guard said. "They'll be here soon."

When the two men in white shirts with red logos loaded her onto the stretcher, she clutched her climbing helmet in her hand. "It was silly to bring it," she told the skinny man who wheeled her through the smudged glass doors.

The ambulance ride was a blur.

One of the men in the white shirts smiled at her. "Not long now."

She waited a long time in a dim corridor of the hospital. She was feeling better, able to sit up. Worried about Gwen standing on the platform in Conway. After an hour, a nurse wheeled her into a little cubicle with a wrinkled curtain. The doctor appeared, pulling the curtain closed. She was a slim woman wearing a white lab coat. Her name was written in blue on a pocket on her chest.

Kathryn had already been hooked up to an electrocardiogram. The places on her chest were still sticky where the technician attached her to the machine.

"Your heart looks fine, blood pressure's back to normal. It seems like it was anxiety, nothing more. Are you under a lot of stress?"

Kathryn wanted to say yes, but instead she said no.

"It might just be the travel," the doctor said.

"It might be the trip from Norway. I didn't want to leave. I was sick on the ship to Newcastle. "

The doctor's smooth hand rested on her shoulder. The heat from her hand.

"Why?"

"I got involved with someone."

"Ah," she said. "You're very young, you'll get over this soon. There's nothing physically wrong with you."

The doctor vanished around the curtain and then reappeared with a whole bottle of valium. "Break them in half," she said, "and you'll be fine."

SHE WAS DIZZY AS the train swayed on the tracks. She thought she might be pregnant. Is that why she felt sick every morning?

She wondered if Olav had driven to the clinic for birth control pills before. Had he driven other lovers along the same narrow road to the clinic? She took them from a pocket on her pack and threw them out, shaking each yellow pill into the toilet on the train.

It was hours before they reached the coast. The blue curve of the sea, caravans parked along the gray sand, children running on the edge of the waves.

Gwen picked her up at Conway, and they drove down narrow roads following the path of a narrow wild river, through little villages with large open barns and sheep thick on the steep green hillsides. One valley road took them past a square castle, sturdy on a rocky bluff. The terrain was more predictable, more medieval than Finnmark.

"You're so pale," Gwen said. "I thought you spent months outside."

Kathryn laughed. "Where's the farm?"

"Two ridges over," Gwen said.

In the morning after breakfast, Kathryn left Gwen's house to walk to the sea. She wanted more than anything to hear Olav's voice. She wanted to go with him into the barn and slip her clothes off in the hayloft, feel his lips on her lips.

Maybe taking valium wasn't a good idea just in case she was pregnant, but it was the only way to keep her heart from pounding furiously in her chest.

She climbed a fence into the grounds of a famous hotel and walked through old trees covered in moss and vines, past a little red Chinese bridge and a graveyard for dogs, and then through the Ghost Garden. She was sweating. The pale trunks of the towering trees grew so close together she could hardly squeeze through. There were bushes with thin leaves so transparent they looked white. A hawk screeched. The sea glimmered beyond the twisted trunks. Gulls cried out above the silver darkness of the woods. It wasn't a garden at all but a maze of branches.

The path up to the headland was narrow, filled with brambles. She'd scratched her hands as she climbed. She sat down on a rock looking out at the water. The tide pulled the waves away from the shore like a peel.

How responsible was she for the boy's death? How responsible was she for anything? Will she feel guilty about the boy in the forest for the rest of her life? It wouldn't have done any good to tell Olav she'd seen the boy with a gun. His face streaked with blood. His dark hair matted. What good would that have done?

That night she pulled her skin boots out of their bag and slipped them on her feet.

51.

AN OFFICER WEARING A black cap with a shiny brim was coming up the track to her cottage. She saw him as she pinned her wet clothes on the line. He was pushing a bike through the puddles on the track. He probably doesn't want to mess up his uniform, she thought. But why was he coming to see her? How did he know where she lived? Gwen must have told him. They had no phone at the farm.

Her heart started to beat faster.

"I have a request for you, miss," he said when he reached the cottage.

She leaned one hand against the stones of the bothy.

"I've been sent to tell you to be in our station tomorrow at noon to talk to a detective from Norway on the phone at the office." He handed her a summons. "It's right by the church. You know where that is?"

"Yes," she said. She'd been shopping in town just the day before with Gwen.

"IT'S NOTHING PROBABLY," GWEN said later when they were eating dinner at her house.

Her boyfriend poured Kathryn a glass of wine and said, "It's curious they're going to so much trouble to track you down. I don't see you as a villainous girl."

"Looks are deceptive. She's surprising, this one," Gwen said. "I'll drive you there. I don't want you walking to this."

Later that night, Kathryn noticed the tiny drops of blood in the shower. Light pink and faint on the soft part of her inner thigh. What if it was a miscarriage? Was she supposed to do something?

THE NEXT DAY, KATHRYN opened the three fences they needed to drive through before they reached the main road. It was a rhythm she liked. A sign she was somewhere where people paid attention to their animals. They didn't want to lose them.

"I'm so lucky," Kathryn said.

"Lucky?" Gwen asked.

"To have you as a friend."

She rubbed her hand on Kathryn's arm. "Everything will be fine."

The station was dusty and hot. The police officer pointed to a desk with a phone and said, "I'll pick it up when it rings and then give it to you. It should be the detective, Hans Sorensen."

It was a name she'd heard before. The detective in Oslo who'd moved away from Finnmark.

She could hardly hear him, the connection was so bad. And he kept asking questions that bounced in her head. A body, a body on the hike, yes, she said, did you know who it was, no, the bomb at the dam, Eric, his beautiful hand. The very cold night, the new skin parka. How will Eric play his music? Jorgens's death, a string of bad news. Her head was spinning, she felt hot then cold. She was having cramps that were so bad, she thought she might be dying.

"Olav," she said. "Is Olav alright?"

"He's fine," the detective said.

"A gold necklace?" he asked. And she didn't know what to answer. The sound in her ears was blowing in and out, in and out like a bellows. Wap wap wap. She could hear the officer asking, "Miss, are you alright?"

I saw the boy with a gun, face streaked with blood, hair matted, she thought she was saying but she was on the floor. The smooth floor cool against her cheek.

"Too much for her, I think," the officer said, and then there was Gwen rubbing her back.

"Oh my god, you're bleeding."

THE DRIVE TO THE hospital was short and fast and Gwen left her off at the emergency room. Kathryn could barely walk. A nurse helped her into a wheelchair with big silver wheels and pushed her to a waiting room.

"I think it's a miscarriage," she said.

She knew the blood had soaked through her clothes.

"She's hemorrhaging," she could hear someone say, and then they wheeled her into a room with a flickering light and a concrete floor with a drain in the middle. The walls were painted light blue, and she knew she was going out fast as they held the anesthesia to her nose.

"It's all over, love," a nurse said.

When she opened her eyes, she was lying half up in a hospital bed. An IV attached to her arm. Gwen sitting by her side in a narrow chair. She was cold. The thin white blanket on the bed was torn on the edges.

She reached out to stroke Gwen's hand. Gwen pulled a tissue out of the box by the bed and pressed it against the tears on Kathryn's face.

52.

SHE WAS WORKING IN a pub near the farm. Some days she helped Gwen with the sheep. It was comforting to be around animals again. Soon she'd begin an art degree in Bangor.

The fields were still green in December. The rhythm of the work with the sheep on her friend's farm reminded Kathryn of her days haymaking. She could hear Gunter's voice suddenly as clear as if he were there with her.

As they lifted the hay and threw it on the wires, Gunter telling her about the grape harvest. About ice wine. The sweetness of the grapes, the way the vineyards cover the entire territory of the little village where he lives. The vineyard hums with insects serenading him as he snips bunches of grapes with the heavy clipper and drops them into the bucket at his feet. His auntie and grandmother are waiting in a truck at the end of the row.

Gunter snips and cradles the bunch of red grapes in their tight skins and then places them into the bucket on top of their cousins. He bends and snips, cradles, and plops. When he gets to the end of the row he climbs up to the trailer, bends and tips the bucket to pour it into the large container on the back of the truck. He can hear his auntie and grandmother talking about a woman in the next village over, how she left her children, seven of them, and went to Aruba with her lover. Now the father is left to take care of the children. Gunter tells Kathryn he thinks he understands that violent longing for another place.

Sometimes he's not careful enough as he picks up the heavy bucket and tips it just so to empty the grapes, and some of the ripe clusters slip down the front of his shirt and land on the ground at his feet. Yellow jackets swarm around him, insistent, stubborn. He's covered with sticky goo.

His grandmother isn't happy to be working with Auntie. There were no men Gunter's age left in the village. The women like his grandmother worked in Auntie's vineyard. Something to do. The old women in their blue flowered dresses laugh at him bent at the base of the vines, snipping ripe grapes. He loves the way the grapes smell, sweet and sharp.

WHEN KATHRYN THOUGHT ABOUT those months in Finnmark as she fed Gwen's sheep or cleared tables in the pub, she liked to remember the hours she spent in the sauna. Sometimes she opened the little wooden window and looked out at the wide river flowing north to the Arctic Ocean. She wound the towel around her head and stepped warm and clean into the night. She wasn't attached to anything. She could be anyone she wanted.

Even in the cold she could smell the sweetness of the tiny leaves and flowers, the tight berries in the forest. The sound of the wind always blowing. If she'd hiked up to the ridge above the village she could see fields sloping to the river and the little track that swerved off the main road down into the settlement with its wooden houses.

Below her were the new low houses with their big windows on the high fields near the forest. Eric's small brown house hugged the field, the river shining below. On the village road the squat white house of the woman who had two lovers on one summer night, the richest reindeer owner in Tana and his brother, a poor man. The woman's sheets were slapping against the wind. And then a few tiny houses. Next Olav's uncle's house, tall and blue with a cluster of birches around the side, and the old shop, another house with two stories where Gunter slept.

Across the dirt road was the Elstads' new house, unremarkable and green, like a house in any development. In the living room, three or four miniature roses, their pink and red buds just unfurling on the windowsill. Near the shop was the barn, large and red. The cows were snorting in the cold air and the white ordinary sheep grazed in nearby fields. The last building was the sports club. A beige concrete place.

KATHRYN TOUCHED THE LETTER she kept in her pocket. A small piece of paper folded once from Olav. He'd typed it on his desk at the shop.

Dear Kathryn,

When will you come to Lismavarri again? We have started the foundation for the new shop. Ellen asked me to thank you for the toy fox. Maren likes it very much. Mother keeps asking when you will come back to us. Are you wearing the pink scarf I gave you?

Love,
Olav

(NOVEMBER)

HANS

53.

Hans caught the late ferry from Oslo to Frederikshavn on his way to Emilie and Gudmund's grave in Denmark.

"I think you need some time to process all this information. It's a web," Malin said. "You've been going nonstop. You can ease up on things. We'll catch up on Monday. You deserve to take a break this weekend."

She picked up Matisse after work and whisked him away in her Volkswagen camper. It was easy to buy the ticket. Arrange the rental car. Pack an overnight bag.

The ferry was filled with Norwegians looking for cheap booze and cheap clothes in Denmark. In the café, two men in dirty sweatshirts were arguing near the bar. Pushing each other against the wall. A few too many beers, he supposed. A waiter appeared and they stopped. The waiter started to wipe a table near them and one of the men picked up a stained rucksack on the table and walked away.

Hans bought a cup of coffee and found a place to sit by a window near the bow of the ferry. The waves foamed up like soap suds as they traveled south. Spumes of water crashed against the ship.

It had been a frustrating day at the office. He'd waited so long to interview Kathryn, but the information she gave him was disappointing. It was puzzling, though, she assumed the body was a male. Wasn't it? Or was it what most people would do? There was no reason for a woman to be alone in the forest. It was odd Kathryn spent time there by herself. Was there something she couldn't tell anyone? Perhaps some kind of deep hurt. How did the delicate necklace end up in the stranger's pocket? What was she holding back? There was so much she wasn't saying.

The coffee was very hot and strong, not the usual kind found on ferries.

He was trying to imagine Kathryn with Gunter and Eric Paulsen when they found the body. The roar of the waterfall. A burning light smoldering through the night. Had they made a pact to protect each other? He didn't think Gunter Schmidt had anything to do with the boy's death.

Lars had hit a dead end with the dispute about leasing rights near Lismavarri. Villagers told him about two Americans everyone had seen going in and out of the Elstads' shop, but no one could tell him much of anything else.

He finished his coffee and threw the cup in a basket near his seat. The ferry lurched from side to side in the rough water.

He had a few of Emilie's letters packed in his duffle. He opened the bag and pulled them out. The first one was crumpled, a little stained.

March 21, 1949

Darling one,

Do you think it's a good idea to be writing about all those years, especially now that my body's reluctant to do anything?

I was so strong. So happy walking or skiing or driving the reindeer. It was mindless like painting, I suppose. Pure instinct. Of course, I had to practice and made mistakes, but after that I could pretty much do many things I'd never done before, and do them well. Sometimes I can't remember the way I felt before we married. More impulsive, certainly braver, and even smarter, I think. I loved those times when I watched the reindeer with Inga. We both fell asleep one day, tired from a long slog over tussocks and through streams and bogs the day before. We were supposed to keep track of the reindeer as they nibbled moss. When we woke they'd gone, so we ran looking for them for hours, it seemed, until we found the herd peacefully grazing a few miles away. We'd been so worried we fell down on the ground and started laughing until we were too tired to laugh at all.

Emilie knew Aunt Inga as a girl. He only knew her as an old woman with long white braids wound around her head.

Copenhagen
March 30, 1949

Darling,

Don't be fooled by these letters. I never tell the truth. Except about that year. The elixir of that year. The taste of snow, metallic in my mouth. The flakes melting on my tongue. The pure joy of being in the wind and watching the reindeer graze, pawing through the crust to get to the brittle moss curled under the surface. The smoke that got through all my clothes and in my hair. The eerie light in the goati at dawn, the dawn that sometimes was no dawn. The three months of darkness. How the wind could blow so hard and then not blow at all.

THE SMELL OF FRIED fish and greasy fries in the café was getting to him. He packed the letters into his duffle and opened the door to the deck. He was the only person braving the wind bashing the bow. Everything was crystal clear: the sky, the green-tinged water, the horizon. Matisse loved to feel the wind on his muzzle when they drove; Hans understood why as he let the breeze scour his face.

He couldn't imagine Emilie dead. Buried. Astrid wanted to be cremated. He fought the idea at first. Just couldn't convince himself that her body should be burned. But she insisted. Easier that way, she said. So much easier. But it wasn't. He took her ashes up to the forest, finally, to a place she loved and scattered them in the woods.

After the ferry docked, he picked up a rental car and drove south to Kauslunde through the miles of flat landscape and big sky on Jutland where Gudmund had spent years excavating old settlements. The large farms with their solid houses and barns marshaling around a courtyard. Small black cows milling in frozen fields, their breaths milky. Hard work in the middle of nowhere. Not much of a life.

It was cold. Cold for Denmark, everyone told Hans when he stopped for gas and filled up the small red Ford Fiesta.

He was near Alborg, the place with a Viking burial ground. Excavated, labeled. He'd seen it once with Astrid. Hundreds of years of burials, the body along with possessions from this life burned on a pyre, surrounded by large stones in the shape of a boat for men, triangular for women. One life piled on top of the next. The village was built around the graves until sand swept in from the fjord and covered it all.

Stands of pines, the old Viking graves. Barrows like loaves of bread repeating now and then on the horizon. A passage from this world to the next. Just your polished bones dry, close to the earth.

He was hearing Emilie's voice again. She thought she was in love, but she wasn't, with his uncle. Beware of all the things you learn about love, beware of how memories of past loves collide in your brain, beware of the seduction of landscape, the feeling of cold wind on your face, the days in bed, hardly able to move. When you're young, you have all this life ahead of you. She wasn't. She was old. She was very old, it seems like now, even though she looked a lot younger, that's worth nothing. Yes, she loved Gudmund, yes, she was disappointed in many things but thrilled with everything else about her life.

He sped along the road, behind a tractor trailer hauling pigs with a cartoon of Porky Pig on the back of the trailer. On the way to the abattoir. He wanted to think it was comforting, the voice of a woman he never knew, but it wasn't.

The truck was slow, so slow he tried to pass at a curve when he thought he could see around the bend. But he couldn't. His foot caught between the brake and clutch, and he wasn't going anywhere, the smoke billowing out from the car. He was too big for such a small car.

He drove until he reached Kauslunde and parked on a hill near a church with a square white tower. A replica of many of the Danish churches he'd passed on his way south. He opened the heavy wooden door. Why was it unlocked? Inside was another door, carved with symbols that were familiar. From the eleventh century. They were the same symbols on the rings his brother sold for so much to tourists.

Hans ran his fingers on the designs, then turned and went outside to search for the grave. Up and down the paths through bordered plots decorated with pine boughs that covered the ground this time of year. Some tied in a fist, an offering for the dead.

A young woman was clearing branches, piling them into a cart. She was bundled up in a heavy coat, a striped hat pulled low over her forehead. "Hello," he said, "I'm looking for a grave. Cold, isn't it?"

"Not as cold as yesterday." She laughed. She had a lovely face. Round, flushed, sweet. "I waited till it got warmer today to do this work."

"You have some time to help me find it?"

"Sure, what's the name on the grave?"

Hans told the verger and she said, "Not familiar with those names, but we can go take a look at the memorial book."

He followed her down a slope to a small white building on the edge of the churchyard. Old gravestones were piled along the outside of the fence. Discarded, lost, unfamiliar. Bodies buried outside the neat green plots, too poor, too sinful?

The book was large, filled with small neat script. Like a card catalogue of deaths and burials. She ran her finger down page after page. "Ah, here we are."

He followed her along a small path through the graves.

Sara had told him Kauslunde was where Emilie and Gudmund lived much of the time during the last years of their lives. Intentionally cut off from Copenhagen in the yellow stone house at the very edge of town. The garden surrounded the house. Their orchard was down the street, closer to the church. They lived just down the street from the school where Emilie's sister had taught for so many years across from the church.

When Emilie looked out the windows of her studio, she would have seen plowed fields this time of year. Dark earth piled in furrows. And beyond the fields, the sea.

"Here you go." The woman pointed. The plot was like the others, but a wrought iron sculpture stood behind the large stone in the center of the plot, surrounded by white gravel. Emilie and Gudmund's names were metal hammered into the stone. Two letters were missing from Gudmund's name, chipped away from the stone. Perhaps it had been vandals or someone who thought Gudmund a traitor, even in his exile.

"It's a special grave," the young woman said moving her finger on the sign. "This says the tree of life is unusual. The only one in Demark. A man in town made it. It's very special. It's a Swedish thing." The sculpture was made of dozens of iron leaves that hung like dark ornaments from the tall support. On the tree were three porcelain plaques for Emilie's mother, father, and sister.

He could read the Danish, but she wouldn't know that. He didn't sound like he was from anywhere near Kauslunde.

"This is great. I appreciate you taking this time from your work."

"It's nothing." She smiled again. "I've got to get to the floor in the church now. I left it half done."

She turned and trotted up the slope to the church. Her yellow striped hat bright against the gray monuments.

It was hard to believe the woman who seemed so alive in her letters could be buried in the frozen graveyard near her house.

Hans crouched down on the pea gravel. The months since Astrid's death disappeared and he felt as raw as he had right after her death. He was suddenly very tired. A kind of exhaustion he hadn't felt since Astrid was sick. And then when she slipped away from him. Even though they tried all the best doctors. All the hospitals where the best doctors worked to make her well. Hans had found a book about how laughter cures cancer. He'd talked to a man who'd used meditation to heal his wife's cancer and said he'd won the battle against his own tumors twice. No, three times.

All those days with his heart scraped out, dissolving. Astrid's hands in his hands. Her shallow breath in the hospital bed. Hair pulled back from her face, in a knot at her neck. Eyes closed. Disappearing as he watched. That day he'd left for a minute, when he got back she was gone. One of her teeth chipped. Her hand still warm as he held it to his lips. He'd just missed her. And then she wasn't there at all.

Minutes passed and then he felt a hand on his shoulder.

"Are you okay?" the verger asked.

Hans was embarrassed. He was crying and stood up, wiping his face before he turned around.

On the ferry home from Frederikshavn to Oslo, Hans finished reading Turi's book. Another day of bumping elbows with drunk passengers and screaming kids. The water was rough, but he didn't mind. On the upper deck, a large family of German tourists tossed bread and cake to the seagulls who were bearing down on them. The children were screeching, and the adults covered their ears.

He sat down on a bench and pulled Turi's book out of his pocket. He flipped back through the pages. Emilie said in one of her letters that Turi felt caught between two worlds. Sápmi was disappearing. Even then tourists were streaming up the train line along with the miners to Narvik.

As he reread the introduction, he realized the description of why Turi wrote the book was an awful lot like the case he was facing. People just didn't tell the truth and didn't understand each other. The best place to meet to solve disputes, Turi wrote, is on the top of a mountain, not closed up in a room, or in a dense warm forest. A Sami has a clear mind when he's on a mountain.

Turi's solution to the problem was to write his book about Sami life and conditions. Then people wouldn't have to lie and "misconstrue" that only the Sami are at fault when disputes arose between the settlers and Sami in Sweden and Norway.

If only Hans could get all the suspects, and all the evidence, and himself on top of a mountain, he could sort out what happened and solve the mystery.

He closed Turi's book. Published in 1910 and nothing had changed. He hadn't seen this at first and he wasn't happy to admit that. The dam was the kind of dispute Turi wrote about. And that dispute had blown off a man's hand and might have been the reason another man was dead, decaying in a ravine in Sápmi.

54.

THE PHONE WAS RINGING inside as he climbed the stairs to his apartment. The lock was tricky sometimes and it took him a minute to open the door.

"Hello, Hans," someone said. "It's Ingrid."

He felt as if her voice was coming from somewhere else, some city he knew in another life. So much had happened.

"Yes?" Trying to sound cool, very cool. Very official. But his heart was thumping. Rattling away.

"Want to grab dinner tonight?" As if they'd been seeing each other for weeks.

Did she know about Jorgen? She must. Someone would have told her. Hans couldn't remember anything in the rules about getting involved with a person who'd been eliminated as a suspect. Crossed off the list. Or was she crossed off the list? It just didn't seem like a very good idea. But he'd been doing a lot worse than that. Passionately kissing a woman he'd just met. Not thinking about Astrid at all for hours at a time.

"Okay. Why not?" He said before he could stop himself. It didn't make any sense: someone else was talking to Ingrid. Someone else who was out of control. He was too tired to do anything else.

"Meet me at my place?"

Ingrid lived in a studio not far from the harbor. She liked the idea of escape. Being close to something liquid. "I suppose I miss the river. I miss the little pools in the forest. Anyway, here's the address. At nine?"

"Sure, see you then."

So he called Malin, not to get permission. He could consider it a follow-up interview, still informal. But he wanted to check on Matisse.

"Oh wow," she said, "how cute. You actually miss him? But I don't mind keeping him a few more days. He's entertaining us. You do look adorable, though, walking him—such a tall man with such a scruffy, charming little dog."

"Fair enough," Hans said, and then confessed. "I'm meeting Ingrid Morland again."

"Officially?"

"I don't think so." He jabbed a pencil into the pad near the phone like a tiny spear.

"Rough waters, Hans."

"I know."

"Be careful."

"I will. And thanks again for taking care of the little rat."

"I'm quite fond of the little rat. And he can hear you over the phone you know."

He wasn't careful at all, it turned out. He realized all his halfway decent shirts were dirty. Tore through the hamper. Smoothed his hair. Pulled a sweater from the wardrobe, the shelves almost empty since Sara's visit.

He stumbled down the stairs of the building and pulled the heavy door open. The sharp damp air of the city. The trees in the gardens clattering against each other in the cold.

He walked to the corner and hailed a cab. He was amazed the driver stopped. Hans gave him the address, and they drove down the hill into the narrow streets of the Center, close to the harbor, to an old squat building near the castle. "Thanks," Hans said, and fished some change out of his pocket. Slammed the door.

He stood for a moment looking at the lights burning around the harbor, the pinpoints of light on the water. In the summer there were chairs along the water.

They were always short summers in Finnmark. On the warmest days Hans swam across the river to Finland when he visited his cousins. It was such a wide shallow river where they lived. The soft ripples of the bottom on his toes. The sun hanging around all night. The shimmer of the water as they swam at midnight. Nothing holding him back from whatever he could imagine. Water like a drug that swept him along. He'd wanted to see other places. Live in a country where it was hot and dark. Strange animals with scales and claws on the floors of wooden houses. You could move through the night and no one would know you were there.

So dark. So warm. The breeze from the ocean stilled. He shouldn't be seeing Ingrid. But he shook his head and stepped off the curb to cross the street to her apartment.

55.

HIS NIGHT WITH INGRID played over and over again as he walked to police headquarters the next morning. Her purple coat on the chair. Her shoes by the door. Like slippers. Such simple shoes. Even though she seemed transparent, she might have lied to him. That might be her trick. She gave away so much information, but left out anything he needed to know.

After dinner, they'd had coffee at the small table in Ingrid's apartment. The apartment absent anything that would tell him more about her. No paintings, no curtains—only a piece of linen she pulled shut at night, nailed in the corners of the windows. It was all too perfect. Too clean. Almost everything hidden. Who was she actually? Was everything packed away in her music? Did she have another house somewhere in the forest where all her possessions were kept?

"You smell like cinnamon," she said.

"Gum."

"Oh, Hans, how funny." She laughed. He was undressing her and it should have been awkward. But he was thinking of her skin. His hands on her skin.

"Better than cigarettes."

"I don't know," she said and started to laugh again.

Her lips, her thighs, her mouth, the tips of her fingers. The light from the street flashed in the small room.

Later, wrapped in his arms, she said, "It was difficult for you, wasn't it, those last weeks when your wife was so sick?"

Hans tried to concentrate. Dull the questions rattling in his head. Horns blared below them on the street.

"Astrid was right. I was a wimp. I lost more and more of her. She couldn't remember people in photographs or names or places. She could hardly walk. I was afraid she'd forget who I was."

"But she didn't?"

"No. She wanted to eat candy. Stand at the window and smell the air. I didn't like it that she was in the hospital. And then, she wasn't there at all."

In the morning Ingrid said, "What's our story?"

"I'm not sure yet," he said.

"I think about that as I'm composing. Whose version of the story do I want to tell? How much can I change the truth?"

"Not a reliable witness, then?" And he thought about what Olav had told him and how some people in the village remembered her in the forest around the time the boy might have died.

"No, not at all. Want some breakfast?"

"I've got to go," Hans said. "Malin wants to go over the case piece by piece. She's been indulging me. Letting me eat up travel budget on these trips."

His cousins had told him stories about how to be smart following the reindeer. If you fall into the water through the ice and go under, try to crawl out on the side of the hole where you fell into the lake. The ice is stronger there. You can kick your shoes off under water. Don't worry though, they said, bodies rise in the summer thaw. You won't be lost forever.

"I DON'T KNOW, HANS, I think you're missing something here," Malin said. They sat at the large table in the office, rain splattering the windows. The city was invisible beyond them.

Hans brought his fist down on the table. Their coffee cups clattered. He was overwhelmed. The bitterness of the last several months, the fruitless wandering in northern Sweden, the night with Ingrid.

"Sorry." His face was hot. "I've gone over all the tracks. I've gone from here to Lismavarri twice, and nothing adds up. Especially Jorgen Elstad's death. There has to be something more to that."

"But not a conspiracy," Lars said, scratching his head. Rubbing his eyes.

"No, not a conspiracy, something more personal."

"Are you missing someone?" Malin asked. "Someone you eliminated at the beginning. This Olav character seems to be a pivotal guy. He only tells you what he wants you to hear. He acts like your buddy, from the notes I've read. But he doesn't give you much to go on. We still know nothing about where Yuri, the Russian kid, went after he left the village in Sweden and set off north on his grand adventure, do we?"

She ran her hands through her hair. "And what about Kathryn? Her answers to your questions seem evasive. Let's outline the whole thing," she said, like a teacher.

Lars picked up the chalk and wrote as she ticked off the details.

"Two or three morons detonate a bomb at the construction of a bridge that will be part of a new hydroelectric power plant. One loses his hand. He's released on bail, flees the country. Suspected of being in the Soviet Union. A public relations nightmare. He's one of the original protestors at Parliament about the dam a couple of years ago. The two saboteurs, though there's no case against the second, who as far as we know wasn't even at the site, come from the same village not far from the bombsite, Lismavarri. At about the same time, reindeer herders find a body."

Malin got up from the table and pointed at the picture of the body on the murder board. She plucked the threads from one photo to another.

"Decomposed, bones scattered by wolves," Lars said.

"Buzzards, probably," Hans said. "Difficult for wolves to climb down into the ravine."

"Clinical, but then it's important to get the details right, isn't it?" Malin asked. "The lab says the dental work is Russian, the body of a male, early twenties probably. How am I doing, Lars?"

"Just fine, boss," he said and added the age of the body he'd drawn in a pit, rounded.

"Not a pit, Lars," Hans said. "A ravine. A kind of gash, like a V."

"Whatever you want. Pit. Ravine, I'm from a tiny island."

"Hans has interviewed Olav Elstad, the one perp anyone can find," Malin said, counting on her fingers. Kathryn Cole, a young American woman involved with Elstad, Gunter Schmidt, a German boy, an almost famous singer Ingrid Moreland, and several other people from the village. He's also talked to the parents of the missing Russian boy and the whole kit and caboodle of people in the little village in Sweden. In the meantime, Olav Elstad's brother either kills himself or is killed on his snowmobile. Drunk, we think."

Lars drew a bottle with bubbles.

"And then there are the suspicious-looking Americans who do or don't want to lease some land from Jorgen Elstad for something to do with a certain kind of rock. Is that right, Lars?"

"Yes," Lars said. "But after his death no one wanted to go ahead with the deal. The Americans evaporated. I had no luck tracking them down."

"It might have been some kind of government deal." Hans said.

"Maybe, but the Minister knew nothing about possible leasing rights in that area." Malin said, walking back and forth in front of the board.

"So, what do we do next? I think Lars needs to get more involved in this. Maybe it was a mistake, Hans, to let you go solo at this point," she said.

He resented being scolded but she was right.

"Interview the singer again," Lars said. "My money's on her."

"Why?" Malin asked.

"Look at Hans's notes. She came out of the forest with blood on her clothes, according to a couple of people in the village. Hans figures it's jealousy, people wanting to build up the story, but it's worth following up. And what about all this stuff with the headless reindeer and the fight with the cousins? Everyone keeps saying they had nothing to do with all of this, but it seems strange."

"Headless reindeer, honestly?" Malin asked.

"You missed that? It's one of the few things I learned from Kathryn," Hans said.

"Dramatic, then, but not important. Lars is right, Hans. We need to interview Ingrid again. I know it's awkward for you, but we'll have Lars do the interview and you can observe. I'm assuming your relationship is just casual."

"With Ingrid?"

"Yes, with Ingrid."

He'd never lied to Malin. Only withheld information until it was absolutely necessary to tell her.

"Yes, casual."

"So there we are. Lars can set up the interview. This time we'll have her come into the station. And then you should call Olav Elstad, Hans, and set up a conference call with Lars. I want backup for you on all this. We need to think about all the pieces in a different way."

The room that always felt so clean, so cool, a kind of pristine hideout in the division of violence and sexual crimes, no longer felt clean and cool.

Hans grabbed his coat and bounded down the stairs. He had to get outside, and flung the large glass door open. Terje, the desk sergeant, was smoking a few feet away from the entrance.

"Can I bum a smoke?" Hans asked.

"Sure," Terje said, lipping one of the long slim cigarettes. He pulled a pack out of his pocket and held it out to Hans.

Hans took a cigarette and held it up to the burning tip of Terje's smoke.

He'd been avoiding this moment for months. One cigarette, he'd be hooked again. He took a deep drag on the abnormally long smoke and his lungs filled with peppermint.

"Are you kidding?" he shouted.

Terje flicked his butt on the pavement and crushed it with his boot. He started to laugh.

Hans threw the cigarette on the ground and stamped on it over and over again.

They were both laughing now so loudly that a woman bundled in a fur coat stopped to look at them. She shook her head and walked away muttering.

Hans was bent over and crying. He couldn't stop laughing.

When he could get a few words out he said, "You were waiting for me, weren't you? You set this up. You know what a fucking bear this case is, don't you?"

Terje said, "No, they were a present from my wife's sister. She got them in duty free on her way back from the States. Some new thing there for the ladies. Virginia Slims."

And they started to laugh again. "Stop," Hans said, "don't do this to me."

"You're not desperate enough to smoke them, I guess," Terje said.

"But you are?"

"You bet. My wife's sister is with us for a week and she's completely bonkers. Never stops talking, criticizes everything I do. Goes on and on about the Americans. How loud and evil they are. But she loves their cigarettes. It's a good way for me to finally break the habit. They're disgusting, aren't they?"

"You can say that again." He slapped Terje on the back. "Thanks for the smoke," he said, and they burst out laughing.

56.

IT WAS DARK AND still outside his apartment hours before dawn. The late drinkers were still asleep on benches. But he guessed it was too cold for them now. He wished he'd picked up Matisse at Malin's. He'd woken up in the middle of the night and couldn't get back to sleep. He made a cup of coffee and sat at the table in the kitchen.

After Astrid's death, he was so angry, but now he felt unmoored, the way he had for many years after his cousin's friends dragged him along the street. He didn't know whether this was better or worse. The police academy, even though it was full of a different kind of bullshit, had anchored him. What he didn't like was being adrift. Everything that kept him in line had fallen away. When he was younger, he felt if he skied harder, studied more, brushed off his father's indifference, he'd get through anything. But he relied too much on Astrid. On Astrid being there for him. And now this loss followed him. Even when he was brushing his teeth and the guy in the mirror looked only vaguely like who he thought he was.

If he drew a map he might be able to figure out answers to his questions.

Hans tore a piece of paper off the pad on the table and started to draw, pressing the pencil hard. The sound of the pencil on the paper was soothing.

When he was young he liked to sketch. Sometimes he put on his pack and walked into the forest. He sat on a rock near the waterfall. It was a safe place away from his brother, and you never knew what would turn up. A willow grouse, a fox, a vole. Once it snowed, he was too busy to draw, and as he grew older it no longer seemed that interesting.

He drew the village of Lismavarri. He was doing something simple, pleasurable. Concrete. There was the river and the riverbank. There was the village road and the main road where they intersected. There was Olav's house and the shop and the sports club lined up neatly on the road.

Olav's uncle's house was by itself, taller in a thicket of birch. He drew the barn and the fields leading off to the river. There was the slope of the hill that led to the forest and there was the place where Jorgen and Ellen would build their house. It was in the forest. To build you'd have to take down some trees. Stake out the plot. Hammer the stakes in with a mallet.

He drew the forest and the paths through the small trees and hummocks leading to the treeless vidda. There was the place where cloudberries grew. There was where Olav told him Ingrid and her sister camped for a few days by the cloudberry man's hut. He filled in the lakes and the ravine where the young man lay dead for weeks.

A day in late August. Already the bushes of the forest yellow and red. The berries ripe.

He drew Jorgen Elstad at the edge of the forest. Olav in the shop. The American girl and the German boy stacking fertilizer bags by the barn.

Ingrid had come out of the forest with blood on her sweater. But they'd all been in the forest off and on that week. The week the coroner guessed the boy had died. And what about the butchered reindeer? The fight that meant nothing.

The growing suspicion that Ingrid had lied to him all along. She knew more than she was telling him.

ON HIS WAY TO work, Hans went to see an archeologist at the university. Someone who'd worked with Gudmund. They met as planned for coffee at a café on St. Olav's Gate. The table was near a window where he could see students slowly pedaling by on their bikes. The whole city seemed to be swirling around him.

"Gudmund Hatt gave up geography," Viggo said, "after the trial. He wanted to be off the radar. He and Emilie lived a quiet life after that."

"I gathered that." Hans shifted in the narrow chair.

"A sad story. No one knew who he was by the time he died. A bunch of students put out a magazine with a dedication to him. I don't think a lot of people forgave him for those radio talks and editorials during the Occupation." Viggo pushed his gray hair away from his eyes. His face was narrow, lined. Compassionate somehow.

"But he was brilliant? He made discoveries in archeology that changed things, from what I've read."

"Brilliant. And lonely, at the end. They revere him on the Faroe Islands. He started their excavations there. I was with him. In my early twenties, traveling to all the wild places I could think of." He passed a plate of chocolate cookies to Hans. Hans shook his head and Viggo set the plate near his cup.

"We took a boat to the place where Trond of Gota from the Saga had his farm. It was my first taste of a dig and after that I was hooked. The next day we found a refuge house, a *fransatoftir* from the 1600s when people would hide from French pirates. We spent several days excavating according to his meticulous standards. His wife Emilie had travelled to the Faroes with him. Lovely. We had drinks each night in the parlor of the hotel. Gudmund and I standing there in our muddy clothes, laughing. They were on their way from Greenland to Denmark. I told her about a woman I loved in Torshavn. How I didn't want to get married, but this woman wanted a child."

A young woman who reminded him of Sara, confident and pretty, parked her bike near the café and opened the door. Cold air blew into the room.

"Emilie told me she loved children but lost two of her own. One, before she was born. Emilie fell off a ladder. She was putting up decorations in their house for a birthday party for one of Gudmund's nieces. The other was stillborn. They brought a bird, a kind of dove, back from St. Thomas that year Gudmund was doing excavations in the Virgin Islands. They loved that dove like a child. Gudmund would play his harmonica and the dove was very happy. The dove perched on Gudmund's shoulder when he was reading in bed. Emilie told me one day when Gudmund had been away for a few weeks, Carl Nielsen came to visit and decided he could entertain the bird, who was lonesome for Gudmund, or at least that's what Emilie thought. She had this uncanny closeness to animals, it seemed. Nothing worked until Nielsen played a piece in a minor note. Then the bird was happy."

"Did you keep in touch?"

"Yes, it was Emilie who wrote most of the letters. When I moved back to Oslo, Hatt and I collaborated on some work in Denmark. Those years after the war were hard. Emilie said Gudmund would disappear into his study. Writing from early in the morning until night. He didn't want to see anyone. He kept away when Emilie gave parties for neighborhood children.

"She grew sick, stuck in bed for weeks, or months sometimes. The cold was bad for her heart. She had several shows of her paintings. She didn't want to brag, she told me, but her work sold well. The artist Christine Swane, a friend of hers, told me it was because of Gudmund that no museum would touch her work. The curators didn't want to be seen as catering to a collaborator's wife. If you want, we can walk back to my office, and I'll show you a watercolor she gave me."

"It's odd," Hans said, "I met a man on a bus in Sweden—I know it sounds like a joke, but he told me he knew my great uncle, Johan Turi. Worked for him when Emilie was helping him write his book, *Muitalus*."

"Emilie said that book was her life for years. Gudmund helped her with the translation when she was depressed about her progress."

"The man I met on the bus said she was pregnant while she was with Turi and then lost a child," Hans said.

"Stories are interesting, aren't they? I don't know. It might be true, but I doubt it. I suppose that's why I like archeology. Digging up the past and then inventing the story to go with what you find. Let's go take a look at Emilie's painting. It will cheer us both up."

"Sounds great." Hans got up to pay the bill.

They walked across the square toward the yellow stone buildings where Viggo had taught for so many years.

"I did get married," Viggo said and laughed. "Tied myself down to another woman I fell in love with, and then had to get a real job."

"A prestigious job."

"Oh, yes, important," Viggo raised his eyebrows. "But some of my happiest moments were when I was working with

Gudmund in those fields in Denmark. Excavating ancient farms in Jutland. He wrote poems, you know."

"That seems unusual."

"He was complicated. I read the draft of a poem he wrote before the war. In it he said Herman Goring should be hanged. But the two anti-Nazi verses were missing in the published version. A friend told me he was with Gudmund when they heard the news that the Nazis had murdered Austrian Chancellor Dollfus. Gudmund exploded, was furious."

"So, he was framed?"

"I don't know about that. I think the evidence was sketchy. The court read it the way they wanted. I heard that British forces asked for Gudmund when Denmark was liberated. He was a big name in academic circles."

They reached Viggo's building on the edge of the square. "Here we are," Viggo said, and led Hans inside. Down a long corridor and up three steps to his office, perched in a turret. It was clean and ordered. Curved bookcases covered most of the walls. A ram's head with curled horns hung over a large chair.

Hans laughed.

"It's from the Faroes. I was young. I wanted something wild. It's a very old breed from the ninth century," Viggo said.

"This is it." He pointed to a small watercolor hanging by itself on one of the curving walls near the window. It was somehow more real than any of Emilie's paintings he'd looked at in Stockholm. Viggo owned this. She'd given it to him. The scene looked like the place Turi described as the summer pastures near Tromso. At the bottom of the painting were rough gray sheds with peaked roofs. But the landscape was what was important. No one yet there. Not the reindeer or the families following the reindeer. Not the settlers selling buttons and cloth. Not the tourists with their cameras. The hills soft and molded. The small forests of the coast shaggy on some of the crests. Taller mountains in the distance against a pale sky. Pastures green with sweet grass.

"She was charming. She smoked little cigars now and then. She looked fifteen years younger than she was. A wonderful storyteller. One night we told ghost stories. We were a little drunk. Hers was so wonderful I asked her to write it down for me. I have it somewhere. I've got a drawing she sent me, too. I keep thinking I'll get it framed. My daughter tells me all her work might be worth something at some point."

Hans stood as close to the painting as he could get. The brushstrokes, the texture, the washes of color. Viggo gestured toward the painting.

"She was an incredible artist. She had piles of writing too. Always working, doing one thing or another. When Gudmund was away she missed him terribly. She sent him fruit when we were in Jutland. Apples and pears from their garden in Kauslunde. Each wrapped in green paper. I can taste how sweet those pears were. A gift each time I bit into one. I was a little in love with her," he said, and smirked at Hans. "But I was always falling in love. And you? Are you married?"

"I was," Hans said. "My wife died about a year ago."

"But you're so young. Too young to be doing all this digging up of the past."

Hans said goodbye to Viggo and headed to the office, late by now, through the winding streets of Oslo. He started to trot down the narrow sidewalk. He wanted to believe Gudmund was innocent but wasn't sure why.

57.

HANS TRIED TO TALK himself out of seeing Ingrid again. Something was gnawing at him. Something in the back of his head. It was almost like a setup. Her call. Her charm. She was so unlike Astrid, who let people know immediately where she stood. Who she loved. He didn't like feeling Ingrid was pulling the wool over his eyes. She had hardly any books, two rugs. Handmade, nubby.

"I know, spare, weird. Like a cell."

"Space to think, right?" he'd said.

But now he wasn't so sure. Why would you strip your life down like this? Maybe if you had something you wanted to forget. Something you wanted to hide.

HE COULDN'T STAY TWISTED in Ingrid's arms. Her breath in his ear. The lights from the harbor flashing in her windows. Salt from the fjord. The hollow feeling in his chest.

She didn't know it was a year since Astrid's death. He tried not to talk too much about her. But the weight of Ingrid's arms. The smell of her skin. Nothing felt right. So he got up.

"Going away?" she asked.

"Just for tonight."

"Going home?"

"Yes," Hans pulled on his shirt.

"Too much?"

"Yes."

"Call me when you get there?"

"Sure."

He left her apartment and walked through the cobbled square, up Kirkegata past the cathedral, empty at two in the morning. Shuttered shops. One car, and minutes later another. Past the train station where brick buildings were going up. Ugly, with empty courtyards at odd angles, wedged in between the curved stone buildings. Sky brittle and hard this time of year, moonless, cloudy. He was brittle too. Unplugged. Worn down by death.

He could stop at Zorba's. Someone was probably still there, and he could beg a cup of coffee. Hans took the turn onto Breigata and saw the light from the café.

HANS WAS LYING ON the sidewalk, blood pooling under his body. The cold, scorching cold night, chilling the blood almost as soon as it ran out on the gritty surface. A man who looked like someone he grew up with, Mikael's friend, bent over him.

He was wearing a ring that Mikael made. It flashed in the light from a passing car. The man was crouched beside him. Holding the knife. A beautiful knife like the one Hans's father used to whittle. Antler for the hilt. A sharp point.

Hans couldn't think of a worse place to die.

THE TALL WAITER WAS standing over Hans, no, he was by his side, moving Hans's fingers away from the blood, pressing something into the gash. Everything was swirling. The walk deep into the forest in Sweden, south of where his mother's family moved so many years ago. The place where Yuri died, or not. How could Yuri have walked such a long way north through bogs and mountain passes and the dark autumn? The smell of pine, hot now, not cold. Why was he hot and not cold? The touch of Ingrid's skin smooth, cold. No, the touch of granite, the statues in the park, bodies twisted and molded. The ducks scooping water with their bills. Stagnant water late summer in the park, old leaves scattered on the shining surface. And Emilie's voice pulling him away from the pain. I never thought I'd be so happy, so happy for so many years. Even sadness sometimes gives way to joy.

No sign of Astrid. Maybe there she was, her cool hand held on his forehead. Her fingers smoothing the hair away.

The flash of Fausto's teeth in the dim light.

"No sweat, Inspector Hans, you'll live if I have anything to do with it. Just a lot of pressure here."

He was cold, so cold, but someone had thrown a blanket over him and now someone was binding up the wound and now he was lifted into the ambulance and now the sirens began.

58.

"Good, you're awake," a nurse said as she carried in a tray of broth and juice.

"I don't think I can," he said. Lying on his back, something he never did at home. The day after Astrid died a year ago. But he was alive, hooked up to an IV. Light coming in the square windows of the hospital room.

"Yes, you can." Her name was Laura. She had taken care of Astrid. She set the tray on the adjustable table near him and pushed the button to raise the head of the bed.

"Strange coincidence."

"No, small hospital," she said. "You almost joined her."

"What saved me?"

"Several whos. A guy at some dive you like to have breakfast at. Stays open almost all night—Malin, your boss, told me."

"Zorba's."

"Maybe, but don't bother explaining why an Italian guy's working at a Greek café."

"Ex-bike racer."

"Anyway, he heard some noise in the street, looked out from the kitchen where he was washing up. He'd taken a break to smoke and saw some guy standing over you. The light from the street, something, convinced him it was you. He said he might not have run out, just called the police, but you needed his help. He could feel it in his bones. He scared the guy holding a knife, a big knife, it turns out. The guy threw the knife down, took off down Breigata, and there you were bleeding to death." She adjusted his pillows and pulled the blanket around him. Adjusted the bag on the IV.

"The waiter took the towel from around his neck and pressed the wound, knew somehow that's what he should do."

"Bike racing," Hans said again. "Fausto knows all about first aid, how to patch himself back together."

"He yelled to someone inside to call an ambulance. You would have bled to death if he hadn't looked out. He was upset, said you were one of the good cops. A nice guy. Your friend Ingrid called the station when she couldn't get you at home. The officer in charge called your colleague Lars, and he met the ambulance. So, do me a favor, eat your breakfast. Celebrate your life."

"Just juice then." He took a sip slowly. "How long am I in for?"

"A couple of weeks and then you'll be fine, everyone thinks, with a couple more months to heal. You're doing great, Hans," she said. "I know it's been a wretched year," she said, as she brushed the hair back from his eyes.

"You need a haircut. You look better with it short."

59.

HANS WAS DOZING. LAUGHTER startled him. A cop stationed at the door. The lights dim above his bed. A woman sat in the chair near him. The other bed was empty. She was knitting bright red yarn, looping each twisted strand over her needles with a soft clacking sound. Hansi, she said. Was it his mother? Had she travelled all this way to see him? But he knew it wasn't his mother. This woman had long white hair pulled back in a bow. She was wearing a *gåkti.* I should have been more forceful with Gudmund, she said. I should have told him no. It would have changed everything those last years.

The room was swirling, and he closed his eyes. He must still have some of the anesthesia in his blood. At least he could blame the vision on that. He felt clammy in his hospital gown and pulled the blanket up.

He remembered the attack now. It was coming back to him in flashes. He knew the man leaning over him was not Mikael's friend but his cousin from so long ago who'd fled to Oslo. Nicke was wearing one of the first rings Mikael had made. It had been years since he'd seen him, but he knew it was him. The same thin face and heavy eyebrows. And he knew he didn't owe him anything. Nicke was brutal even when Hans was a kid. He could have stopped his friends from trying to kill Hans. He still had nightmares about that night, the searing pain, the frigid cold.

All the anger he should have felt when it happened was shooting through his body. Burning, sharp. His cousin laughing, the hollow thumps of Nicke's friends kicking and punching, Hans's arms held over his face. The way he wasn't completely in his body he was so drunk. It was dark and cold and the drumbeat of the kicks echoed in the frigid air.

Malin was standing over him smiling. She had the stack of *New York Times* crossword puzzles from his apartment in one hand and a toy seal in the other.

"To keep you company," she said as she propped the seal up on the tray near his bed.

"I know who it is," he said. He was sweating. He knew his mother wouldn't be happy with him. She must have known Nicke was still in Oslo but didn't want to tell him.

"We've already grabbed him. He was in our files. He's been in and out of prison. Your friend Fausto sat down with the Photofit tech and developed a composite good enough to find a match. We know he's the one who attacked you with the plank too. The partial fingerprint matches the ones on the knife. Not very smart to toss it so close to you. Fausto saw him run away and recognized his coat. A red parka with fake fur around the hood."

"It's all snapped together this morning. I recognized the ring but thought it belonged to a friend of my brother's. Then I realized it was one of the first rings Mikael made, and he made it for my cousin Nicke. A lowlife who fled to Oslo when I was fourteen. He lived with his father, a small-time pusher. We lost track of him."

"He's kept track of you. What's he have against you?"

"History. A long story. I think he's just a vicious customer. He probably blames me for his exile in Oslo. His mother threw him out and his father was the only one who wanted him."

"I've given Lars the Alta case. Your doctor says it will take at least a few weeks for you to start to feel better," she said.

"That makes sense. You think you might like to keep Matisse for a couple of months? I don't think I can handle a dog right now."

"I don't think you can either, but are you sure?"

"I'm sure."

"Fine, then. Soren loves him, but you have to promise to come visit when you're better. Probably a month or more for you to heal. A good time to step back from all this. You weren't honest with me either, were you? You're more involved with Ingrid than you said. Though I think she helped save your life. She and Lars made sure the emergency room took you right away."

"I figured it wouldn't make any difference, but I feel guilty about it."

"You did leave out some crucial information." Malin said and tapped his arm gently.

"It didn't make any difference. Did it?"

"No, Lars talked to her, and it seems like your notes make sense. She had the same story. He believed her. He followed up with calls to the villagers you mentioned, and they said, of course they could have been wrong. She's very a nice girl, even though she's so famous now. They didn't like it that she dumped Olav Elstad."

"Any follow up on Jorgen and the cousins?"

"A bit. Lars ended up at the same dead end you did. No one wants to talk about it. It was nothing. Just a flare up sometime in the summer. A party for a cousin going away. Oh, and by the way, Lars says hi and to tell you he's glad the perp missed your brisket. Wherever that might be." Malin said and raised her eyebrows.

60.

THE CLICKING OF MACHINES, hollow noise of the intercom, smell of boiled cabbage.

"Hans," she said and held her face close. He tasted the perfume she wore. Light, like wildflowers. He struggled through sleep to open his eyes. Layers of bad dreams.

"You're here."

"Yeah, they wouldn't let anyone in yesterday except your supervisor. 'Still critical,' they kept telling me."

"I'm lucky, the doctor said."

"Yes, a few more minutes and it would have been all over," Ingrid said. "You're very dramatic, Hans. You didn't have to go through all this to make sure I cared about you." She touched his hand and sat down by the bed.

"Sorry I left."

"I got worried."

"I'm glad." But he wasn't happy about the way things were working out. She's kept something from him. Not lying maybe, just not telling everything she knows. Yuri meant nothing to her. A boy doing something dumb. Getting lost in the forest.

"But there's something going on, isn't there? I can see it in your face. You've pulled away, haven't you?" Ingrid said.

"I don't have much to do. Just think. And I started to think you were pretty vague about your days in the forest. The days you spent with your sister. You told me about the trip to Alta, but not much else. You told me enough to make me think I knew you. But how could I? You didn't tell me everything about the days when you and your sister were in the forest, did you? My colleague, Lars Dokken, doesn't think you had anything to do with the boy's death."

"But you do?"

Ingrid wrapped his hand in her slender hands. She was beautiful like a medieval princess.

He should have listened more carefully when she'd told him her story. After all, people had seen her with blood on her sweater when she came down from the forest. But he'd believed her when she told him it was fish blood and not human. He was worse than those TV detectives, so stupid.

She shifted on the plastic chair. "I wanted to let you think I was someone else. Someone who didn't seduce trouble wherever I went. It seemed like a simple deception. I was in too deep. I couldn't tell you, once we'd been together. I didn't want to end up in jail, festering there for not telling you everything I knew."

Hans touched her face with his other hand. Pushed the dark hair away from her eyes.

"We'd been picking cloudberries with my uncle's family. You know, by Grandmother's Lake. He has a hut there and we'd slept over for about a week. It was my holiday before we left for Oslo and the concerts there. It was a lovely week. The air was mild, and my sister's children were with us picking in the bog. They had a tent. Some days we were covered with the sticky berry juice. At night we caught fish and grilled it. I'd forgotten what it was like to be so free and relaxed. I'd forgotten the taste of sweet fish grilled on sticks over the fire. I wondered what my life was doing to me."

Past the open door a nurse pushed a rattling cart of medical supplies. Ingrid took a deep breath.

"When we were ready to go home, we decided to take the long way back by the waterfall above Lismavarri where the eagles nest. Olav probably told you about that."

"Olav told me some things, yes, but I'm beginning to think he didn't tell me about everything."

"Oh, he's like that." She laughed. "Always something up his sleeve. I hadn't been there in a long time, and I loved to sleep on the edge of the cliff, listening to the sound of the water. We sent the children home with my uncle who had a tractor to haul the boxes of berries back to the village."

Ingrid moved her right hand toward the cup of water she'd poured from the jug on the tray by his bed. She brought it to her lips for a second. Her throat moved as she swallowed the warm water.

"We had a wonderful time. Walking across the vidda in the little tracks. The trees were starting to turn yellow when we reached the campsite above the falls."

"The same campsite that Eric and the American girl and the German boy would use a few weeks later?"

"Yes. It's just the right distance if you want to get back by morning the following day. We were tired and put our sleeping bags out quickly and set the teakettle to boil when a man appeared from nowhere. He was staggering and had a gun in his right hand. He was almost on the edge of the cliff. We watched him stumble over the edge. Everything happened so quickly. I ran to the cliff and saw him lying by the edge of the river. If the water rose up, it would sweep him away. It was too steep to climb down."

"It didn't make sense for you to go near him. If he had a gun."

"I thought if I told anyone there would be an inquest. I didn't know what a stranger was doing wandering around in the forest. I knew someone had hurt him. Or he'd fallen somewhere else. I knew somehow that it wasn't a good thing—a stranger with a gun wandering in the forest above Lismavarri. I thought maybe people I loved were involved. I didn't want to ruin my career or get anyone else in trouble. Do you understand that?"

"Yes," he said. "You should have reported his fall to the police. And you could have told me the truth days ago."

"I didn't know what would happen. I was in over my head."

"You didn't know if he was dead?" He couldn't forgive this and the thought made him shift in the bed. Take a sip of the water through the straw, he told himself.

"No. But how could he be alive after falling like that on the rocks? My sister and I packed up our gear and headed down the path through the forest to Lismavarri."

"You were trying to protect your friend Eric?"

"Yes, there's that, too. He was so determined to make a point. I miss him terribly. He's given up so much for such a small gesture."

"You didn't see Jorgen Elstad in the forest, did you?"

"Jorgen, no. You don't think he had anything to do with this?"

There was something about the way she said this that made him wonder if she was telling the truth.

"The whole thing is such a mess. So tragic." She bent down and touched his cheek with her cold lips. "You won't let this get out of hand, will you?"

He closed his eyes and listened as she got up from the chair and walked out the door. He would have to tell Malin what she had told him. But he wasn't sure Ingrid had told him everything.

Later he called Olav. Hans needed to understand how much he knew. How much he'd known all along. "Ingrid filled me in."

"Told you everything?" Olav asked.

"Yes. I'm on leave now, but I've spoken to Kathryn and Gunter." He thought Olav might ask about them. But he didn't say anything. Hans heard a baby crying. Someone shutting a door.

"Can you tell me anything else? I'm still trying to put the pieces together. Is there any way Jorgen could have met the stranger in the forest the day he was staking out the plot for his house?"

"What if Jorgen did tell me something about that? Perhaps this is what happened. Jorgen was at the edge of the forest, pacing out his plot, putting stakes in. He was angry, the Russian threatened him. The Russian came out of the forest with a gun. He seemed like he was going to shoot Jorgen. You know they're very thick, strong stakes to go into the forest soil. Maybe he smashed the Russian's head with the mallet he was using to hammer the stakes in and the fellow staggered off. Jorgen could have been killed. There was nothing he could do. He didn't want to tell the police. Perhaps you're right. Maybe he was torn up by his guilt. The man hadn't fired the gun. We may have looked in the forest and found no trace of the man. He disappeared. We never found the gun. We thought perhaps he was the deserter who may have fled into Kirkenes from Russia."

Olav coughed and then hesitated. "And maybe Ingrid kept her own secrets, or maybe she told Eric. Everyone's life got caught up with the dead Russian."

"Why didn't you tell me about this?"

"Ah, but you didn't ask. And I'm not sure this is what actually happened."

"But the Russian was a boy," Hans said.

"Yes, that's the tragedy. We thought he was a Russian deserter. We forgot to remember he was only a boy."

61.

He told Malin about Ingrid's encounter with the man near the waterfall when his boss called the next day. How Ingrid and her sister watched the Russian disappear over the edge of the ravine. Ingrid knew she should've told the police, but she was afraid it would disrupt Eric's plans. There'd be cops all over the village asking questions.

"She doesn't realize we could still charge her for obstructing the investigation?" Malin asked. He was hot and his ears started to throb.

"I don't think she thought about that. She only thought about Eric. And, well, there's more. I followed up with Olav who told me in his roundabout way Jorgen probably hit the boy with the mallet. Jorgen thought the guy was going to kill him. He panicked. Later that day, Olav and Jorgen searched for the boy and didn't find anything. They couldn't have known he would make it as far as the ravine."

"Probably? There's no proof. That's the problem, isn't it?" Malin said and took a deep breath.

"Yeah. Does it matter at this point?"

"It would have been helpful if we'd gotten a better description of the man from Ingrid and Jorgen. Each would have been close enough to identify him."

"And we would have been able to tell Yuri's parents that their son was dead or he was still missing."

"Yes, tragic, whatever the identity of the person in the morgue."

HANS WAS LUCKY, EVERYONE kept telling him. His attacker missed all those important organs. Didn't twist the knife. Just stabbed cleanly. Weeks in the hospital. And then the long rehab.

After he got home, he heard from the police in Sweden. "I'm on leave," Hans said, "Lars Dokken's in charge."

"There's not much news, but we'll pass it along to him," the officer said.

Hans was afraid he'd tell him they'd identified the remains and the body was Yuri's. But it was inconclusive, the officer said.

Yuri's father had found out about a deserter who might have slipped into Kirkenes. A submarine crewman. So Olav was right, the dead man could be the Russian deserter. The man was about Yuri's age. The dental work was expensive, though, something that matched Yuri's teeth. So it would have to be someone with parents who could spend money on his teeth. Someone like a party boss.

Annika Johnson called and told him reindeer herders found a skin pouch in the snow, like the one she gave Yuri. Soft and small, full of coins for varro muorra. But it was found in another direction. Not north. It looked like the tracks went toward the old summer pastures near Tromso. So Yuri could have made it safely to the sea and hopped on a boat to Canada.

Was it better that it might be another boy, one around the same age, but living a very different life in Kirkenes, cleaning his gun each morning, the pieces spread out on a cloth?

In some ways it didn't matter who hurt the Russian boy first. Or second. He was lost to his family. To the people who loved him. It mattered that no one had helped him, but how could they? He was waving a gun and raving in a language they didn't understand.

Hans had been an idiot with Ingrid. It was a kind of magic trick. Her trek into his heart. Was Ingrid just a way to feel like he was someone else? Someone who didn't love Astrid. Someone who hadn't watched her slip away until the world was almost completely empty.

It didn't matter who the heart loved, the body craved, it all came down to sore knees, split skin, the weathering of the body like rocks in rain. Rain so many years, over and over again.

(FEBRUARY)

62.

HANS LEANS AGAINST A seat. Children near him are clutching their metal skis and poles. They're all laughing and shouting. Hitting each other on the head or bumping into passengers as they get on at each stop.

The train moves quickly up to the mountains. The forest disappearing. The sky almost the same color as the slopes. His muscles don't ache. No persistent throbbing. He's on his way to Hemsedal to rent some alpine ski touring gear and climb as far as he can on the tracks up the glacier. The sun should be up by the time they reach the station. The days are getting longer finally. Late February. Two more weeks and he'll be back to work.

AFTER HE WAS DISCHARGED from the hospital, he went to see his aunt. She'd had a dowry of reindeer when she married his uncle. She'd told him how her father bought another man's herd when the man was old and moved south to be with his daughter. "They were beautiful reindeer," she said, "and your uncle was very pleased. He wasn't the only one who wanted to marry me, though. I had many suitors who gave me silk scarves and brooches."

"Like the pin you're wearing now," he said.

"Yes, this is one your uncle gave me. The others I gave back when I chose him."

"What was your wedding like?"

"Very jolly. There was a woman from England who was traveling through Finnmark then with Beartu, your uncle's cousin, and she came to the wedding. She gave me a cheap glass necklace. I was embarrassed, but I wore it to make her happy."

"And was she happy?" Hans asked, laughing.

"Yes, I think so. She took pictures with a camera she had with her. I suppose they showed up somewhere."

"Somewhere, you're famous."

"Yes, somewhere I'm famous."

She was ironing as he ate her delicious waffles. "And your Uncle Johan, he was very famous, wasn't he?" he asked.

"Oh, for a time, yes. We didn't see him very much. He'd gotten so famous he built a house for himself. People from the south paid him money to take them into the forest hunting, or on trips, like the woman from England."

"And what about his book? What did they think about that?"

"No one talked about it. I think they hoped it was just one of his silly ideas that would disappear."

"I've read it," he said.

"Ah, I know. Your mother told me. I thought he was very clever. I liked the drawings he made. He had a funny dog who was my companion sometimes. A little white dog with one black ear. Some people thought Uncle was telling everyone our secrets, but Papa said it didn't matter. Uncle was afraid it would all be lost. And I suppose he was right. It was."

The Oslo train creaks to a stop and the kids explode out of the cars. A school trip, he guesses. Hans hauls his canvas bag over his shoulder and steps onto the platform, the light blinding him. The train from Bergen pulls away. A woman with short blonde hair strides toward the station. Her touring skis on her shoulder, poles clasped in one hand, a pack slung over her arm. She stops to adjust her gear.

For a minute he thinks it's Kari. But how strange. He hasn't heard from her in months. She turns and there she is looking straight at him. It takes her a second to recognize him in the bright light, but when she does, she waves. He doesn't expect her to be happy to see him.

He nods and walks fast across the wooden platform to where she's standing.

"I heard what happened to you," she says.

"I wanted to write to you."

"But you didn't. Going skiing?"

"Yeah."

"Catch the minibus with me?"

"Sure, and I can tell you the story." He laughs and they walk toward the taxi stand. His arm brushing against her hand, resting on the skis.

ACKNOWLEDGMENTS

Thank you to my dear friend Awel Irene who has enriched my life in so many ways. Her home has been a safe harbor for me from the very beginning of our friendship.

I'm grateful to my wonderful friends who guided this book on its journey. A warm thank you to Barbara Colin, Karen Donovan, Patricia Eakins, Ann de Forest, Ted Kerasote, Sharon Kirsch, Peter Money, Elaine Terranova, and Carolyn Yalkut. My former Temple University colleague Keith Gumery graciously entertained me in Copenhagen, along with being my tour guide. Mette von Buchwald was my lifeboat in Svendborg and translated several of Emilie Demant Hatt's letters for me. Many thanks to Charlotte Høgh, my fellow artist on Hirsholmene, along with Elisabet Diedrichs and Vibebeke Rostrup Bøyesen who made me feel welcome. Max Nicolaisen, Kirsten Skou, and Søren Lind, took care of me at Brecht's house. Several people graciously opened museum collections to me in the Nordic region: Maria Maxén, Cecillia Hammarlund-Larsson, and Connie Hansen. Steffen Strumman Hansen, Dorte Smedegaard, and Helle Askgaard, were especially helpful with this project in Denmark. A big thank you to Evan Sorg, my brilliant former student, for a conversation about his experience as a New York City police officer.

Special thanks to Ricklundgarden in Saxnas, Sweden; Brecht's House in Svendborg, Denmark; The Council of Danish Artists, Hirsholmene, Denmark; Creator in Residence, Hillswick, Shetland, especially Geoff Jukes for including a perfect artist retreat in his beautiful house and gallery, The Weaving Shed; along with the Caselberg Trust, New Zealand, for residencies; and a fellowship from the Summer Literary Seminars, Vilnius, Lithuania.

Thank you to my talented colleagues at Betty: director and editor-in-chief, Peg Alford Pursell, Magdalena Bartowska, Leah Browning, Elizabeth Casillas, Leah De Forest, Ilze Duarte, Johanna Choi Kalbus, Janis Hubschman, and Marianne Villanueva.

And love and thanks to Graham Masker, my baggage handler and general factotum during a research trip to Norway and Sweden. Scott Masker is my jolly navigator and driver wherever I am.

I used two editions of Johan Turi's book while writing *If the Owl Calls*. The first is a 1966 reprint of E. Gee Nash's English translation of *Muitalus Sámiid Birra*. The second version is Thomas A. DuBois' 2011 translation of Mikael Svonni's new edition called *An Account of the Sámi*.

photo credit: Joseph V. Labolito

ABOUT THE AUTHOR

SHARON WHITE is an award-winning author whose work spans nonfiction, poetry, and fiction. Her books include: *Vanished Gardens*, the AWP Award in Creative Nonfiction winner; *Boiling Lake*, winner of the Italo Calvino Prize in Fabulist Fiction; and *Minato Sketches*, a Rosemary Daniell Prize winner. An Associate Professor Emerita at Temple University, she has dedicated her career to writing and teaching, with her work appearing in numerous literary journals and anthologies. A passionate traveler, Sharon White draws inspiration from landscapes and cultures, weaving themes of nature, place, and memory into her stories. She lives in Philadelphia.

ABOUT BETTY

Founded in 2023, Betty is an imprint of WTAW Press, with a mission to publish books of prose by women for everyone. Betty aims to showcase and celebrate the diversity of women's voices.

By focusing on the voices of those who identify as women, Betty can contribute to a more nuanced understanding of women's experiences and foster empathy, understanding, and dialogue on important issues.

WTAW Press is a 501(c)(3) nonprofit publisher devoted to discovering and publishing enduring literary works of prose. WTAW publishes and champions a carefully curated list of titles across a range of genres (literary fiction, creative nonfiction, and prose that falls somewhere in between), subject matter, and perspectives. WTAW welcomes submissions from writers of all backgrounds and aims to support authors throughout their careers.

As a nonprofit literary press, WTAW depends on the support of donors. We are grateful for the assistance we receive from organizations, foundations, and individuals. To find out more about our mission and publishing program, or to make a donation, please visit wtawpress.org.